DOCTOR HUGUET

A NOVEL

BY

EDMUND BOISGILBERT, M. D.

(IGNATIUS DONNELLY), *1831–1901*

Author of "ATLANTIS," "RAGNARÖK," "THE GREAT CRYPTOGRAM,"
AND "CÆSAR'S COLUMN."

"Mere puppets they, who come and go,
    At bidding of vast formless things,
That shift the scenery to and fro,
    Flapping, from out their condor wings,
Invisible woe."
— *Edgar A. Poe.*

———

6-33726

N/DD

CHICAGO:
F. J. SCHULTE & COMPANY, PUBLISHERS,
298 DEARBORN STREET.

CONTENTS.

DOCTOR HUGUET.

A NOVEL.

CHAPTER I.

MYSELF.

" There's one at the gate.
Ah, marry, what is he ? "
— *Twelfth Night, i. v.*

I HAVE made up my mind to tell the whole dreadful story, let the consequences be what they may. I know there are those, among my friends, who will consider it a species of degradation for me to make public the facts which will appear in these pages; while there are others who will urge that the world will never believe so improbable a story as that which I am about to tell. But it seems to me that I have been chosen, by some extra-mundane, superhuman intelligence, out of the multitude of mankind, and subjected to a terrible and unparalleled experience, in order that a great lesson may be taught to the world; and that it is a duty, therefore, which I owe to the world, and which I must not shrink from or avoid, to make known all the facts of that experience, at whatever cost of shame or agony to myself. Blessed is the man who can feel that God has singled him out from among his fellows, and that the divine hand has shaped his destiny; and yet such men usually bear on their hearts and minds a burden of life-long woe. Those whom God so honors he agonizes.

My name is Doctor Anthony Huguet. I am a native of South Carolina, and have lived here, in this city of C——, ever since I was born, except during the years I was abroad and in the North, perfecting my medical education. My ancestors were French, and among the first Huguenot settlers in this State; my grandfather was a planter, and laid the foundation of the fortune which I now enjoy, by large cotton crops in the old slave-days, and judicious investments of the money so made in real estate. I am an aristocrat of the aristocrats. My education was as thorough as wealth, on the part of my parents, and great industry, on my own part, could make it. I have been, by inheritance, a leader in the best society in my State and city. My house and grounds are the admiration of all who behold them. I take my physical constitution and stature from my French ancestors. I have never exceeded one hundred and fifty pounds in weight, and I am five feet six inches in height. My complexion is fair. In disposition I am, by nature, somewhat reserved and exclusive, and with a certain degree of *hauteur* in manner. My tastes are refined and studious, with a strong love for music and poetry. I have but little personal ambition. My opinions, naturally enough, have taken color from my surroundings. I have been a Democrat in politics, and a strong supporter of the South on all national questions.

I mention these facts that the reader may form some conception of the person with whom these pages will largely deal. Let him bring before his mind's eye a small, spare, sinewy, French-looking, aristocratic gentleman, of thirty-five years of age, with gold spectacles and heavy mustache; and he will have a pretty fair picture of what I was when the misfortune befell me of which I am about to speak.

My house stands on one of the most beautiful avenues in C——; it was built more than one hundred years ago, and has been occupied for several generations by my ancestors. The furniture is a history in little, as it were, of the family: each article has a story of its own which renders it all the more dear to me; from the few plain, solid pieces brought over from France by the founder of the family, down through each generation, including the rich additions made to it by my dear mother. And this is as it should be. The dwellings of the "new rich" look like warehouses of furniture-dealers: all is spick and span new, until one is almost tempted, as he wanders through this resplendent grandeur, to look around for the salesman and inquire the price.

Broad verandas, shadowy and social, surround the house, in the Southern style, and the whole is framed in a semi-tropical garden, the finest in the city, where the very trees are bowers of blossoms in their season, and every bush and shrub gives out to the warm air its gorgeous tribute of flowers and perfume.

I am a bachelor, and my household consists simply of servants and of such friends as may from time to time do me the honor to visit me.   My income is so large that I have pretty much withdrawn from the practice of my profession.   I read a great deal, and lead a quiet, pleasant, happy life.

Little did I think that upon this placid existence would be suddenly obtruded the most extraordinary experience that ever fell to the lot of man.

CHAPTER II.

MARY RUDDIMAN.

" In maiden meditation, fancy free."
—*Midsummer Night's Dream, ii. 2.*

WHEN a citizen of the United States has plenty
of money and nothing to do, he naturally drifts
into politics.   If he has not himself any predisposition
in that direction, he will be sought out by the professional politicians and forced into such a career — not, it
may be, from any admiration of his talents, for he may,
perchance, possess none; but from a desire to get their
nands into his " barrel," as it is called in the vernacular
of the day, or into his " pocket," as our ancestors
would have said.   The advance of the world is shown
in the fact that the " pocket " has grown into a "barrel."
Civilization enlarges everything, even corruption.

Being rich and with fair abilities, I was naturally
sought out by the leaders of my party and urged to
become a candidate for this or that public position.
To all these suggestions I had invariably turned a deaf
ear.   As I said before, I have no ambition to shine,
and I looked upon public life as discredited, if not dis-
honored, by the kind of men who ruled it.   It appeared
to me as a sordid and debased struggle of little creatures
for honors that faded from the memories of men almost
as soon as they were won.   Out of the thousands of

public characters who have taken part in our national life, one can count upon the fingers of his two hands the list of those statesmen who have really left any impress on their age; while a still smaller number will be remembered beyond the termination of the century in which they lived. I turned, therefore, from the temptations of this shallow and barren life to the quiet of my own library, and communion with the mighty souls of the past —

> " Those dead but sceptered sovereigns who still rule
> Our spirits from their urns"—

as one might turn from the sprawling and con-temptible contentions of dogs to a banquet of the gods.

But a change had come over me. For the first time in my life I was in love. I had experienced that " pull of the heart " which drew me toward a fair maiden; and a cold and critical analysis made by my mind confirmed the wisdom of my inherited passion. For love, after all, is simply a primal instinct imposed on humanity for the perpetuation of the race. We are all *automata*. Civilized man submits love to the super-vision of his judgment, and there can be no permanent love where the natural physical affinity is not supple-mented by the approval of a trained and cultured intelligence.

Colonel Ruddiman lives ten miles from the town of C——. He is a planter, the last of a long line of planters, old settlers in this section, a man of fine mind and education, who won wounds and honor in com-mand of a South Carolina regiment in the War between the States. The defeat of his section almost broke his heart, and he returned home, at the close of the war, to find his negroes free and his plantation laid waste and woefully dilapidated. He possesses none of the traits of a business man. He would much rather entertain his neighbors than make money off them. He has scarcely enough selfishness to protect his own interests. He is hospitable, generous, a good liver, and fond of joviality and conviviality. For some years after his return from the war he had all he could do to provide a bare living for his family. But he hunted and killed his own hogs, which had run wild into the adjacent forests during his absence, and raised corn enough for his own use.

He has three sons and one daughter. The sons are gallant, high-spirited, fast-riding gentlemen, like their father; fond of all sorts of field sports, and not much given to study; and yet, withal, honorable, intelligent men, on whose faithfulness one might at any time stake his life. Hot partisans of the South, and worshipers of the memory of Lee and Stonewall Jackson, they at the same time are men of just and kindly views toward the people of the North.

The philosophers tell us there is "a law of variation" in nature, whereby its sameness and uniformity are broken up, and new species or varieties are created. If it were not so, "like would produce like" to the end of the chapter, and the dead-level of commonplace would spread, like a stagnant ocean, everywhere. But by that "law of variation" *freaks* occur everywhere;

and people are born whose pedigrees will be searched in vain for any prelude or prophesy of their coming.

Mary Ruddiman was a *freak*. True, she had inherited all the courage, daring, high-spirit and honorable impulses of her parents and ancestors; it would be impossible for her to commit a debased or degrading act. But she was something that none of her predecessors had ever been. There were plenty of *intelligent* Ruddimans; but Mary was the first of her race that was *intellectual*. She had displayed, from childhood, a ravenous appetite for knowledge, and a memory that was abnormal. The Colonel possessed a good-sized library, the result of the accumulations of several generations; and an odd conglomeration of books it was — romances, histories, narratives of travel, religious works and scientific treatises. The latter were a generation or two old, and of little practical value; for it is the peculiar and distinguishing characteristic of science that every ten or twenty years its conclusions are all reversed and set aside, as ridiculous absurdities, and a new set, brand-new, adopted, to be in turn cast overboard, but to rule with pope-like infallibility while they are accepted. Mary devoured everything in this old library, even to the prosiest sermons of forgotten divines who had proved conclusively, to their delighted congregations, that all the human family, except a favored portion of their own little segment of a creed, were hurrying, at railroad speed, to everlasting damnation.

In those days, before my own terrible experience, there was, to me, something dreadful about that old theology. Its advocates conceived of God as a cruel monster, waiting on the other side of the fence of life for the trembling and cowering soul of the dead man to pass through the rails, that He might pounce upon it and plunge it, howling and shrieking, into everlasting flame. It never seemed to have occurred to them to ask why Omnipotence had to stay on the other side of the fence — why He did not invade the domain of life and roast and burn the sinners before our very eyes. But they held rigidly to this horrible belief, in the face of a thousand facts which testify to the benevolence of the all-merciful Father, and the adaptation of His creation, in a million details, to the comfort and happiness of His creatures.

But an old library is, indeed, a sad object to contemplate. It represents so much of abandoned errors and disappointed ambitions, that to examine its shelves is very much like walking through an old church-yard. And what can be sadder than to look upon the graves of the dead and consider that houses, lands, furniture, goods, gold, silver, horses, cattle, books, grief, merriment, love, hate, are all taken away from the departed, and they are all brought down to a little, ghastly, erect stone, and a memory that grows fainter and fainter every day, and at last disappears utterly in the awful abyss of universal oblivion.

Thus an old library is a sort of intellectual graveyard: we find in it hundreds of forgotten books by forgotten men, who sought to drag a fragment of remembrance out of the black waters of Lethe, and fondly hoped that their works would live and occupy the minds of mankind for many generations. How marvelously the living creature shrinks from annihilation! And yet Time will obliterate the memory even of Homer. That universal maw spares nothing that is or was.

> "Time hath, my lord, a wallet at his back,
>   Wherein he puts alms for oblivion;
>   A great-sized monster of ingratitudes:
>   Those scraps are good deeds past, which are devoured
>   As fast as they are made, forgot as soon
>   As done."

But, as the bee finds its honey in almost every flower, so the eager mind of Mary Ruddiman extracted nourishment from all the dead and dusty tomes of her father's library. While her brothers were hunting and fishing or horse-racing, she was seated on the porch, or in a window recess of the library, in the ancient stone house, poring, with bent head, diligently, over her precious volumes. She grew up a tall, angular, shy girl, with fine dark eyes, and an awkward and constrained manner. As such I remembered meeting her some years before the date of this story; and I remember, too, that I scarcely gave her a second glance.

But the negroes had come back to work — they had to work or starve; and, like white men, they would rather work than starve; and, like the average white man, nothing could make them work but the fear that they would starve. And the Colonel received a share of the crop; and the store-keeper and the usurer got nearly all that was left, except enough hog and hominy to keep the ebony machine in operation, and enough cheap goods to cover its nakedness. And so the Colonel prospered again, to some extent, and Mary was sent to an academy in C——, there to be finished off and polished up, after the manner of all eligible young ladies of good families.

Now, it so happened that Miss McGlynn's academy occupied the next house to my own; and I knew her very well, and she stood very high in my estimation. She was a tall, spare, spectacled maiden, of fifty-odd summers; an intelligent, kindly-hearted, good woman. She had three sisters, all unmarried, like herself, who had charge of different studies in the academy, while Miss McGlynn looked after the business management of that flourishing institution. Her sisters were shorter and stouter than herself; cheerful, dapper, kindly little women. It has always seemed to me a reflection on the good sense of the male sex that so many of the very best of the other division of mankind, of each generation, are left unwedded, while a weak and silly creature may be encumbered with suitors and bury three or four husbands. I suppose the average man is not willing to marry a woman he " must look up to." He would rather sit on the pedestal himself, and be worshiped by shallowness, than to kneel at the feet of the noblest creature God ever made. And thus the best of the race cease to be mothers, and humanity is so much the worse off thereby.

One day Miss McGlynn came in to see me, and, with many apologies and hesitations, said she had a strange request to prefer. She had a pupil who was an exceedingly bright young lady, and a great reader. She had gone through every book in the limited library of the academy, and was now ranging up and down, seeking

2

something to devour. The poor girl was really unhappy for want of mental food; and it had occurred to one of her (Miss McGlynn's) sisters, that if I would be kind enough to lend her some works out of my large library, it would be a kindness to them and a real charity to the pupil. I, of course, replied that I would be very glad to do so, and I asked the young lady's name. Miss McGlynn replied that it was Mary Ruddiman.

" What," I said, "the daughter of my old friend, Colonel Ruddiman ? "

" The same," she replied.

" Why," said I, "I am really obliged to you for preferring the request. I have met Miss Ruddiman. I did not know she was in your academy, or I should have called and paid my respects to her ere this. I will lose no time in doing so now."

I escorted Miss McGlynn back to her own house. In a few moments Miss Ruddiman made her appearance in the reception-room. I was surprised to find her greatly changed. Instead of the angular, awkward girl I had seen at her father's house, there came to me a tall, graceful, beautiful woman, with all those rounded outlines and subtle charms which cunning Nature confers upon the other sex for the entrancement of man. Her manner, while self-possessed, was modest and retiring; but intelligence beamed from every line of her fine face; and her eyes had the bright glow of youth and the strength of energy in them.

I took her hand and welcomed her to C——; I spoke of her father and family, and concluded by assuring her that every book in my house, and the owner of them, for that matter, was at her service, and I begged her to make my library her own; that she would find it a quieter place to read and study than the noisy academy, with its drumming pianos and turbulent voices.

She thanked me cordially and promised to accept my invitation. After some further conversation I took my departure, pleased at having been able to render a civility to the daughter of my old friend Colonel Ruddiman.

CHAPTER III.

" SEJANUS. "

" I, thus neglecting worldly ends, all dedicated
To closeness and the bettering of my mind."
—*Tempest, i. 2.*

BUSINESS of importance called me out of town for a day or two. On my return I went straight to my library. Ben — my negro " boy," a man of twenty-five, grandson of one of my father's former slaves, very black physically and quite bright mentally — met me at the door. He pointed significantly with his thumb over his shoulder, and whispered:

" Miss Mary dar. Bin here most of the time since you's gone."

It took me a few seconds to remember who " Miss Mary" was. I looked, and there, in an easy chair, near a window, with her back to the light, and her head bent over a book, I saw a slim, graceful figure, utterly absorbed in her occupation, and unconscious of the presence of Ben or myself. I stepped forward.

" Miss Ruddiman," I said, " I am delighted to see that you have availed yourself of my invitation. You are most welcome — for your father's sake as well as your own."

She blushed and said something about her " intrusion," and explained that she was afraid to take val-

uable books into the academy, lest they should be injured by her careless fellow-students.

I assured her that there was no " intrusion" whatever;
that I was only too glad to have her visit me; that she
must make herself perfectly at home, and that we
would not interfere with each other's pursuits in the
least. I begged her to go on with her reading, and that,
if she would excuse me for a few moments, I would
write a letter to a friend upon a matter of some
urgency.

I took my seat at the table to write, and Miss
Mary was soon again buried in her book.

There is something peculiar in the sensations which
are experienced by a bachelor when he finds himself,
for the first time, under the same roof — his own roof
— with a beautiful young girl. And so my pen
stopped its monotonous scratching, and, as I looked
over at the shapely, stooped head, I fell into meditation.

What a strange fancy for one so young and fair to be
such a book-worm? Was it an affectation? No, for
I had heard that, even as a child, she had been a diligent reader. But did her reading profit her any? As
a physician I knew there were diseased conditions of
the system when the patient consumed very large quantities of food, and remained thin and sickly in spite of
it all, or perhaps because of it all. The appetite was
insatiable, but there was no assimilation of that which
was absorbed. So there were minds that read, and
read, and read, and profited nothing. A mass of information swept over the surface of the brain, but nothing

stuck. There are novel-readers of this kind, who can remember not one thing of or about the romance they read a month ago; who can scarcely keep in their recollection the names of the characters of the novels which they are perusing. Was Miss Mary one of these? Indeed, as a bachelor, — coming in contact with so many shallow creatures in every-day life, chattering, giggling ninnies, — I held the female mind in a kind of contempt. I looked upon the whole sex as pleasant creatures, whose function it was, in the economy of Nature, to keep the male part of humanity from dying out — a kind of agreeable, necessary evil for the maintenance of a race of men. And so I said to myself, I will have some amusement sounding the shallow depths of this young girl's mind.

"Pardon me for interrupting you, Miss Mary," I said, "but you seem to be very fond of reading."

"Yes," she replied, "I am, indeed, very fond of books. Indeed it is a passion with me."

"Why, may I ask?" I inquired.

"A good library," she answered, "seems to me to be a collection of the great personages of all ages, — that is, of their minds, — and the mind is, after all, the better part, the only enduring part, of the individual."

I was struck with astonishment at this reply, uttered, seemingly, without any consciousness of its pith or point. She continued:

"In every generation there are, it seems to me, but a few great souls, and one may go through life without meeting with a single one of them. It has never been my good fortune to encounter any person who stood much above his fellows. But here, in this library, are all the great souls of Greece and Rome, and modern Europe and America, down to the present day. It is as if they sat around this table, ready to talk to me; ready to give me their choicest and most select thoughts — the distilled wisdom of their lives. I can't help but think how many millions of boobies and envious detractors time has swept away into oblivion, while it has left this galaxy of greatness undisturbed. It is the privilege of genius to survive whole generations of maligners. The conflagration of time, which consumes the mean, illumines the great."

I listened with increasing astonishment. This was no dyspeptic of the mind; this was a *thinker*. So young, so fair, and yet so wise! Where did this mind come from? Colonel Ruddiman and his ancestors never thought such thoughts as these. How did this young philosopher spring out of such a generation of fox-hunters and warriors? Like does not, then, always produce like. If it did, there would be absolute uniformity among all human beings; and there is absolute non-uniformity. Neither were these sentences uttered in a pretentious or pedantic manner. Though oracular in their nature, they came from her lips modestly and hesitatingly, as if she feared to put her thoughts into words; as if she did not realize their merit.

I grew interested. I stopped my letter.

I drew my chair nearer to her.

" May I ask," I said, " what work you are reading?"

" Certainly," she replied; " I am reading, for the third time, Ben Jonson's *Sejanus.*"

" Indeed," I said, " that is rather an out-of-the-way and neglected book, nowadays. The world goes wild over Jonson's great contemporary, Shakespeare, — in fact, he is the rage and the fashion, — but it gives little attention to ' rare Ben,' his fellow actor and playwright."

" True," she replied, " and yet there are many passages in his poetry that sound as if they had been written by the pen of Shakespeare himself, while, on the other hand, in his prose writings, especially his *Discoveries*, there are sentences that have all the depth and profoundness, the pith and point, and even the very color, of Bacon's compositions."

" Indeed," I said, more and more astonished with this school-girl. " Have you read Bacon's works? "

" Oh, yes," she said, and she smiled with enthusiasm; " they have been my daily study for years. I found an old edition in my father's library and devoured it years ago. I brought it with me to the school. I have made more than a hundred pages of annotations upon it."

" To publish? " I inquired.

" Oh, no," she said, with a slight blush; " I never thought of anything of that kind. I made them simply for my own instruction and pleasure."

No wonder, I said to myself, that the great philosopher of Verulam said that his thoughts would fall, like seeds, in the minds of those, of future generations, who were fitted to receive them! Here was this American girl, brought up upon a solitary plantation, who eagerly sought out that which generations of her ancestors had neglected to notice; which they had been, indeed, incapable of understanding.

"I had not supposed," I said, wishing to draw her out still farther, "that there was any resemblance between Ben Jonson's prose and Lord Bacon's writings."

"Oh, yes," she said, eagerly, "listen to this:

"'Language most shows a man. *Speak that I may see thee.* It springs out of the most retired and inward parts of us, and is the image of the mind. No glass renders a man's form or likeness so true as his speech.'

"And this," she continued:

"'A fool may talk, but a wise man speaks. . . . It is easier to do many things and continue, than to do one thing long. . . . As when a man is weary of writing, to read; and then again of reading, to write. . . . Though ambition itself be a vice, it is often the cause of great virtue. . . Let them look over all the great and monstrous wickedness; they shall never find those in poor families. They are the issue of the wealthy giants and the mighty hunters: whereas no *great work, or worthy of praise or memory, but came out of poor cradles.* . . . I have considered our whole life is like a play: wherein every man, forgetful of himself, is in travail with expression of another. . . . Placed high on the top of all virtue, they looked down on the Stage of the World, and contemned the Play of Fortune. For, though the most be players, some must be spectators.'"

"Really," said I, "you astonish me. Are you reading from Ben Jonson? Why, the sentences have all the pith, condensation and wisdom of Bacon. And how curiously that last sentence agrees with the rhymes that have come down to us by tradition; where Shake-speare was asked, in reference to the expression, 'All the world's a stage, and all the men and women merely players,'

> " 'If but stage acting all the world displays,
>   Where shall we find spectators for our plays ? '

" And the answer given:

> " 'But little of the much we see we do;
>   We are both actors and spectators too.'

" That," said I, " is the very thought you have just read; 'the stage of the world,—the play of fortune,— for, though the most be players, some must be specta-tors.' It is all very strange. You give me a new in-terest in Ben Jonson's writings."

" Indeed!" she replied; " I am astonished that an intelligent age has paid so little attention to them. The *Discoveries* alone is a mine of profound and original thought."

" You have spoken of passages that have reminded you of the pen of Shakespeare. Can you give me any instances? I have supposed Jonson to be rather a tame and prosy poet, distinguished more by learning than genius; that, at least, is the common verdict of our modern critics."

" It is altogether an error," she replied; " take these verses, for instance, from *Every Man out of his Humor*, the very opening of the play:

> " 'Who is so patient of this impious world
>   That he can check his spirit, or rein his tongue ?
>   Or who hath such a dead, unfeeling sense,
>   That heaven's horrid thunders cannot wake ?

> To see the earth cracked with the weight of sin,
> Hell gaping under us, and o'er our heads
> Black, ravenous ruin, with her sail-stretched wings,
> Ready to sink us down, and cover us.' "

" That is a grand figure of speech," I said. " ' Black, ravenous ruin, with her sail-stretched wings.' There is surely imagination enough in that."

" Yes," she said, eagerly; " listen to this picture of Sejanus' exultation:

> " ' Great and high
> The world knows only two, that's Rome and I.
> My roof receives me not; 'tis air I tread;
> *And at each step I feeel my advanced head*
> *Knock out a star in heaven.* Reared to this height,
> All my desires seem modest, poor and slight,
> That did before sound impudent. 'Tis place,
> Not blood, discerns the noble and the base. '

" Is that in Ben Jonson?" I said. " You astonish me. Its splendid extravagance reminds me of some lines in *Henry V.* — ah, here they are:

" ' I will not change my horse with any that treads but on four pasterns, *ca, ha!* He bounds from the earth as if his entrails were hairs; *le cheval volant,* the Pegasus, *qui a les narines de feu!* When I bestride him I soar, I am a hawk; he trots the air; *the earth sings when he touches it: the basest horn of his hoof is more musical than the pipe of Hermes.*' "

" Splendid !" she cried, enthusiastically; " it is grand; it is the same magnificent daring of gorgeous metaphor. The very words are the same ! ' 'Tis air I tread;' ' he trots the air.' "

" And what a grand adjuration," she continued, " is this, put into the mouth of Arruntius:

> " ' Still dost thou suffer, Heaven! Will no flame,
> No heat of sin, make thy just wrath to boil,
> In thy distempered bosom, and o'erflow
> The pitchy blazes of impiety
> Kindled beneath thy throne? Still canst thou sleep,
> Patient, while vice doth make an antick face
> At thy dread power, and blow dust and smoke
> Into thy nostrils! Jove, will nothing wake thee?
> Must vile Sejanus pull thee by the beard,
> Ere thou wilt open thy black-lidded eye
> And look him dead? Well, snore on, dreaming gods;
> And let this last of that proud giant-race
> Heave mountain upon mountain 'gainst your state.' "

" And you really think *Sejanus* is a great production?" I asked.

" Magnificent," she replied; " in its description of the corrupt life of the Empire it is terrible! It represents a most dreadful contrast between Sejanus entering the Temple of Apollo, with the senators cringing most servilely before him, paying him the adoration due a god; and the same Sejanus, after the Emperor's letter has been read, and he falls never to rise again, torn to pieces by the very mob that was just howling his praises. And how, like a running commentary from our own thoughts, come in the utterances of the honest but sarcastic Arruntius. As he looks upon the servile courtiers cringing around Sejanus, he says:

> " ' Gods! how the sponges open and take in,
> And shut again! Look! Look! Is not he blest
> That gets a seat in eye-reach of him? More
> That comes in ear or tongue-reach? Oh, but most
> *Can claw his subtle elbow, or with a buz*
> *Fly-blow his ears.'* . . .

> " ' See, see! What troops of his officious friends
> Flock to salute my lord, and start before
> My great proud lord! to get a lord-like nod!
> Attend my lord unto the senate-house!
> Bring back my lord! like servile ushers, make
> Way for my lord! Proclaim his idol lordship
> More than ten criers, or six noise of trumpets!
> Make legs, kiss hands, and *take a scattered hair*
> *From my lord's eminent shoulder!* ' "

" What observation," I said, " is revealed in that last touch! It brings the picture distinctly before the mind's eye. Read on."

" And then," she continued, " listen to this dreadful picture of the doom of the fallen favorite an hour afterward:

> " ' Sentenced by the senate
> To lose his head; which was no sooner off,
> But that and the unfortunate trunk were seized
> By the rude multitude; who, not content
> With what the froward justice of the state
> Officiously had done, with violent rage
> Have rent it limb from limb. A thousand heads,
> A thousand hands, ten thousand tongues and voices,
> Employed at once in several acts of malice!
> Old men not staid with age, virgins with shame,
> Late wives with loss of husbands, mothers of children,
> Losing all grief in joy of his sad fall,
> Run quite transported with their cruelty!
> These mounting at his head, these at his face,
> These digging out his eyes, those with his brains
> Sprinkling themselves, their houses and their friends;
> Others are met, have ravished thence an arm,
> And deal small pieces of the flesh for favors.
> The whole and all of what was great Sejanus,
> And, next to Cæsar, did possess the world,
> Now torn and scattered, as he needs no grave;
> Each little dust covers a little part:
> So lies he nowhere and yet often buried.' "

" What a dreadful picture!" I exclaimed. " I can recall nothing in literature equal to this violent contrast between the base servility of mankind and its horrible cruelty; and the worst of it is that the story is historically true. One is tempted to cry out against human nature for this worse than beast-like baseness."

" Oh!" she replied, " the whole play is wonderful. The minute, accurate knowledge which it reveals of the daily, familiar life of the Roman people of that age is only equaled by its loathing of the infamy of mankind. It seems to have been written by one who had suffered great wrongs, and was embittered against his kind."

From this our conversation flowed on to the other great writers of that wonderful Elizabethan age; an age when men's minds seemed to have been broader, and their thoughts more intense than they were in any succeeding generation; and I was astonished to find that this school-girl was familiar with them all: Shakespeare, Beaumont and Fletcher, Massinger, Spenser, Marlowe, and all the rest. She seemed to have read everything, and to have remembered everything; and I was surprised to find that her criticisms were always wise and thoughtful.

CHAPTER IV.

GROWING TOGETHER.

> " So we grew together
> Like to a double cherry, seeming parted,
> But yet an union in partition."
> — *Midsummer Night's Dream, iii. 2.*

EVERY day Miss Mary, as soon as her school duties were finished, found her way into my library. Every day we held lengthy conversations together. Every day my opinion of her mind and character was heightened. On Saturdays and Sundays we took long walks together, into the fields, when I discoursed to her upon my favorite study, botany. She was an apt scholar.

To my surprise I began to note the fact that when she was not with me I had a vague sense of something lacking. I was restless, uncomfortable, almost unhappy. Every day the pleasure of greeting her shone brighter from my eyes, and it seemed to me that every day her welcome of me grew warmer. " And why not? " said I to myself. " We are the only beings in this place who share the same thoughts and the same studies." To the average man and woman around us the era-making Elizabethan period was but a name. To us it was the visible interference of the hand of God in the affairs of men, through the mediumship of

mighty intellects, who have affected the minds of all
subsequent generations, and whose power will increase
with the growth of population and the development of
civilization on the earth.

And so we read and studied together, and talked
together; and before I was aware of it, I — the ascetic
bachelor, Doctor Anthony Huguet — I, who despised
all womankind — was deeply in love with Colonel
Ruddiman's fair and wise young daughter. And I
could not fail to see, with all modesty, that my feelings
were fully reciprocated. The very tendrils of our being
seemed to be intertwining and interlacing with each
other, like the roots of two plants growing closely
together, in an inseparable, undistinguishable mass. I
realized, for the first time, what the despised passion
called love really meant. I perceived that it was a
going out of one's self — a divine unselfishness; a
grand necessity imposed on humanity by Him who
made us all; a merging together of two minds, souls,
natures; a lifting up, a glorifying of the whole creature.

I could realize that God had forced upon us this
passion, for His own purposes; He did not vilely enslave
us to it, but treated us as His friends and co-workers;
and covered our instincts with splendor and beauty,
in which the hard lines of fate disappeared, buried in
flowers.

Every day the passion grew upon me, until I found
myself absolutely wretched separated from my love. I
met her with dancing eyes, and in reply her eyes danced
again, brightened by the red blushes that swept over
her.

But why prolong the story of this most charming period of my existence — for even its pains graduated into such delights that the pains became pleasures?

Suffice it to say our hearts spoke to each other by a thousand subtle modes of speech, long before our tongues dared frame our thoughts. The course of true love, in our case, ran smoothly indeed. There were no rocks in the channel to torture the current into the foam or spray of tears. Many a time afterwards, from the depths of the blackest and most horrid despair, did I look back to that golden, sun-lighted period, as the followers of Lucifer, " the fallen star of the morning," may, in the midst of the black stench of sulphur smoke, and the red-flashing, terrifying flames of hell, have recalled the unspeakable delights of the glorious, flower-covered valleys of Paradise.

I loved. I was beloved. There were no family objections to be raised on either side. We were social equals. I was rich. It seemed to me that Heaven, unwalled, lay spread before my feet. I had but to advance and take possession of it.

Little, little did I dream of the awful barrier that was soon to rise up and shut me out from my Eden.

CHAPTER V.

AMBITION.

"By that sin fell the angels; how can man, then,
The image of his Maker, hope to win by it?"
— *Henry VIII., iii. 2.*

I HAVE already said that I am not naturally ambitious. The scrambles and squabbles of public life have no charms for me. I have no respect for that kind of honor which belongs not to the man himself, but to the place he occupies; and which leaves him as soon as he is sundered from the place. It seems to me to be the smallest and the most unsubstantial of all human glories. Who can recall the long list of Roman consuls? And yet they were mightier than kings in their day — dreaded to the uttermost limits of the civilized world. But they are gone and forgotten, while the memory of Homer, of Plato, of Socrates is still fresh upon the tongues of men, and they stand out, limned upon the background of the ages, as distinctly as the living heroes of our own era.

And yet I had no claim to be regarded as a philanthropist. I wished well to the whole human family; but I loved my leisure and my pleasures too much to go forth and do battle for it. Life was very delightful to me. My home, my friends, my garden, my books, and now, above all, my love! Who would think to leave all these and wrangle and wrestle in the mud of politics, for the temporary honors or the vile spoils of public life? I felt like setting the dogs on the men who called upon me to tempt me into the dirty puddle of this unclean strife.

But Mary Ruddiman was ambitious. Not for herself; but she had, in her partial love, formed an estimate of me and my abilities far beyond what I deserved. She believed she saw in me a great man, a great orator and statesman, sunk and lost in sybaritic retirement and luxury. We had many an argument upon this subject. She told me I must shake off my lethargy. I must rouse myself and do justice to my genius. The South — the new South, the unhappy South, darkened by the shadows of its great disasters; humbled in the eyes of the unthinking nations by failure; overwhelmed by the numbers, wealth and intellectual power of the North — needed such men as I, to lift her up, and guide her to greater and brighter destinies. The standing of a country did not depend, she said, upon mere population, or the number of bales of cotton it produced; nor even upon the splendor of its cities, or the wealth of its people, but upon the God-given intellects of which it could boast. We must prove to mankind, she exclaimed, that our warmer skies do not, as some have claimed, lessen the mental capacities; that the fibre of the brain may be as firm in the land of the magnolias as in the lands of snow and ice; because the greatest intellects of past ages were nourished in climates as sunny as our own. " Rouse thyself," she cried, "from thy torpor — let thy weak, wanton indifference be shaken to air, like the dew-drop from the lion's mane! Be just to thyself!"

It was beautiful to see her enthusiasm. She grew eloquent upon the theme of my greatness. She quoted Ben Jonson:

> "'Tis place,
> Not blood, discerns the noble and the base."

It is one of the easiest things in the world for even a modest man to be persuaded that he is really greater than his own estimate of himself. Especially when the argument is enforced by a graceful, youthful form, a pair of glowing, glorious eyes, a couple of shapely, ruddy lips, and the eloquent gesticulations of the most charming arms and hands in the world, reinforced by all the love and adoration that can muster in a man's heart. And so, day by day, I began to think, more earnestly, that the world was, indeed, really longing and waiting for me to serve and save it; and that it would be a crime against my race and my country, and especially my section, to longer delay the revelation of my greatness.

Mary planned it all out. She said I must first go to the House of Representatives in Washington. My wealth, my social standing, my education, my talents would entitle me to that. Then I must pave the way to enter, in a few years, the Senate of the United States; — and forthwith she drew a vivid picture of herself sitting in the gallery, listening to me pouring forth the eloquence that would delight and enthrall the world. I was fool enough to believe it all.

Then, with her usual energy, she wrote at once to

her father, giving her plans and views. The Colonel, like all men of his class and caste in the South, was an instinctive politician; and it seemed moreover that he was an influential one, and resided in the same Congressional district with myself. The Colonel was a whole-souled man, and he had taken me warmly into his heart of hearts, as the accepted lover of his only daughter; and he and his sons entered at once with zeal upon the task of smoothing my way to the Democratic nomination.

It was then approaching midsummer. The school was to close for a few weeks; and Miss Mary was to return home. I received a cordial invitation from the Colonel to visit the Ruddiman mansion; and I accompanied my beloved in the stage which bore her to the parental roof. It was a hot and dusty ride, over a country parched by the excessive heat of the season; but such is the charm of love that, as I look back upon it, it seems to me I rode through the valleys of the Hesperides, fanned by cooling breezes from the Holy Mountains, the whole landscape ablaze with many-hued flowers and foliage.

CHAPTER VI.

LAWYER BURYHILL.

" Get thee glass eyes,
And, like a scurvy politician, seem
To see the things thou dost not."
— *Lear, iv. 6.*

THERE was a cordial Southern welcome for me, from
the Colonel and all the family. It must be admitted that our people are a big-hearted, hospitable race,
who can never do too much for those they respect or love;
or, I might add, too little for those they dislike. Their
loves and hates partake of their summer suns: all their
opinions are convictions; all their feelings passions.
But the strong sense of personal honor has survived
here while it seems to be dying out under the blight of
the commercial, trading spirit of the North. Beyond
Mason and Dixon's line politics are an individual grab
for profits; in the South they are devotion to ideas and
theories of statecraft, which may not be correct, but
are always respectable from their sincerity. One of
the most beautiful traits of Southern character is its
fiery devotion to the great men of its section. The
South stands by them with passionate partisanship, ex-
aggerating their best qualities and ignoring their weak
ones. It honors them living and worships them dead.
In the North to be a great man is simply to invite un-

sympathetic criticism of every detail of the individual's career and character; to become the conspicuous target for limitless abuse and insult while living, and to receive halting, grudging praise when dead, with the promise of a monument which is rarely built. The South regards genius with grateful eyes, lifted to heaven; the North with its nose in the air, to smell out the faults of its victim.

The prosperous Southern plantation is a sort of little kingdom in itself, and largely self-supporting. It runs in a circle. As a Southerner once said: " We raise corn to raise the hogs; we raise hogs to raise the negroes; and we raise the negroes to raise the corn." But the directing white intelligence reserves to itself a small percentage of the net profits, for the luxuries of life and the adornments of civilization, including books and newspapers; and thus the higher life of the world is scattered, in points of light, through vast regions of country, gradually penetrating to wider and wider circles in the darkness of primeval ignorance. And thus He who runs the whole great automatic machine is carrying out His purposes, and gradually lifting up mankind.

The life of the plantation is so monotonous and isolated that an intelligent man, with new ideas and new facts, coming from the outside world, is a God-given boon and blessing. The brain, weary with contemplating the same fields, buildings, barns, pig-pens, animals, trees and hills, rises, with absolute delight, out of its ruts, and is conscious of new sensations and new capabilities. And so we sat, by the hour,—the Colonel and his sons and I,—upon the broad porch, smoking and discussing the affairs of the whole world. The porch is the Southern academy.

And the neighbors, to whom the Colonel's grand scheme had been communicated in confidence, began to gather, returning late at night on horseback, or sharing the hospitality of the household for the night. And the young ladies of the neighborhood, bright, attractive, high-spirited girls, called to gossip and chat or ride with Miss Mary.

It was a very bright and pleasant life — kindly and social and generous. No man was trying to outwit or plunder his fellow. The discussions of politics — apart from the natural, local prejudices — were all conducted on a high plane — the good of their section. There was, to be sure, a sort of half-expressed feeling that the South had been caught in a kind of eddy of dead water full of the drift-wood of old opinions, far remote from the great, surging, swollen, rapidly-advancing stream of the world. And yet they felt, too, that that stream was covered with the *débris* of selfishness, and its shores lined with cruel wreckers; and that its waters poured over the drowned caves of abysmal and multitudinous want; and that — in comparison with it all—their lives were honorable and sweet and idyllic.

There was Major Archibald McFettridge, who had lost his left arm at Gettysburg. A Scotchman, with all the best traits of his great race—shrewd, kindly, capable; ready to die for his opinions, but with an open eye in the meantime for the main chance. His heart was as broad as his accent. He owned the next plantation and was universally liked and respected.

And there, too, was Captain William Braynton, who had lost two brothers in the war, and had been severely wounded himself, more than once. He also was a planter, a high-mettled, chivalric, but undemonstrative and quiet gentleman.

And Major Berrisford came too, a neighbor with a large family of handsome daughters, rather " under the harrow," as they say, financially. But he also had a fine war-record, and was much liked. In fact, a good war-record in our section is equal to a coat-of-arms of the nobility in other countries.

And occasionally Doctor Magruder, an intelligent physician of the old school, of the neighboring village of N——, drove over and took part in our discussions. A well-to-do man, of resolute character, and generally liked. He was a Northern man by birth, but fully in sympathy with the people of his new home, while not permitting any disparagement of the land of his nativity.

It was pleasant to sit, in the cool of the evening, on the piazza, and listen to the war-stories of these old heroes. To the philosophic mind they illustrated what a curious fighting animal man is, and how singularly, under high excitements, he considers life and limb as of less consequence than insistance upon his own opinions. It seemed to me strange that a man should be willing to go out of the world to improve the world, when, after he goes out of it, the world can be of no further interest to him. The presence of vast war-passions, in great bodies of men, inciting them to dash themselves to death, is one of the marvels of the world. I suppose those passions are the survivals of emotions and habits possessed by our remote savage ancestors, when every particle of food a man swallowed had to be fought for, and one man lived only by another man's death. The human being, as all wars testify, is, when you take off the crust of social refinement, simply a ferocious wild beast.

I was interested especially in one story which was told, and which illustrated how familiar one can become with the horrors of battle. A Confederate general, with, as it seems, a ghastly sense of humor, rose from the battle-field, where he had been sleeping, after a hard-fought fight, and drew his cloak around him, for the morning was chilly. His place of slumber had been close to an extemporized field-hospital, and all around him lay dead bodies and amputated legs and arms. He saw one of his colonels approaching him through the mist of early morning, and, stooping down, he picked up an arm which had been taken from some poor fellow, and, hiding it under his cloak, approached his friend.

"Good morning, Colonel," he said, extending the dead hand from beneath his cloak.

"Good morning, General," replied the Colonel, grasping the cold, dead member.

The General stepped back, leaving the naked hand and arm in the grasp of the Colonel, who turned white with horror, and almost fainted when he perceived what he held. And the General broke into a roar of laughter which was interrupted only by the renewal of the battle. Think of it! Men on the very verge of eternity practicing such jokes with the mutilated fragments of mortality.

There was one man who sometimes came over to our conferences on the porch, in his handsome carriage, driven by his black boy, who, although always made welcome and treated with uniform courtesy and hospitality, never failed to cast a chilling shadow over our intercourse. This was Lawyer Buryhill, of C——. We all have our instincts, and mine warned me against this man from the very first. And yet he was not ill-looking. He was a medium-sized man, of dark complexion, active in his motions and pleasant in his manners; but there was a look out of his furtive, rapidly-rolling black eyes, as if they would grasp everything they encountered — a greedy, cruel look. And his hair stood up, especially upon the middle line of his head, in a way that reminded me unpleasantly of the bristles I once observed on the back of a hyena in a menagerie. The suavity of his mouth and the softness of his mellifluous voice were strongly and promptly contradicted by the hardness and the greed of his eyes, which, as from a watch-tower, looked out over the sham of his face, and seemed to say to the observer, " Do not be deceived by these wrecker's lights; here is the real man. Beware of the rocks." Indeed, it always seemed to me that he regarded those about him in a sort of rapacious, proprietary way, very like a man-eating tiger who drools a little at the mouth as he contemplates the group of unconscious Hindoos he is about to spring upon. So when Buryhill looked at his fellow-man it was as if his softly working mouth tasted the pleasant flavor of *property*.

He was from New York. He was not popular. It was said — but no one knew with how much truth — that he had been what is called a " Tombs shyster," but, becoming involved in some transactions too disreputable for even that corrupt atmosphere, he had removed to the South. He had made a good deal of money dealing in tax titles, buying up outstanding claims to real estate and making them good by litigation, and in other questionable ways. He had no friends, but was generally feared for his capacities for evil. And, moreover, it is the rule with Southern gentlemen to treat a man in the most courteous manner up to the point where they find it necessary to shoot him.

I did not understand at that time the reason of his visits to Colonel Ruddiman's house. I ascertained afterwards that he had fixed upon the Colonel as one of his victims. He regarded him as a careless, jovial, generous sort of man, a fool in his eyes, who owed a good deal of money and neglected to look after his own business in his zealous devotion to public affairs. And so he proceeded to quietly buy up the mortgages against the Ruddiman plantation and certain outstanding tax titles in the names of third parties, and was steadily weaving his net around the unfortunate man. But behind his natural rapacity there was another reason for his visits. He had noticed Mary Ruddiman's charms of form and face; he contemplated them in very much the same spirit with which he would regard the fine points of a handsome race-horse. They showed *blood*, which he sadly lacked, and his marriage to her would, he knew, give him a standing in the community which he could never win by his own merits. To Miss Mary, as might be expected, he was utterly loathsome: she shrank from him instinctively, as a child shrinks from a reptile, although at this time she did not dream that he had turned his proprietary gaze upon her. But he was a man of wealth and professional prominence, and therefore to be treated as a gentleman, for in the South (as in England) the professions and the land furnish the gentlemen.

CHAPTER VII.

ABIGAIL.

"The musky daughter of the Nile,
With plaited hair and almond eyes."
—*Holmes.*

AMONG the servants at the Ruddiman house I met with a surprise.

It was the second day after my arrival. I was passing along the corridor, soon after breakfast, when I came face to face with a young girl. At the first glance I thought she was one of Miss Mary's visitors; but, as I stepped aside to let her pass, a second look showed me that she was one of those unfortunate beings who, while nearly white, hold in their veins a mere fraction of negro blood, sufficient, however, according to our social prejudices, to damn her white blood to unlimited public contempt. Even I—gentleman as I claim to be—found that the hat which I had raised to her, as a Saxon, instinctively fell as I realized she was an octoroon. And yet many an Egyptian Pharaoh had taken to his breast, and covered with his crown, beauties that were many shades darker than the skin I looked upon. Cæsar, and Cicero, and Pompey, and Cato, had loved and wedded women more dusky of hue than this fair creature. In the abandon of our pride over the whiteness of our skin, bleached by thousands of years of northern storms and ice and snow, we forget that the greatest part of mankind, including all the great nations of antiquity, Egyptians, Hindoos, Assyrians, Greeks and Romans, were much darker than ourselves ; that it is only of late years that the pale-faced Goth is leading the advance of the world ; and that, if we take out of the accumulations of the past those arts, inventions, works and thoughts derived from people as shadowy in hue as our own mulattoes, there would be little left for our civilization to boast of.

These thoughts did not come to me at the moment, for I was lost in astonishment. Perceiving that she belonged to the inferior caste, I replaced my hat and stopped to talk familiarly with her. She said, in answer to my question, that her name was Abigail. I learned afterward that she was the natural daughter of one of Colonel Ruddiman's brothers, now deceased, and acted as waiting-maid to Miss Mary. She was of medium height and plump of figure; the lines of her person flowed into each other everywhere with graceful curves; the wrists, I noticed, were large; the hands small and soft, the breasts large, the limbs taper; the whole figure was beautiful and suggestive of luxuriousness. Her eyes were large, long and black, and the pupils seemed to cover the iris; the face was exceedingly handsome; only in the fullness of the lips and chin, and the non-Gothic, almond-shaped eyes were there any indications of the *bar-sinister* in her pedigree; her hair black and flowing, but in graceful curls. Her countenance was modest and betokened unusual intelligence. In fact, there was such decorum and fitness in her replies that I found myself forgetting that she belonged to the proscribed class, and when we parted I lifted my hat to her as I would have done to a duchess. I learned subsequently from Miss Mary that Abigail possessed a fair education, and had even picked up some knowledge of music. They had been very much together as children, and, although the relation of mistress and servant had always existed between them, Miss Mary had become greatly attached to her. Indeed, the original and strong mind of that young lady had risen, to some degree, above the prejudices of her caste; and she saw the white of Abigail and not the fraction of the negro, and treasured her for her affectionate nature and many good qualities. Indeed, she often spoke to me of her sympathy for the poor girl. Abigail had many gloomy moments which her mistress knew well how to interpret. The seven-eighths of her blood protested against being dragged down to servile life by the other eighth. She well knew what a dreadful barrier of prejudice stood in the way of her becoming the wife of any respectable white man; while she shrank, with Saxon horror, against descending still lower in the social scale to marriage with one of the darker stock. And yet she was fair and graceful and intelligent, and fitted to make any man happy. But society had placed gyves on her feet, and manacles on her hands; she could fall, but she could not rise. The inextinguishable taint of the slave was upon her; a taint more dreadful than leprosy; more fearful than the mark which the Lord God branded on the brow of the murderer Cain. High walls of caste were built around her, and she could not see the sun of hope shining into her prison-house, even at high noon. The whole world was banded against her — against her, a white woman! All that was bright and cultured and beautiful in the world pointed her downward to the abyss of dishonor, and with jeers and mockings told her that her white womanhood was fit only for degradation. The humblest foreign immigrant — poor, ignorant, starving — might rise; his children, in another generation, might be lords in the land; nay, his son might ascend to the topmost chair of state: for them and theirs there were no social limitations; but for the man or woman marked with the ancient brand of abhorrent slavery, surrounded by century-old prejudices, there is no future, no hope; life is a grave; the eighth, the sixteenth, the thirty-second part of the despised blood is enough to mark their ostracism. This is the only case in America where the majority does not rule; where the smallest minority overwhelms the largest plurality. I might aptly quote Hamlet:

> " So oft it chances in particular men,
>   That for some vicious mole of nature in them,
>   As in their birth (wherein they are not guilty,
>   Since nature cannot choose its origin);
>   By their overgrowth of some complexion,
>   Oft breaking down the forts and pales of reason;
>   Or by some habit, that too much o'er-leavens
>   The form of plausive manners; — that these men, —
>   Carrying, I say, the stamp of one defect,
>   Being nature's livery or fortune's star, —
>   Their virtues else, be they as pure as grace,
>   As infinite as man may undergo,

> Shall in the general censure take corruption
> From that particular fault; — the dram of bale
> Doth all the noble substance off and out
> To his own scandal."

Many times Mary and I conversed together about poor Abigail and her hard lot; and I must say that I began to conceive therefrom new ideas touching the negro race. I had never been hostile to them, and had always treated those I came in contact with kindly; but it seemed to me that, thinking over Miss Mary's poor handmaid, my heart commenced to soften toward them more than ever. I realized, as I had never done before, the vast burden they carried of prejudice and injustice. Ah! little did I think that the time was not far distant when I should realize the pressure of a heavier burden in most dreadful fashion.

CHAPTER VIII.

THE DEBATE.

> " When mind meets mind
> To blend and brighten."
>
> —*Mrs. Sigourney.*

ONE pleasant afternoon a group of us sat upon the Colonel's broad veranda, smoking and talking, when the conversation chanced to turn upon the all-pervading negro question. There was a good deal of fiery invective upon the subject.

This is how it came about: Colonel Ruddiman expressed the conviction that only the Anglo-Saxon was fit for self-government, and that attempts to that end, by any other race, could only end in bloodshed and anarchy; and he pointed to the French Revolution and the Reign of Terror in justification of his opinion.

I was lying back in a hammock, watching the smoke curling in wreaths from my cigar, when, from pure wantonness and idleness, I took issue with him. I replied by pointing to the fact that the French people had, for some years past, succeeded in maintaining a very respectable republic, with peace, order and progress; and I expressed the opinion that the Reign of Terror was a godsend to the oppressors of mankind, for it had been their stock in trade for nearly a century. I further said that the French Revolution was the great-

est blessing that had ever fallen to the lot of the French
people; in fact, it had lifted up all Europe.   A man,
I said, had only to read Arthur Young's description of
the awful condition of the French peasantry, just before
that great outbreak, when he saw them coming down,
half-naked and half-starved, out of the mountains, to
pay the government tax on salt,—the only thing out of
which the King and courtiers could wring an income,
because it was the last necessity of the barest and most
wretched animal existence,—to realize the justice of
that revolution.   All the European nations, I said,
were of one stock—or, strictly speaking, of two stocks,
a dark and a light one, commingled in varying propor-
tions; and the real differences of men depended on their
environment and conditions.

Major McFettridge, who was something of a radical,
and had read the history of the French Revolution and
the Napoleonic wars with the attention and interest of
a soldier, confirmed my view.

"Indeed," he said, "it was vera plain that the ancient *régime* could na gae langer at the auld gait.   It
was royalty and not the people that brought about the
Reign o' Terror.   There was nae way out o' it but rav-
elution.   When a sma' minority owned a' the land and
the great majority paid a' the taxes, the eend was certain.   I do na wonder that Robbie Burns sympathized
wi' the French people; every honest man wad do so.
Hear Robbie:

> " 'May liberty meet wi' success!
>   May prudence protect her from evil!
>   May tyrants and tyranny tire in the mist,

> And wander their way to the devil.
> Here's freedom to him that wad read,
> Here's freedom to him that wad write!
> There's none ever feared
> That the truth should be heered,
> But they wham the truth wad indict.'

" God bless Robbie," said the Major, as if to himself; " when he says a thing there is nae use of onybody else trying to say it any ither way after him."

" But, Major," said I, " it seems to me that you are not consistent; you do not apply Burns' noble sentiments to any but the French and Scotch and other foreign nations. How about the negroes? "

The whole company looked at me with astonishment.

" Is it the black de'ils?" asked the Major.

" Certainly," I said, seeing I was in for it; and, like Macbeth, I was

> " Stepped in so far, that, should I wade no more,
> Returning were as tedious as go o'er."

" Why, surely," said the Colonel, " the principles that apply to white men do not reach those wretched creatures; they are hardly human."

" Simian," said Lawyer Buryhill, who had a smattering of scientific knowledge.

" They prove the truth of Darwinism," added Major Berrisford; " they are one of the links that bind our own race to the animal creation."

" No, no, gentlemen," I replied; " do not be unfair to them: a race that could produce a Toussaint L'Ouverture is not simian. You cannot rank a coal-black negro, like Toussaint — who compelled the surrender of a French army, under Brandicourt; took twenty-eight Spanish batteries in four days; and, with half their force, compelled the surrender of an English army — with the monkeys. He brought Napoleon's brother-in-law, Leclerc, to his knees, and was only overcome at last by treachery. The darkest page in the history of the great Corsican is his treatment of that magnificent negro. He kidnaped him by fraud and left him to die of starvation, and be eaten by the rats, in a French prison. If he had treated a white general in that manner, the whole world would have risen up to denounce him; but Toussaint's dusky skin justified everything."

"But will you not admit," asked Buryhill, who was more Southern than the Southerners in his intolerance of the blacks, "that the negro stands nearer to the brute world than all other races?"

"No," I said; "I do not admit it. But, even if it were true, there is a vast, an impassable gulf between the lowest man and the highest ape; a gap which only the creative presence of the great God, with vast designs for the human race, could fill. And, if the taint of the brute origin adheres to the negro, does it not cling to us all? If the son of a murderer stands disgraced, does not his grandson inherit something of the shame? If the white man is but a bleached negro, what right has he to mock his dark progenitor? The credit is due, not to him, but to the cold and clouds of the stormy north, or the darkness of the troglodytes' caves, during myriads of years. But, after all, the matter must be considered from a higher level.

What right have we to question God—the recipients of whose bounty we are, for life itself and all its blessings—and ask Him why He sees fit to put other men on this planet, and paint their skin a different color from our own? It would be better for us to thank Him, on our bent knees, for sweeping away the ape-like intermediate forms—half man and half brute—with all a man's cunning, and all a brute's ferocity—which once occupied the earth in swarming multitudes. Fancy a world thick with such soulless monsters, and man contending, in the midst of them, for a foothold on the planet. Civilization would have been impossible."

"Oh," said Buryhill, with a sneer, for he had observed Mary listening at the open window, "the best intelligences are now agreed that the belief in God is one of the fables of the world's youth; and that there is nothing in the universe but this self-acting, self-perpetuating thing we call Nature."

"Indeed!" I said, warming up, for I too was conscious of Mary's presence. "Indeed! why, you use the very intelligence which God has given you to deny that there is an Intelligence in the universe. You conceive of a great work-shop without a master mechanic. You perceive a million delicate adjustments in nature, and you conclude that those adjustments adjusted themselves. You would have design, but no designer. Consider it but a moment. To permit you to deny God, with your thoughts and your tongue, there have to be ten thousand curious and cunning inventions applied to your own body, so subtle that science has not yet been able to apprehend, much less explain, but a few of them. The process of thought is inexplicable on any physical basis. How can a mass of pulpy matter, which we call the brain, dart out lines of something that shall travel to the remotest borders of the milky way, and weigh, as in a grocer's balance, the very planets and suns? If you would deny God, you must begin by denying yourself, for the power to think that there is or is not a God implies a thought-power somewhere in the universe of which your intellect is a fragment or fraction. It is impossible to conceive a vast creation without a general intelligence; a creation possessing only spots of unconnected intelligence, scattered here and there, self-born, self-luminous, and mortal."

"Vera true," said Major McFettridge; "if it was na for some great power, — as Burns says,

"Some power supreme, whose mighty scheme
These woes of mine fulfill," —

this weel-ordered universe wad fly to pieces before you could raise up your han'. You are right; Doctor, I hold ye're right in that."

"But," said Captain Berrisford, "we are wandering from the subject — the negroes. Do you pretend, Doctor Huguet, that the black man is equal to the white?"

"No," I replied; "I do not say what the black race may come to be in time, under favorable conditions, but at present I admit that they are an inferior people. It must be remembered, however, that for countless generations they have occupied the most malarial and unhealthy lands in the world — lands in which no white child can pass the age of puberty, in which no white adult's life is worth a year's purchase. The relations of *bacteria* to the races are as yet but little understood. We have simply progressed far enough in knowledge to understand their existence. It may be established hereafter that our white superiority of brain and beauty of body are due to the fact that our ancestors dwelt for long ages in lands so cold and inhospitable that microbe-life could not endure it. The negro race has lived for possibly hundreds of thousands of years in regions where every breath they breathed was full of hostile forms of life. Their black skins, their swollen faces, their depressed noses, represent the physical degrada-tion of ages of such conditions, with the pressure of brutal ignorance and insufficient food."

" Yes," said Doctor Magruder, " I see it is now claimed by a new school of scientists that the mental inferiority of the negroes is due to the fact that the sutures of the skull close at an earlier age than those of other races, and the thick skull, thus becoming solid, arrests the growth of the brain."

" Precisely," I said; " and the school-teachers will tell you that the negro child, up to a certain age, is fully as bright, and as capable of receiving education, as the white child; but then a change comes over him; he grows stolid, stupid and indifferent."

" What is it causes the greater thickness of the skull of the negro?" asked the Colonel.

" It is simply the result of an effort of nature," I replied, " to protect the brain from the intense rays of the tropical sun. There is no doubt that, if the black

race continues to dwell in temperate climates for generations, the skull will lose this unnecessary density,
and the brain will continue to expand, with the demands
made upon it, as with the white race.   It is a wonderful thing to think of, that the mental superiority of this
great conquering, colonizing white race may be due to
the fact that their ancestors lived for generations in
lands where the sun's rays were feeble, and the skull
grew thin and plastic to the growth of the brain.   The
negro's intellect has been, as it were, a helpless captive
in a prison of bone.   And yet upon these physiological
effects of climate has depended the history of the
world: — they have made one race a race of masters,
and another a race of servants.   There is scientific reason to believe that the first inhabitants of Europe were
negroes, and that they were, in part, our own ancestors.
It is claimed that the long skull, the *dolichocephalic
skull*, of the white man, as contra-distinguished from
the *brachycephalic* or short skull of the Mongols, was
derived by us from remote negro ancestors.   The
Neanderthal skull, the oldest European skull, is strikingly
negroloid.   If this theory is correct, the white man
is, to some extent, a climatically modified negro; but
vast lapses of time were necessary for this transformation.   The extreme north — in lands perhaps now sunk
under the sea — was the original habitat of our wonderful race."

   " I don't like to listen to such views," said Buryhill.
" The idea that the white man's ancestors were negroes!
Pardon me the expression, Doctor, but it seems to me
absurd."

" I know," I replied, " that it runs counter to your prejudices — I will not say your inherited prejudices — for I believe you are from the North."

Buryhill winced, for he does not like allusions to his Northern origin. He is rather ashamed of the fact. Like the chameleon, such men take color from their surroundings.

" Is it any more strange," I continued, " than the fact that the reddish-brown Arabs, according to Burckhardt and others, have become black in Africa. In fact, equatorial Africa has swallowed up scores of lighter-colored races, the Abyssinians, Mandingoes, Joloffs, Gallas, etc., and turned them all black. Why, we see the same physiological effects even in this country: the people of malarial regions grow darker in color than those of the colder sections; already, in a hundred years, there have been developed marked differences between the man of Maine and the man of Louisiana; there is no mistaking one for the other. You can even observe an unlikeness between the Canadian and the man of the Ohio valley. Some argue that the white race is slowly approximating the characteristics of the red man; this is the more marked in those whose ancestors belonged to the dark Iberian stock, miscalled Celtic. The progress toward the Indian type is so rapid in these that one is often inclined to ask, even in the North, whether a dark-skinned, lank-haired, black-eyed, lantern-jawed individual, of supposed pure European blood, has not a large contribution of the Indian in his pedigree. It would almost seem like an ancient type gravitating rapidly toward its original, when restored to the original habitat."

"What conclusions, Doctor," asked Berrisford, "do you draw from all these facts?"

"Why," said I, "it seems to me that all men are men, and none of them monkeys; and the rights of a man should not depend upon the shade of his complexion. If that is to be the standard, how, let me ask, are you going to graduate it? Will you argue that the fair-haired Finlander should have more rights than the dark-haired Frenchman, or the tawny Spaniard or Italian? Who would be willing to proscribe the Portuguese as not white men, and yet perhaps there is not a single individual of that race who has not some remnant of Moorish, and therefore negroloid, blood in his veins."

"And do you think," said Buryhill, with his nose in the air, and a frown on his brow, "that the negroes should have the same political rights as the whites?"

I was aware that I was advancing upon ticklish ground, but I could not get clear of my logical faculty, and so I replied:

"Why not? Political equality does not imply social equality, or physical equality, or moral equality, or race equality. When you go to the ballot-box to vote you find a group assembled of white men, originally of different nationalities — Yankee, French, German, Irish, Scotch — of different complexions, conditions, mental power, education and knowledge. No two are alike; no two are equal in any respect, and yet they all peacefully unite in expressing their political preferences. The right to participate in the government, in a republic, is like the right to breathe the atmosphere. No man feels degraded because the air he inhales has already passed through the lungs of his fellow-man, differing from him in every respect and condition. We must all breathe to live, and we must all vote if the republic is to live. Because a man votes beside me at the polling-place, it does not follow that I must take him into my house, or wed him to my daughter, any more than those results follow because we breathe the same air."

I observed that the Colonel's brow grew troubled; and there was a triumphant sneer on Buryhill's face. There was a movement at an upper window, and I caught sight of a dress which I knew belonged to Abigail, and I felt sure she had been listening to the conversation.

" If these views are not true," I continued, " if the right to participate in the government which governs one depends upon the possession of European blood, how much of that blood, in an individual, will be necessary to give him the standing of a man? How small a portion of negro blood will deprive him of his humanity? Will you make liberty a question of preponderance of ancestry? Must every man bring his pedigree to the polls? If the major portion of his blood is of white origin, will the majority rule and the man be accounted a white man? Or will you hold that if it can be shown that one one-thousandth part of his blood is African, that therefore the white man is a negro? In twenty-one generations we have one million ancestors whose blood is in our veins:— will you inaugurate a new gospel of human rights, and declare that if one of those million ancestors was a negro he was prepotent enough to overwhelm all that white man's blood and reduce the citizen to a brutish condition, unfit to be free where all the rest are free?"

"Guid God, Doctor," cried Major McFettridge, excitedly, "ye dinna mean to say that a mulatto is a white man!"

"Not in the judgment of society," I replied; "but, Major, you know that society's judgments have not always been wise or conclusive. You remember how Robert Burns, when invited, because of his resplendent genius, to a gentleman's house, was put, when dinner-time came, to eat with the servants in the kitchen; and you remember how his outraged soul burst forth in immortal verse:

> "'For a' that, and a' that,
>   Our toil's obscure and a' that;
> The rank is but the guinea's stamp,
>   The man's the gold for a' that.
> Then let us pray that come it may,
>   As come it will for a' that,
> The sense and worth o'er a' the earth,
>   May bear the gree, and a' that.
> For a' that, and a' that,
>   It's coming yet, for a' that,
> That man to man the world o'er
>   Shall brothers be for a' that.'"

The Major's eyes lighted up with fine enthusiasm as he listened to the familiar lines.

"True, true," he said, in a softened tone, "but there is nae comparison between the Scotch peasantry and the black de'ils. When did the negro plowmen ever produce a Burns?"

"Granted, Major," I replied; "granted that the white race is the masterful race of the globe; and, in the presence of their tremendous achievements, no man —black, brown, red or yellow—can doubt it. They are the biggest-brained, the boldest-hearted, the most capable subdivision of mankind that has ever dwelt on the planet. I grant you all that. But are we to do justice only to our superiors, or our equals? If so, it yields us no honor, for our superiors and our equals are able to enforce justice from us. Generosity can only be exercised toward those less fortunate than ourselves. Power has no attribute grander than the god-like instinct to reach down and lift up the fallen. If we can plainly perceive in the progress of humanity the movement of a great Benevolence, every year adding to the comfort and happiness of mankind, why should we not, to the extent of our little powers, aid Him in His tremendous work? How divine a thought is it that we are participating in the purposes and work of the Almighty One! That, as he has dragged man up from reptilian barbarism to this splendid, this august era of peace and love, we are able to help the flagging footsteps of the laggards and stragglers who have dropped behind in God's great march ! In such a work we become the very children of God — fired with his zeal, illuminated by his smile. How base and brutal it would be if we were willing to be fed with all the countless fruits of God's beneficence, and, in the midst of our full content, commend only poison to the lips of those whose sole offense is that Heaven has not given them our blessings!"

I had risen from the hammock and spoke like **one** exhorting. Mary's eyes flashed with delight, and the Colonel's face was a study. Pride in his prospective son-in-law contended with the astonishment with which he received such unheard-of doctrines.

" Really, Doctor," said Buryhill, with a sneer, " you should have been a preacher."

" Every honest man," I replied, " who perceives abuses in the world, should be a preacher, in the broad sense of the word. There are, of course, wolfish natures, whose only instinct is to sneak and leap and devour. To these men mercy is a mockery, and humanity but another name for food. They are the cannibals of civilized life, and live upon their fellows."

Buryhill grew red in the face, and his eyes glared the rage he did not dare to speak; but I felt that he hated me as bitterly as I despised him.

Major McFettridge was silent. The appeal to his higher nature was too much for the gallant Scotchman. He sat lost in sober thought, until his cigar went out.

" But seriously, now, Doctor," said Major Berrisford, " you don't mean to say that we should not protect ourselves from the domination of a horde of ignorant negroes, led by poor white demagogues, or adventurers from the North? Look at the condition they brought the Southern States to, after the war, under the carpet-bag *régime*, when plunder was the first object and the people were overwhelmed with bankruptcy. You are not in favor of another Governor Moses *régime*, I hope?"

" Certainly not," I replied. " I think the intellect of the South should rule the South; it will not be well governed unless it is governed by its best and wisest. But there are many ways to reach this end besides murder. The present system, practiced in some places, of brutally killing a man because he attempts to peacefully exercise the right which the laws of the land confer upon him, is, to my mind, revolting and dreadful, and a disgrace to the Southern people. To fill a man with lead, to tear his vitals to pieces, simply because he attempts to put a piece of paper in the ballot-box, when the law says he shall have the right to do so, is a horrible travesty on our civilization and Christianity; and I am glad to know that our best people repudiate it. It is the work of ruffians, of low-down, degraded ruffians, who would kill white men as quickly as black men, if public opinion made it safe for them to do so."

" But what are you to do?" asked Buryhill. " In many places the negroes are in a majority, and if you let them vote they will govern, and experience has shown that they are not fit to govern."

" Do you mean to tell me," I replied, " that this cunning, crafty, long-headed white race, which has dominated every darker people it has come in contact with, is unable to control a horde of ignorant black men without butchering them? How do they control their own people? Look at the vast populations of laboring men in the cities of the North. They have the ballot; they are united by a sense of real or fancied wrongs; they enthusiastically resolve every year to take the

5

government into their own hands; they are the vast
majority. Did you ever hear of the bankers and
brokers and lawyers shooting them down at the
polls? Not a bit of it. And yet the professional
classes and the corporations, comparatively insignificant
in number, always rule the cities and the States. How
do they do it? They divide up the laborers. They
buy up their leaders. They set them to battling on
side issues. They adopt what the philosophers call
'the expulsive power of a new affection.' They be-
wilder and befuddle them, and govern them. They
establish newspapers among them to direct them; and
they take possession of them very much as the negroes
of Africa capture monkeys. They leave beer for them
to drink, and when the quadrumanous little fools are
pretty well overcome by intoxication, one negro steps
forward and takes the leader by the hand; the imita-
tive creatures follow this example, and all clasp hands
in the same way, and the colored gentleman leads them
all off, in a long line, happy and contented, to cap-
tivity. If the South desires to control its labor vote,
it should take example from the astute North, where
politics are reduced to a science. But firing bullets
into their lungs and stomachs and hearts! Pah! that
is brutal and barbarous, and marks an undeveloped
state of society. In fact, force is always the remedy of
men who cannot reason. You kill a man because Nature
has not given you brains enough to convince him.
What a lovely time there would be in one of those
great Northern cities if the wealthier classes turned out,
on election day, and murdered a few workingmen

for trying to vote! How much of that town would be up in the air in the form of smoke before night-fall? How many of those intelligent bankers and brokers, and lawyers, and railroad presidents, would be ready to adorn a grave-yard before supper-time? But let us go a step farther. Let us suppose that the ruling class not only tried to keep the workingmen from voting by murdering them, but went so far as to shut up the school-houses and deny them education, and employ the whole power of the civilized state to make them brutes and savages? What a hell-upon-earth would they prepare for themselves! What a cheerful place that would be for a cultured gentleman, of quiet and refined tastes, to reside in, where the vast majority of the people around him, male and female, were uncivilized monsters, as enlightened as gorillas, and as bloodthirsty as thugs. Why, the shallowest-pated fool in the whole North would under-stand that such a course would bring down the entire fabric of society in undistinguishable confusion and ruin. And yet this is just what the inhabitants of some portions of the South are doing. The negroes are the most patient and forbearing and gentle people in the world.

" Imagine a body of white slaves, during our late civil war, in charge of the plantations, with the women and children at their mercy, while their masters were at the front fighting to decide whether their slavery should end or should continue forever! If they had been Englishmen, or Irishmen, or Germans — or even Scotch-men, Major — the heavens would have been lurid with midnight flames, and the Southern soldiers would have had to rush home to find the calcined bones of their best beloved shining white in the ashes of their habitations.　Nor was this from lack of native courage on the part of the blacks; for, when armed by the Northern generals, and placed in the field of battle, they fought like demons.　No; it was natural goodness, and it should make every Southern father and husband feel more kindly to these poor black creatures, who had everything at their mercy and refused to shed a drop of white blood, or bring shame and despair to the face of a single white woman.　The history of the human family does not afford another illustration of like forbearance under like circumstances."

"Vera true — vera true," said the Major; " I have often thought of that mysel'.　Indeed, they raised the vera crops to feed us while we fought to keep them in slavery.　And vera well they kenned what was going on, too."

"No, gentlemen," I said; " whatever may be our prejudices, every fair-minded man must see that the true course for the South is to educate and lift up this people.　We must have a labor-force that will till our fields in the face of our blazing sun and miasma.　Where can we find one so sturdy, so patient, so tractable as the negroes?　How long do you think white men — foreigners — would toil for so small a reward?　Let us be kindly and just and gentle with these unfortunate people.　If you had visited the Northern interior cities, as I have done, and seen how education and good living are modifying the very forms and features of the race, even where the skin retains its original black-ness, you would see that America is to do some good even to the least fortunate of her inhabitants. I have seen black men there with features as perfect and as regular as the most cultivated Caucasian; and the streets of a Northern city, of a Sunday afternoon, are as gay as a many-colored garden, with the handsome daughters of Ham, of all shades of complexion. The truth is, that when you refine the mind you refine the features. Take brutality out of the brain, and it leaves the lips. Raise the heart and soul of man, and the bridge of his nose rises. If the negroes progress as rapidly in the next century as they have done in the last twenty-five years, they will be as handsome as any race on earth. It is the province of this great continent, reserved by God for that purpose, to lift up all the races of Europe to heights of perfection never dreamed of by our ancestors; and who will be mean enough to grudge a little of the universal advancement to our poor, dusky co-toilers from Africa, who need it so much more than we do?"

"Well, well, Doctor," said the Colonel, advancing and taking me by the hand, "you have given me some new ideas; your enthusiasm for humanity is noble; but you must excuse an old man like me if I cannot overcome in an hour the prejudices of a life-time. But come, gentlemen, I hear the summons for supper. And here is my daughter to show us the way."

CHAPTER IX.

THE TEMPTATION.

SEVERAL days passed after this discussion, and I observed, with some surprise, that none of our neighbors dropped in for the afternoon chat on the piazza. I grew tired looking at the magnolia trees and listening to the chirruping song of the birds. I yawned and took to reading. I noticed, too, that Miss Mary seemed troubled; but Abigail met me with shining face and a peculiar light in her eyes, and all the negroes on the plantation smiled and bowed very low whenever they met me. The Colonel was the same as ever, but he did not renew the discussion upon the negro question. At last I could not fail to see that something had gone wrong; and so I said to Mary, one day, as she sat beside me with a book in her hand:

"Mary, what's the matter? Why do Major McFettridge and Captain Braynton and the rest not call as usual? And there is some trouble in your eyes, too, Mary?"

"Well, I suppose your radical and liberal views, as to the negroes," she said, "have offended our neighbors, and the more they think over them the more they dislike them. I hear, too, through some of the house servants (your conversation on the porch was overheard), that their friends, servants on other plantations,

inform them that Buryhill has been going around telling
the white people that you are a fanatical advocate of
the negroes, and want to go to Congress to put the
government of the country in the hands of the blacks;
that you are indeed a Republican, in disguise, of the
most radical kind. All this, of course, is terribly in-
jurious to your chances of success."

"But, Mary," I said, "you heard the discussion. Do
you think my opinions deserved any such denuncia-
tion?"

"Certainly not," she replied, warmly; "I heard every
word, and you were clearly right, and — and — I was
proud of you. But even the truth must not always
be spoken, when it runs counter to prejudices which
cannot be overthrown. And you know our people —
kind, and noble, and generous as they are, upon all
other subjects, they have an ineradicable feeling against
the negroes, inherited from that day when the planters'
wives, with pale faces, told their children of the danger of a slave insurrection. The negro has been, indeed, the *bête noir* of the white people, from childhood.
Individually the planter would treat any of them with
kindness, nay, with affection; but collectively they are
the *incubus* that sits upon his breast when he sleeps; the
hobgoblin that is ready to start out at him from every
bush. The strongest instinct he has is that they must
be put down, kept down; — shot down if they cannot
be kept down in any other way."

"You do not seem to share that feeling, Mary ?"

"No," she replied; "I did to some extent, until I listened to your eloquent words; but now I see that the white

man has no reason to fear that the black man will surpass him in the battle of life. But you remember that our neighbors, while men of fair, average intelligence, are not readers or thinkers, or philosophers ; and when you talk to them about the possibility, as a scientific theorem, of the white race being descended from an aboriginal negro stock living in Europe, many thousands of years ago, they cannot follow you. They take your reasoning, upon scientific probabilities, as a bare statement of fact, that the whites were originally black. And when they think it all over, at home, away from the magnetism of your voice and presence, they will, I fear, — pardon me, — they will regard it as ridiculous, or — worse — as high-treason against our Caucasian blood and lineage."

" Do you so regard it, Mary ? "

" Oh, no," she said ; " to one who has read Darwin's *Origin of Species* and *Descent of Man* no such proposition can appear absurd. Both science and religion teach us that ' God made of one blood all the races of men that dwell on the face of the earth.' The white race must have come from somewhere ; it must have been developed —if the theory of evolution is true — out of some inferior branch of the human family ; and it is not unreasonable to suppose that it may have received the shape of its skull from an outlying colony of the negro race, ages before it fell under those climatic influences which changed — as you suggest — the color of its skin. All nature teaches us that God does not move *per saltum*, by a leap or jump, but that His highest creations creep slowly up out of lower forms, and retain in their con-

formation the history of their ascent. But, apart from
all this," she continued, and she spoke timidly and hesitatingly, " there is another question, — pardon me, —
was it wise to have uttered your inmost thoughts as you
did ? I might say with Hamlet, your favorite, ' All of
which, sir, though I most powerfully and potently
believe, yet I hold it not honesty to have it thus set
down.' I fear that you have lived so isolated a life,
immersed in your library, mingling but little with the
people, that you do not appreciate the depth and intensity of the white prejudice against and fear of the negroes.
I have heard it at my father's table ever since my childhood, and I therefore can comprehend it."

" But, Mary, what would you have me do ? " I replied.
" Surely you do not advise me to encourage my fellow
citizens in a course which I know to be most destructive of their true interests. Now, if I went out, and
talked these things upon the platform, I might overcome the unreasoning bigotry to which you allude."

" No, no," she said ; " you would destroy yourself
and all your future capacity for usefulness. You would
be hated, despised, persecuted ; your utterances would
be distorted, exaggerated ; you would be regarded as
a demagogue or a lunatic."

" But," I said, " some one must die for the truth.
Some one must gather the spears into his breast, like
Arnold von Winkelried at the battle of Sempach, that
over his dead body the forces of liberty may rush in to
victory."

" But can you, by your own ruin," she said, " overthrow error? This is not the battle of Sempach,

This is the age-long conflict of truth and falsehood. And think of the grief and sorrow of those who love you"— and her eyes grew moist—" when they see you cast yourself away in an unavailing struggle! No; no; it seems to me that you must obtain position and influence first, and then gradually mold the minds of men to your views of right. Remember this is a *race* conflict, and the contentions of races with one another are always more bitter than the battles of rival religions, for every physical attribute which separates the combatants accentuates the ferocity of the struggle. In a battle of the birds and beasts only the bats, hideous, misshapen creatures, can be indifferent. One must go, right or wrong, with his class."

" Then," said I, " if one side is right and the other wrong, there must be an eternal division between them; if wrong has the majority, it is to triumph forever. No voice can be raised for the fallen. No allies can march from one camp to the other. Justice is to be terrorized by fear. No, no; my dear Mary, that cannot be right."

" Remember," she said, " the course of that wisest of men, Francis Bacon. He did not cast himself headlong against the adamantine wall of popular bigotry and ignorance. He bowed to the tempest, but he never abandoned his views of right. He saw that truth had to be *'insinuated'* — that was his phrase — into the minds of men, that ' that old arbitrator, Time,' was a mighty factor in the correction of abuses; that progress selected the brain tenements in which it would dwell, and marked them off with white clalk. He has vastly advanced the world, but he has therein imitated nature, which, as he said, 'innovateth greatly, but yet by degrees scarce to be perceived.'"

"Why, my dear Mary," I said, "you talk like a philosopher. Almost thou persuadest me to be a — hypocrite!"

"No, no," she said, earnestly, "not a hypocrite, but a statesman. A true statesman is one who adapts righteousness to circumstances; as the Swiss peasant builds his house, irregularly it may be, but strongly, against the crooked inequalities of the mountain. He could not erect a symmetrical Greek temple upon the face of the precipice, but he secures an humble home, where love and peace may find shelter in the midst of Alpine tempests.

"And think," she continued, "of the folly of throwing away the glorious career we had determined upon for the sake of so wretched a race as the negroes. When I heard you pouring forth that stream of eloquence the other day on the porch, my heart lighted up with joy, for I saw you, in my imagination, in the Senate chamber, with the whole world listening to your burning periods."

"Yes, my dear temptress," I replied, "but under your guidance I could not fulfill the grand picture of the English poet:

> "'The applause of listening senates to command,
>   The threats of pain and ruin to despise;
>   To scatter plenty o'er a smiling land,
>   And read your history in a nation's eyes.'

I would simply mislead the people by confirming

them in their prejudices; and while they praised me
now they would curse me hereafter. The people need
prophets, not panders — bold-hearted men, ready to
fight the surging torrents of popular error, rather than
mealy-mouthed, sweet-tongued, empty-hearted demagogues, who will float, like rotten drift-wood, along
the ill-smelling, turbid current of the world's common
delusions. The people need:

> " ' Men whom the lust of office does not kill;
>   Men whom the spoils of office cannot buy;
> Men who possess opinions and a will;
>   Men who have honor; men who will not lie;
> Men who can stand before a demagogue,
>   And damn his treacherous flatteries without winking;
> Tall men, sun-crowned, who live above the fog
>   In public duty, and in private thinking:
> For while the rabble, with their thumb-worn creeds,
>   Their large professions and their little deeds,
> Mingle in selfish strife, lo! Freedom weeps,
>   Wrong rules the land, and waiting Justice sleeps.' "

" But, my dear friend," she replied, " while all that
is true, from a poet's standpoint, it seems to me that
in a republic the statesmen must represent the race and
sectional bigotries, or they will not represent anything.
The only hope for the republic is that the people, being
free to advance, will gradually move forward out of
their errors. The public school system and the enlightened spirit of our age are gradually lifting all men up into
higher and purer levels of thought. In that lies the
hope of mankind. One man can do nothing."

" One man can do much," I said. " Look at the history of the anti-slavery movement. In 1783 six obscure
Quakers met in London and organized the first society

which, in all the history of mankind, had been created to protest against the slave trade and labor for its destruction. In the same year there was a lawsuit in London against certain ship-owners for the throwing into the sea and the drowning of one hundred and thirty-two Africans, by the master of a slave-ship, to defraud the underwriters. No penalty was inflicted, because they were slaves! And yet, in twenty-four years, the movement, inaugurated by the six Quakers, had grown so strong — in the consciences and souls of men — that a bill passed Parliament to abolish the slave trade. In twenty-three years more every Christian nation in Europe and America had prohibited the commerce in human beings; and in thirty-five years more slavery itself had ceased to exist in nearly every country on earth. All this horrible prejudice against the negro; this desire to drive him from the ballot-box with shot-guns; this passionate and vehement determination to keep him down, to trample him in the mud, is but a survival of that old-time feeling when an English court and jury could justify the murder of one hundred and thirty-two human beings because their skins were darker than that of the average Englishman. Why should I not follow the example of those six obscure Quakers of 1783? Why should I not inaugurate a movement in behalf of fair play and Christianity, and throw all my wealth, and intellect, and station on the side of justice and right? God has not swept away slavery in nearly all the lands of the earth, from frozen Russia to burning Brazil, for nothing; he has not been busy, through all these centuries, by his cherubim and seraphim, winning battles for liberty, drowning great armadas in terrible tempests, and overruling even the passions and follies of men in behalf of mankind, to permit this fair land of America, under the very shadow of the stars and stripes, to make her own soil bloody with the heart's blood of men whose sole offense is that they desire to exercise their legal and constitutional right to participate in the government of the republic. No, no! It is not natural; it is not human; it is not Christian; it is not American. Some one defined the Turkish government as an absolute monarchy, tempered by assassination. Here we have a free republic, subordinated to and modified by murder! A commingling of free ballots and bullets! Free thought and shot-guns! The very devils in hell might grin over such a combination."

Mary said:

" I love to hear you talk thus, when you become excited; but we women are not, as a rule, subject to such enthusiasms. God made the males for leaders and fighters. Perhaps as a matter of abstract right you are correct. I think you are. But let us look at the practical aspects of the question. By the course you have suggested, you would doom yourself to private life forever; for, right or wrong, the white race is determined to rule this land, or perish in the attempt. In private life you can do nothing. You have not the commanding pedestal to speak from. Your voice would sound as from a cellar. You might become, to use Bacon's phrase, 'some sorry book-maker;' but your eloquence would pass away from earth unused. If, on the other hand, you could speak as the mouth-piece of South Carolina, with our noble State and all its glorious memories behind you, you would command the attention of mankind; and you might do more good for the interests you have at heart in that way than in any other. You might be able to modify public sentiment without losing your hold on public confidence."

How sweet is the voice of flattery when it sounds from the lips of those we love!   While I knew what was right, my sybaritic devotion to peace and luxury echoed in my heart the sentiments of my beloved. I feared the dislike of the vulgar.   I could not face public ostracism.   I was rather proud of my oratorical gifts, or the warm flow of language which I mistook for such, and I hungered for the applause of my race. The poor blacks!   What did they know of eloquence? Would they even be grateful for any sacrifices I might make for them?   And, after all, is any man justified in following the emotions of his heart against the dictates of his common sense?   Is not that the final arbiter of action?   Did not great enthusiasms lead to the stake and the scaffold?   Who was to draw the line between unregulated fanaticism and insanity?   All this I said to myself, but away back in the depths of my inner consciousness, in that part of me where the God-in-man dwells, there was a still, small voice that whispered: " All this is reasoned well, but you are a coward! You do not dare to use your gifts for the purpose for which they were given you.   You are a recreant — you are a *nidering!*"

And I was ashamed of myself, even while I boasted, and my love praised me.

"I have been talking to father," Mary continued,— she had been attentively watching my face,— "and he says that Buryhill's stories will so prejudice the Democrats against you, that you will not be able to carry the convention, unless ——" And she paused.

"Unless what?"

"Unless you can make a speech, and publish it in the papers, in which you will take ground that this is a white-man's government and must be ruled by white men, or something of that sort."

I winced.

"It is hard enough," I replied, "to suppress one's convictions, even with good intentions as to the future, but to belie them; to denounce them; to strengthen the very evils one is opposed to, that is too much to ask. Not that I do not believe that the white man's intelligence shall rule this State; but that is not what the politicians mean. It is not white domination they seek, but negro degradation; they are not satisfied to rule the blacks — they must ruin them; not content to deny the colored people leadership, they would reduce them to beasts. I do not speak of the whole people, but of a faction, who rise to office on the shoulders of public prejudice. They are not teachers of the people, but betrayers of humanity. I shall remain in private life."

"But for the sake of your own genius," said Mary, pleadingly, laying her hand upon my arm, "for the sake of your friends — for my sake, you must make the sacrifice. What is it to bow to the inevitable—to submit to the unconquerable — to yield to the force of public prejudice and thereby rise to a position of incalculable power for good? You will not strengthen the race prejudice. It is invulnerable now. It will triumph with you or without you. It is simply a question whether you will stand upon it and direct it, or be crushed under it. Is it better to step aside and let vulgar, merciless demagogues rule the hour, or lend to the cause of the state your cultured mind and your benevolent heart?"

Never did any man endure the pressure of stronger pleading. I knew in my own heart of hearts that I could not reform evil by yielding to it — by indorsing it. And yet all my poor human frailty cried out on the side of my ambition — vanity, pride, affection, all wrought in me. I looked in the bright eyes and excited face of the woman who loved me, whose sense of right was even darkened by her love for me; I caught the spell of her enthusiam; I took her hand; I yielded. I promised to abandon my convictions and throw the weight of my station and my intelligence against the poor wretches who were already borne down to the earth by the accumulated weight of their misfortunes.

And something, away within me — a hundred miles within me — sneered at me and reviled me — yea, spat at me. And in my heart of hearts I stood at the altar of my soul, with downcast head and shamed face, sore and sorry, humiliated and wretched. It seemed to me that I was an outcast from myself—that my conscience spurned me out of its doors into the wilderness.

6

But my fair and lovely and innocent temptress, who had led me away from my higher nature, through excess of admiration and affection, rejoiced and was happy, even to tears; and she hurried away to tell her father the glad tidings.

And I — well, it seemed to me that every day I beat down my conscience with a club until it bled; and every blow I struck it hurt my heart;— I, making excuse that I must return to my library to prepare my speech, hurried away to C——, an utterly wretched man.

It was night when I reached my residence. Ben admitted me. The quiet and peace of the house was grateful to me. I hurried to my bed-chamber.

CHAPTER X.

THE VISION.

> " Angels and ministers of grace,
> Defend me !"   —*Hamlet.*

I FELL asleep,—fanned by a gentle night breeze, laden with the perfume of flowers. My last glance was upon my beautiful and luxurious room, as my sense of discomfort and distress gave place at length to dreamless and profound slumber.

I must have drifted thus peacefully over the silent waters of oblivion for some hours, for it was early when I retired.

I awakened with a start. There is no doubt I was awake. No noise disturbed me; but there was, within my brain and in all my quickly pulsating blood-vessels, that inexplicable sense of *a presence* which so many have felt. Never before had I experienced such a sensation. I was alarmed and felt as if I was beneath the stroke of some impending danger.

A bright light covered all the eastern part of the room. I remember I was sufficiently collected in mind to study it carefully. It was neither sun-light nor lamp-light. It was not a glare, but a softened glow. It seemed like a thing—a substance—a luminous mist, through which I could dimly perceive the wall and the outlines of the articles of furniture. At first it had covered with equal effulgence all the eastern part of the room, reaching nearly to where I lay. But as I looked a change came over it. It receded toward the wall, and, at the same time, seemed to gather in greater brightness toward one central point.

As I gazed intently upon this spot, to my extreme astonishment, I perceived that the light was slowly taking upon itself the outlines of a human head and face; vaguely at first, but gradually growing more and more plain, until at last the lines of the countenance glowed with great distinctness. It was a face painted in light—I might almost say, in fire. A marvelous face! A face never to be forgotten. A face I had never seen before. I had often thought how much of diverse character and meaning could be implanted on the few square inches of the human countenance; but here was a face that transcended my highest dream of all such possibilities.

It was a massive head. The forehead was broad—very broad—high and serene. Beneath it glowed wonderful orbs that looked as if they had sounded all depths of thought and feeling—even to the dreadful verge of despair. There was in them infinite power, sorrow, kindliness and compassion; and yet it was a strong face; the mouth mobile, but the chin square. The face was very fair; the hair bright golden, falling in masses to the shoulders, and from it radiated luminous beams, pulsating and ever moving, like the throbbing rays of the aurora in the lands of polar snow. This was the source of the light that illumined the whole room.

I had never beheld, anywhere, any picture of this countenance, and yet something within me whispered to me:

" This is THE CHRIST ! "

As I gazed, awe-struck and motionless, the eyes, which had been fixed on me, moved slowly from side to side, and I was then able to withdraw my fascinated eye-balls from the countenance of the vision and look at its surroundings. As I did so I rose terrified and awe-stricken half-way from my couch.

Around the face, just outside the pulsating *nimbus*, there seemed to be a dark, moving mass, in great and, apparently, endless circles. The trembling light from the hair beat over its margin, but it was some time before I could discern what it was. To my extreme astonishment I at last perceived that it was made up of millions of dark hands, all clasped in the attitude of prayer, and all directed toward The Christ. Something within me told me that they were the supplicating hands of negroes. They were of all sizes and shades of darkness, from ebon black to those no browner than the hands of the peasants of southern Europe. There were the plump hands of children, the tapering hands of women, the coarse, rude hands of workmen, seamed and calloused with toil; the gnarled and knotted hands of decrepid old men and feeble women. All were bent appealingly toward the central figure, and they moved, with a continual movement, as if they sought to reach and touch Him, but could not. The walls of the room afforded no limit to the sight — it was an universe of hands, shading off into infinity,

The great, slowly-moving eyes regarded me again with a look of melancholy reproach, and then swept that vast circle of piteous appeal. Two bright tears flowed slowly down the fair face; the lips parted, and, in a voice sweeter than the sound cf rippling waters, the vision spake:

"THESE, TOO, ARE MY CHILDREN. FOR THEM, ALSO, I DIED ON THE CROSS!"

Scarce had the words been spoken when the vision began to fade. First the outer multitude of hands disappeared; then those nearer the figure became confused and clouded; then the magnificent face itself grew less luminous, and slowly disappeared, until at length only the great wonderful eyes shone out of the darkness; and it seemed to me a threat mingled with their look of sorrow. Then these too faded away, and I was alone. No, not alone; for the room appeared to me to be full of whispering *presences*, and I thought I could hear the soft beat of innumerable wings.

I was overwhelmed — awe-stricken. I fell on my knees. I trembled. I could not understand the meaning of the vision; but the last look of those gentle yet awful eyes terrified me. I prayed long and fervently to God, if I had done wrong, in any wise, to pardon me; not to put forth His limitless power against me; and I asked Him to remember what a poor, abject, helpless worm I was. I begged Him not to roll His universe upon me, but to have pity on my weakness, my misery and my insignificance. I wrestled with God. I argued my case with Him. Why did the eyes of His Son threaten me? What had *I* done? For in my terror and confusion I did not connect those multitudinous dark hands with anything in my own history. And again and again I cried aloud for mercy.

My inner nature was stirred to its deepest depths. Feelings I had never before experienced rushed over me, like high-mounting tidal-waves, crested with terror. My innermost soul rose above the thought-producing faculty, and dominated the conventional being I had known since childhood.

I lighted a lamp. I looked at the spot where the vision had appeared. It reproduced itself clearly in my memory; but there was no physical trace to mark what had been. And yet I had no doubt that I had looked upon the very Son of God, in the exact likeness he had worn eighteen hundred years ago, in Galilee, when he walked among men, commanding reverence by the Godhood in his countenance.

What did it mean? I paced the room. What did it mean? The Christ surrounded by millions of dark hands. Why *dark* hands? Where were the hands of my own race? And why did this vision come to *me?* What had *I* to do with the negroes? Could it mean that I had been false, in my heart, to God and my fellow-men?

I walked the room and thought and thought, until at last, wearied and exhausted, I cast myself upon my bed and slept.

CHAPTER XI.

THE TRANSFORMATION.

> " Elements, near me,
>   Be mingled and stirred,
> Know me and hear me,
>   And leap to my word!
> Sunbeams, awaken
>   This earth's animation!
> 'Tis done! He hath taken
>   His stand in creation."
>   —*Byron.*

HOW long I slept I know not. It must have been an hour or two—an hour or two of disturbed and uneasy slumber, troubled with dreams, in which I saw again and again those reproachful, threatening eyes.

Then came a feeling as if I was smothering—choking. I gasped and was awake. But the smothering sensation did not leave me. It seemed to me as if the air was exhausted; as if I was shut up in a vault or—coffin! And then I noticed a strong, *negro-like* smell. My first thought was that a negro burglar had entered my room and was leaning over me. I threw my hands up; they encountered nothing. I was in total darkness. As my arms fell one of them came near my face, and the negro-like smell grew stronger than before. Instinctively I placed my bare arm close to my nose, and I then perceived that the strong odor came from my own person. What could it mean? I felt with one hand my other hand and arm. The arm was larger than my own — much larger! The hand was coarse and huge — the palms calloused and rough; — little, fine filaments of skin projected from the frayed callosities, as in the hands of those worn with hard work. My God! What does it mean? I quickly brought both hands to my face. The negroloid smell was stronger than ever. I felt my face. Instead of my own clean-cut features, my hands encountered a flat nose and a pair of swollen lips. Was I dreaming some dreadful dream? I bit my hand until the blood came. No; I was wide awake. The bed was not my own. It was lumpy, and stuffed, apparently, with straw. I felt out on both sides of me. My left hand encountered a huge, sleeping body.

Where am I? What in God's name does all this mean? Am I insane? Has some dreadful disease — like the Indian *elephantiasis* — overtaken me, in my sleep, and swelled my limbs and features to twice their natural size? But that would not account for the changed bed and the sleeper by my side. I must find out where I am. I put my feet out of the bed and stood erect. In doing so my head struck the ceiling with such force that I made an exclamation of pain. There was a movement in the bed, and a voice cried out, shrilly and fiercely, and in the unmistakable speech of a negro woman:

" Hi there! Sam Johnsing, you d——d nigger! What you gittin' up for now? Does you think yer gwine steal Colonel Jenkins' shirts agin and pon 'em?''

There was a bounce out of bed, on the instant, and the next minute a match was struck and a tallow candle lighted. It revealed to me an astonishing sight. I was standing in a negro cabin, between the bed and the wall, my head touching the sloping roof. On the other side of the bed, holding the lighted candle in her hand, and glaring at me savagely, was a huge, coal-black negro woman. In one corner was a cradle; in another a wash-tub; and across the farther end of the cabin were some lines, on which hung an assortment of washing — stockings, shirts and underwear. All this my astonished eyes took in at one glance. I looked down at myself. A torn fragment of a shirt revealed to me the large body, arms and legs of a negro — the huge, splay feet resting on the mud floor of the cabin.

For a few moments I was as one paralyzed. My mind seemed torn from its moorings. I could not put the facts together. I had fallen asleep in my own luxurious room. I had awakened here in this wretched hovel. Who was this woman? I had never seen her before. Who was this man, standing, almost naked, against the wall, with eyes revolving wildly, taking in his surroundings? It could not be I, — Doctor Anthony Huguet — the gentleman — the physician — the cultured scholar! Oh, no! That thought was too dreadful — too impossible. I smiled.

The woman noted the expression, and said:

"What you grinnin' at, you d——d nigger — you chicken-thief. You knows dat you got up to steal de clothes, to buy more whisky. But I'll crack yer d——d skull first."

With this she picked up an ironing-board and assumed a threatening position, advancing toward me. The bed was between us.

And still my brain worked, and still I couldn't understand what it all meant. How did I come here? Where was I? What had happened to me? Who was this standing against the wall, with stooped head, watching the advancing virago? It was not I, and yet *I seemed to think within it!* How did I come to be within this black figure? And then came to me a dreadful thought:

" *My God! has my soul been placed within the body of this black man?* "

And then I thought of those menacing eyes; of that reproachful face; of those millions of black, pleading hands, all pointed toward The Christ.

I shrieked out aloud in terror; and, springing over the low bed and pushing the woman rudely aside, I rushed to a broken mirror, that hung upon the wall, and gazed into it. The glass gave back to me a terrible revelation. There before me was the large face of a black man:— the low, retreating forehead;— the clustering, woolly hair;— the flat nose;— the thick lips;— the eyeballs yellow where they should be white;— the glossy, oily, ebony skin;— the colossal throat.

" Oh, my God! " I cried, " I am lost! *I am a negro! I am a negro!* "

I leaped up and down with rage and terror. I clutched at my flesh, as if I would pluck it from my bones and release the imprisoned spirit. I opened my mouth and looked down the great red throat, as if I would seek out myself within this body of damnation.

There was a yowl from the cradle, and a woolly head protruded, and a pair of bright, bead-like black eyes contemplated me with wonder.

The woman stood astonished at my extraordinary movements and outcries. They were something beyond her usual experience.

I groaned I swore, I even wept; then I danced with rage.

"See here, you Sam Johnsing," the woman said, "what de debbil you mean by dis kind ob work? Dere you've done gone and waked de baby. What's de use ob shoutin', 'I's a nigger! I's a nigger!' Ob course you's a nigger, and de meanest nigger in South Car'liny. An' I knows you're up to some new game! You're after dat 'ar washin'! I knows you, drat you. If you don't git right into bed I'll break dis board ober your black head sure's my name's Emeline Johnsing."

And she came toward me with the ironing-board uplifted.

My rage found a new vent. I turned upon her savagely, and with startling rapidity tore the board from her hands and dealt her a fearful blow upon the head. She fell like an ox under the axe of the butcher, for I had smitten her, not with the muscles of Doctor Huguet, but with those of Sam Johnsing, inspired by the intellect and rage of Doctor Huguet. I rushed for the door, overturning the cradle, and leaving its dusky occupant sprawling and howling on the floor.

CHAPTER XII.

OUT OF DOORS.

" Ay, marry, now my soul hath elbow-room ;
It would not out at windows nor at doors."
— *King John, v. 7.*

I RAN wildly along the open road, dimly lighted by the stars, past numerous, closely-clustered negro cabins. It was the dead of night, and no one was abroad. I ran and ran, as if I would run away from this hated body which inclosed me. Now and then I stopped, as the thought recurred to me, " It is all a horrible dream ; it cannot be true. I shall waken soon!" No, no. I examined again and again my arms, hands, limbs. I felt my face. The glass had spoken truly. *I was a negro.* I leaped up in the air as if I would spring out of myself. I rolled in the dust. I shrieked; I cried. Then I prayed. Down on my knees — down on my very face, I prostrated myself, and cried out, in the midst of the silent night, to the merciful God to spare me and lift this curse from me.

" Smite me with sudden death, O Lord God !" I cried aloud; " cover me with leprosy; rot me with consumption; infect me with all the racking pains that flesh inherits; plunge me in poverty to the very lips; overwhelm me with shame and dishonor; but give me back my body, my *race*, my white skin — that loftiest testimony of dignity and greatness, throughout all the habitable world. Let me stand, if you will, O God ! at some street corner, lame and blind and sick and sore, with outstretched hand, living upon the pitiful and contemptuous bounty of my kind; but give me back my white manhood ! Spare me this awful, this incomprehensible, this unprecedented affliction. And, O Christ ! have your pitying eyes no glance of mercy for me? You died on the cross, but you died a white man? This is a living cross, a life-long crucifixion, compared with which the nails and the spear were merciful. Why, why, O Mighty One, have you selected me for this dreadful doom? True, I was false to the black man in my thoughts. But how many others have persecuted them with the utmost cruelty? Where are the slave-drivers, the men of the slave-ships, the men who parted husband and wife, and mother and child, on the auction block? Where are the scourgers who made their backs run red with blood — the murderers of men, the despoilers of women? Of all those millions of black hands which surrounded you, in the vision, not one, living or dead, O Christ! can be raised against me in imprecation for wrongs done them. I have been kind and just to all men. Why, then, this awful doom? I, Anthony Huguet, buried, imprisoned in the abhorred carcass of a negro! Compelled to look up to you, O Christ, through these bestial yellow eyes; to speak to you through the swollen and distorted features of a chicken-thief ! Have mercy on me, O Christ; have mercy on me !"

I paused, I listened; I scanned the heavens above

me for some answer to my prayers. There was none. The indignation mounted in my heart like a sweeping tide; and I cursed the Unknown Powers who stood behind the veil of life, ruling the destinies of us poor puppets; making us the mockery and sport of their inhuman humor. In my ferocious rage (I shame to say it), I blasphemed my very Maker. I argued with Him! I told him that the right to make me did not imply the right to subject me to such tortures; that there were limitations of fair play even to Omnipotence! And then — horrified at my own thoughts — I fell upon my face again and cried aloud for " mercy, mercy, mercy!"

I sprang to my feet. I ran like the wind. Rapid motion seemed to be a relief to my mind. On a hill-top I caught sight of long, parallel, converging lines of twinkling light-spots. It was the street of a town.

I stopped. Where was I? If a transformation had been wrought in me whither had I been carried? The dialect of the woman showed that I was in the United States — probably in one of the Southern States — but where?

And then another thought thrilled me, and a flash of joy came over me. Why could I not get back to C——, to my own house, and, despite my fleshly covering, convince my friends that I was indeed Doctor Huguet? Might there not be some power, known to science, by which I could be relieved of this dreadful spell? And then there was Mary Ruddiman!

At this thought I groaned aloud in anguish of spirit.

" Oh, Mary, Mary!" I cried, to the night wind, " fair and lovely and loving! Am I divorced from thee for-

ever? Are my golden dreams blasted and shriv-
eled? With all the attributes of the soul I am still
your accepted lover, but this beastly habiliment of
flesh! This — this — separates me from you by an
abyss wider and deeper than the grave — wider and
deeper than oceans — yea, than the planetary spaces."

And now the full extent of my calamity burst upon
me. Home, fortune, station, race, friends, family — all
these were dreadful losses; but what were they to the
loss of the fair and loving creature whose spirit had
permeated mine, and dwelt within me, side by side
with my own soul?

At least I could die !

That would end it all. A few moments of agony
and the imprisoned spirit would escape from its horrible dungeon; this dungeon which it carried around with
it; this walking grave!

But how? I had no weapon. I was almost naked.
There was no river or pond in sight.

I would go on in the direction of the lights. As I
walked a new thought came to me:

"What! should I die a negro? My life a failure!
To be buried in a negro's grave! Mary lost forever! No, no!"

And then, again, there rose before me the wonderful
vision. I saw the mournful, merciful look of that
divine countenance; even when the fading eyes threatened me, they seemed to pity me. I said to myself:
"No, I will live; this curse will pass away. This trial
is for some good end."

CHAPTER XIII.

THE ARREST.

" She laughed so long and she laughed so loud,
   That Dame Ulrica often vowed
      A dirge were a merrier thing, by half,
      Than such a senseless, soulless laugh."

— Praed.

I ADVANCED toward the city. I would, at least, find out where I was. I drew near the lights. I passed a cottage I recognized. Thank God ! I was still in C——. I will go to my home and make myself known to Ben. He would conceal me and care for me until I had time to think.

A faint light overspread the eastern sky. The day was about to dawn. I must hurry home and hide my nakedness.

The houses grew more numerous. I knew the streets. I passed a tavern; the door stood open, casting a flood of light upon the pavement. Some roysterers were about to break up an all-night revel. I hurried past. They caught sight of me. They were wild with liquor. My dishabille offended their sensibilities. A great shout of laughter broke forth, and unsteadily they rushed forward, with many insulting outcries, and pursued me. I fled from them like the wind, and should have escaped but that, by ill chance, I rushed headlong into the arms of a policeman.

I tried to break loose from him. I must get home and avoid exposure! The policeman held me fast. We struggled together. I was immensely strong. The officer, finding I was about to escape, beat me over the head with his club. At the second blow I became unconscious. When I recovered I found myself handcuffed and my legs tied together, lying on an iron bedstead in a cell of the police station. My head was tied up in a cloth, and my face pasted over with dried blood. A physician had his finger on my pulse. As I opened my eyes he turned to one of a group of policemen, and said:

"Here, Billy; he's all right. But if his skull had not been an inch thick you would have finished him."

"The d——d nigger is as strong as an ox," replied Billy. "If I hadn't given it to him he would have got away."

"Do you know him?" asked the doctor.

"Know him? Of course I do. We all know him. His name is Sam Johnsing. He's been before his honor twenty times: a quarrelsome, drunken cuss, and a petty thief. Lives down in 'Nigger Hollow.' His wife's a decent woman and washes for a living. She's an honest woman; but Sam's a bad 'un."

"See here, Sam," said one of the officers, "what were you doing out at that time of night, without your clothes?"

I tried to rise from the bed, but they threw their weight upon me, and held me down.

"Come now," said Billy, "keep still, you d——d

rascal, or I'll give you another taste of the *lignum vitæ.*" And he flourished his club in the air.

"Gentlemen!" I said, "this is shameful treatment. I shall complain to the courts and the newspapers. I am Doctor Anthony Huguet."

The burst of laughter which followed this announcement it would be difficult to describe. They laughed so loud, and they laughed so long, that all the policemen in the station-house, with some of the usual hangers-on, came rushing into the room.

"What's the matter? What's the matter?" they cried.

It was some minutes before the others could recover their breath. The doctor, at last, with tears of merriment rolling down his face, his speach interrupted by bursts of uncontrollable laughter, managed to gasp out:

"He!"—pointing to me—"He!—ha-ha-ha—he says—he's—ha-ha-ha—he's—Doctor—Anthony—Huguet!"

And then he grasped his sides to keep from bursting, while the roof rang with shouts of stentorian laughter from all present.

And surely, when I think of it now, I cannot wonder. Who could see in that huge, burly, black, naked figure, handcuffed and manacled, lying on a prison-bed, with two policemen sitting on him, the small, neat figure of the cultured aristocrat, Doctor Anthony Huguet?

An old black woman, whose office it was to clean up the cells, came running to the door, and, poking in her alarmed face and grizzled mop of wool, asked timidly of the nearest policemen — for the policemen are the gods of the humble:

" Honey, what's de matter?"

" Matter! Why, this d——d nigger chicken-thief, Sam Johnsing, says he's Doctor Anthony Huguet!"

The old woman's mouth covered half her face; she howled with laughter, and ran off, dropping her mop and slop-pail, to tell her neighbors about the last marvelous and miraculous lie of Sam Johnsing.

I lay there paralyzed. It had been taught me that the *mind* is the man; but now I perceived that the *body* is the man. I was unquestionably Doctor Anthony Huguet. My intellect, my modes of thought, my acquired knowledge, my disposition, my feelings, my affections, everything belonged to Doctor Huguet. It seemed to me that all these should shine through the apparel of the flesh, like a light through a porcelain shade. But no; the world saw no further than the skin; men judged their fellows by their appearance. The convolutions of the brain are covered by the osseous plate of the impervious skull. And then I thought, why did not God place the character and mold of the mind on the *outside* of the head, so that men could recognize the intellects of their fellows, when they pass them in the street, as they now recognize the shape of their noses or chins? How many lovely forms inclose a mental *vacuum!* How many grand souls look out through distorted, Socratic features! But the human spirit dwells, unhappily for itself, behind a mask — an impenetrable mask.

While I thus philosophized, the crowd swelled and

the laughter continued. Each new comer had to be told the extravagant and improbable lie; and then the merriment broke forth afresh. At length the doctor said to me:

" Well, Sam! you have risen to a higher dignity in the estimation of your fellow-men. Heretofore you were simply Sam Johnsing, the purloiner of chickens and the appropriator of garden-stuff. You are now a recognized genius. You are the most colossal liar in South Carolina; and *that's saying a great deal!*"

And then they all laughed again; for the doctor had a large income, from his profession, and his jokes were always regarded as excellent.

I remained perfectly quiet, looking from one of the howling mob to the other. Then with my manacled hands I reached down and pulled the dirty bed-clothes over me; for, although the body was not mine, I took shame of Sam Johnsing's nakedness. And I thought —thought. And my thoughts were dreadful. For I said to myself: "If my claim, that I am other than I appear, meets with such inextinguishable merriment, it would be better that I remain silent. I cannot convince mankind against the evidence of their own senses. I must be prudent, and yield for the present to the uncontrollable." And then I thought, " Am I to yield forever? Is there to be no end to this thing? Can I ever convince Mary Ruddiman that this bloated form incloses the mind and soul of her fair-faced lover? " And, forgetting everything around me, I groaned aloud.

The doctor reached over and felt my pulse. It was

dancing wildly in tune to the passions that swept through me.

" Come, sergeant," he said, " darken the windows and let this poor devil alone. He is threatened with fever."

They did as he desired, and withdrew. I heard the clank of the bolt as it shot into the lock behind them.

My thoughts were blacker than my body. My soul was chained even as my limbs. But my brain worked and beat like a steam-engine.

" Prudence, prudence!" I exclaimed aloud; " you can do nothing by violence. You must put the white-man's intellect at work to get clear of the black-man's body. You must get away from here and go home."

And then came, like a flash, a new thought:

" If my soul had been taken out of the body of Doctor Huguet and transferred to the physical system of the negro, *what had become of the body of Doctor Huguet?* Should I, when I came home, *find myself a corpse?* Should I be in time to attend my own funeral? Or should I find that body simply unconscious, lying in my great bed, in a trance condition? How could I convince even Ben that the living negro was the dead or insensible white man?"

" But"— and the thought was so dreadful that, man-acled as I was, I got out of bed and stood erect —" *what had become of the soul of Sam Johnsing?* HAD IT ENTERED INTO THE BODY OF DOCTOR HUGUET ? Would the base wretch succeed to my name — my station, my home, my wealth ? Would he — awful thought! — *would he marry Mary Ruddiman?* "

I jumped, shuffled, fell, crawled to the door of my cell, and, rising up, pounded upon it with my great black fists, and screamed, until one of the policemen came running.

"Let me out! Let me out!" I cried; "I am Doctor Huguet! I am Doctor Huguet! I am being robbed —plundered—this very hour:—my life, my home, my love—that cursed wretch, Sam Johnsing, has taken them all! Let me out! Let me out! Or I shall break down the door."

"What's the matter, Bob?" cried another policeman, hurrying up.

"Matter?" replied Bob; "matter enough! Why, this poor devil has gone crazy—crazy as a bed-bug. Listen to him."

"The doctor said he had a high fever," replied the other; "he's not crazy, but sick. Send for the doctor."

I beat the door until my hands were raw and bloody; I sprang against it; I struck it with my head; I fell at last to the floor.

How long I remained unconscious I know not. I recovered to find myself on the cot-bed, two or three policemen around me, and the doctor leaning over me, forcing some medicine down my throat, between my clenched teeth. My manacles had been removed.

I glared wildly around me. Memory came slowly back to me, and I realized once more my awful position, and a groan escaped me.

"How do you feel now, my man?" said the doctor

kindly, for he was a good-hearted gentleman. " Here,
take the rest of this medicine.   It will quiet you."

" Doctor," I said, " my name is Anthony Huguet.
I am"——

" Yes, yes," said the doctor, with a sidelong look
at the others. " Yes; we know all that; but say no more
about it now.   Go to sleep, and we will talk over the
matter when you are better.   Go to sleep."

And as he spoke I felt, despite all my wrongs and
sorrows, the powerful influence of morphine stealing
like a mist over my senses; the room grew dim; the
voices sank to whispers; the figures around me became
shadows, and I slept.

CHAPTER XIV.

DISCHARGED.

"Fly, while thou art blest and free,
Ne'er see thou man, and let me ne'er see thee."
— Timon of Athens, iv. 3.

"COME, get up," said Billy; "you must go to court. Put on these clothes."

He handed me a rough shirt and trousers.

"Can I wash myself?" I asked.

"Well, Sam," he replied, "you're mighty pertic'lar this morning; never knew you to be so before."

But he stepped out and soon returned with a basin of water, a piece of yellow soap and a coarse and not overly clean towel. I removed the bandage from my head, and washed away the clotted blood, and cleaned my hands and face the best I could. The instincts of the gentleman triumphed over all the abasements of utter misery.

Billy ushered me into the prison van, where I found two men and a woman, not yet recovered from last night's drunken debauch; they were red, sour, ill-smelling and blear-eyed, and hardly yet wide awake. But they cursed and complained, as the wagon jolted along, at having to associate with a d——d nigger, the language of the woman being even fouler than that of the men.

Wretched creatures! They were white, but, negro as I was, I drew as far away from them as possible. We mutually repudiated each other — they for my skin, I for their degradation.

"Call the next case," said the judge.

The police judge was a fat, cross-eyed, half-bald man of low instincts and mean countenance; a pettifogging lawyer, who owed his elevation to the bench to his popularity with the saloons, and his capacity to drink whisky and pack caucuses. He was morally only one degree above the petty offenders he every day passed judgment upon.

"Call the next case."

"Sam Johnsing!" shouted the clerk.

"What's the charge?" asked the judge.

"There isn't any," replied the clerk.

"Who made the arrest?" inquired the judge.

"Billy Winters," said the clerk.

"Stand up," said the judge to me.

I rose in the dock. I stood nearly six feet high. I was barefooted — my feet were of prodigious size and very flat. My skin was of inky blackness. I made this inventory of myself as I stood there waiting.

"Well, Sam," said his honor, familiarly, "is it chickens this time or laundry work?"

I made no reply.

"Come, Billy," said the judge to the policeman, "what has Sam been doing?"

"May it please your honor," replied Billy, "I just can't say. This morning about three o'clock, or, maybe, half past, I was going down Semmes Street, when I hears a big uproar, and there comes a gang of drunken men chasing Sam, and Sam a-runnin' for his life. He was so scart he didn't see me, and ran plumb into my arms. He had nothing on but a short shirt which reached to his waist. I grabbed him, and he fought like the devil to get loose; and I had to club him sorter gently to quiet him. I asked the drunken men what he had been a-doin', but not one of them could tell; and so I took him to the station-house. I thought at one time he was dead, and I had to send for the doctor, but he soon came to."

" Did he give any account of himself ?" asked the judge.

" No, but he got off the darndest lie I ever heard — we all laughed for half an hour. He-he-he."

" What was it, Billy?" asked the judge.

" He said — ha-ha-ha — he said he was — ha-ha-ha — he was — Doctor — Anthony — Huguet !"

" Doctor Anthony Huguet !" said the judge; and then he smiled; and then he looked at me, standing there in the dock — six feet tall, with my shock of black wool, and my black skin; with a shirt and trousers several sizes too small for me; and great splay feet and huge hands and thick lips and yellow eyes;— and the smile broadened into a grin, and the grin into a laugh, and the laugh into a roar, and the whole court-room joined in, till the building shook.

" Why, the man's crazy!" said the judge, as soon as he could catch his breath.

" That's just it, yer honor," replied Billy, " for after

we left him in his cell, he stormed and raved and but-
ted the door with his head, until he was all one gore
of blood; and he kept howling that he was Doctor Huguet, and askin' us to let him out — just like a mad-
man."

" How is he this morning?" asked the judge.

" Better," replied Billy; " he acted quite sensible
and came along very peaceable-like; and he washed
himself — a thing I never knew Sam to do before."

" See here," said the judge to me, " who are you?"

The words, " Doctor Huguet," sprang to my lips,
but I glanced down at my feet, and stood silent
and bewildered. Was I Doctor Huguet? Was I *not*
crazy? And if I said I was Doctor Huguet would
they not roar with laughter again, and send me to the
insane asylum? And was it not necessary that I should
be free, to look after the real Sam Johnson and Mary
Ruddiman? Had I not better lie against my own
conscience?

" Come! answer," said the judge, " who are you?"

" I am Sam Johnson," I replied meekly.

" Where do you live?" asked the judge.

" Down in ' Nigger Hollow,' " I replied.

" What were you doing out last night, without your
clothes?" asked the judge.

" I don't know," I replied.

" Had he been drinking, Billy?" asked the judge.

" No, yer honor, I can't say as he had been. I
couldn't smell any on him. The doctor said he had a
fever."

" Well, that may account for it," said the judge;

" he may have rushed out of a sick-bed in a paroxysm of the fever. But as there is no offense charged against him I suppose we must discharge him. See here, you black scoundrel," he continued, addressing me fiercely, " you can go now, but if you are caught again in such a scrape I'll send you up — sure's shoot-ing. And I say — Doctor Huguet!" ——

I started and said " Sir," and thereupon the judge laughed, and the obsequious court shouted with merriment.

" Let him out of the pen," said the judge.

CHAPTER XV.

AT HOME.

" 'Tis sweet to hear the watch-dog's honest bark
Bay deep-mouthed welcome as we draw near home."

—*Byron.*

BEN was in the garden.

I must use cunning. I will approach him diplomatically.

Ben was training my favorite rose-bush over the latticed walls of a summer-house, looking very much absorbed in thought.

" Good morning," I said respectfully.

" Mornin'," said Ben, eying me askance, with no very friendly expression; and I must admit I was not a prepossessing figure, hatless and shoeless, and in that undeveloped suit of clothes; and Ben, be it said, held the poor of his own race, at all times, in undisguised contempt.

" Ben," said I, " is Doctor Huguet at home? "

" Now see here, nigger, I don't want you to come hyar *Ben*-in' me. I don't know you; and I guess de less I knows o' you de better for dis 'stablishment. Cl'ar out! Whut you want with Doctor Hugay? Doctor Hugay don't know no sich niggers as you."

" Well, you might answer a civil question,— is the Doctor at home? " I asked.

There was something in my mode of speech so different from my appearance, that Ben answered, sullenly enough:

" No; he's gone fishin'."

" Gone fishing," I replied; " isn't that something unusual for the Doctor?"

" Yes," he said, " fust time in ten years."

" Now see here, Ben," I asked, " what else did you observe unusual in the Doctor this morning?"

Ben laid down his gardener's knife on a bench, and turned and came up to me, and said:

" See here, nigger, who is you? You look like a nigger and you talks like a white man. And how'd you know dat de Doctor done suthin' oncommon dis mornin'? Is you a Obiman? Is you Voodoo?"

I grew giddy. I saw plainly that the soul of that wretched chicken-thief had indeed been transferred to my own body at the very moment my spirit had entered his.

" Go on, Ben," I replied, and I fixed him with my eye.

Ben's manner had become respectful, not to say timid. His superstitions were all awakened : — he felt he stood in the presence of some one possessing supernatural knowledge ; for out of fidelity to his master he had not disclosed a word of that which was harrowing his own breast, and I — a total stranger — seemed to know all about it.

" I don't know who you is," he proceeded, but I 'spects you is a conjurer, and I might as well tell you all I knowt. I goes into de Doctor's bed-room dis mornin' to wake and shave him. He was sound asleep. I opened de curtains. As soon as de light struck his eyes he gin er start, an' den he kicked out vicious to de left, an' he said : ' H'yar, Emeline, get up. It's mornin'.' He seemed kind of s'prised that his kick didn't reach any one, and so he kicked again, more vicious than befoah and furder to de left. Then he got up on his elbow and looked at de place where he had been kickin', and, findin' no one dar, he looked around de room. I never seed no man so s'prised in all my life. Den he sot up in de bed an' looked an' looked, fust one way, den anodder; den he looked at de bed and felt of de bed-cloze; den he caught sight o de hand he was feelin' de bed-cloze wid; an' he hil it up an' stared at it, an' den at de odder hand; an' den he pulled up de sleeve of his night-gown an' looked at his arm, and de more he looked de more s'prised he got. An' den he bit his finger right hard, and opened his eyes very wide an' looked around de room ag'in, more s'prised dan eber. Den he caught sight o' me, as I stood dar, wid the hot water in my han', an' he stared at me for a minute or two. An' den he said, kinder soft an' low an' humble:

" ' Come yere, mister.'

" He acted like he was afraid; and still his eyes kept rollin' around de room, and stoppin' ebery now an' den to rest upon his gold watch and chain, dat was lyin' on a table near de bed.

" I went up to him.

" ' Mister,' said he, ' who is I and where is I ?'

" ' Why, Doctor,' said I, ' is you crazy ? Or is you just playin' a game on Ben ? '

"An' still he looked eberywhere and studied me hard. An' again he spoke, sort o' low:

" 'I don't remember you. Who is I an' where am I?'

" 'Well,' I said, 'dis *is* a game. Why, o' course you's Doctor Anthony Hugay, and dis is yo' house, an' dat is de bed whar you went to sleep last night. An' I is Ben Magruder, your body servant, sah. An' it's time for you to get up and dress yourself.'

"And I went and closed de door ob de room for fear some ob de oder servants would hear his queer talk. An', would you believe it! when I came back dat gold watch and chain was gone. It turned out afterwards he had slipped it under de pillow, but what he did it for I can't make out. An' still the Doctor kept rollin' his eyes around dat room, or lookin' at his hands, and studyin' me. Suddenly he said :

" 'Bring me dat lookin'-glass.'

"He pointed to a hand-mirror on one of de booros, an' when I give it to him he hil it up and looked into it for several minutes, kind ob studyin' his own face. An' den a cunnin' look come into his eyes, and de wonder went out ob them, and he got up and said, loud and sharp:

" 'Help me ter dress.'

"De Doctor never spoke dat way to me befo'. I dressed him and shaved him, and all de time he axed me de cuisest questions — what was de names ob de servants, when he knowed them just as well as I did; and how much income he had; and what property he owned; and whether I could bring him a lot o' money. 'Fo' God,' I said to myself, 'de Doctor has done gone

8

plumb crazy.' An' den I brought him up from his desk about a hundred dollars in gold and silver and bank notes; and he was just like a child: he would run his hands through it, and count it over and over agin, and watch me like he thought I would steal it; and then he would put it in one pocket of his cloze, and den change it to anodder; and den divide it up so's to have some in ebery pocket. An' he would laugh. Lord, how he would laugh! An' strut before de big glass and look at his cloze! An' den he took de watch and chain out from under de piller and put 'em on, spreading de chain out so's it would show bigger; and den he would strut ag'in and smile an' smile an' laugh and laugh. I never saw a critter act so in all my life. An' den he walked around de room an' 'spected eberything, an' all de jewels and pretty things and brick-brack he puts into his pockets, until da bulged out. And den I took him down-stairs to breakfast. An', Lord, how he looked at eberything! An' ebery now and den he would ask me: 'Does I really own all dis?' An' when I told him ober and ober again, yes, how he would laugh! And den he would look at me kind of cunnin'-like, and say he was on'y jokin'. At de breakfast he eat like a starved dog: — he didn't 'pear as if he'd had anything to eat for a week. An' den old black Hannah, forty years old, an' as ugly as sin, comes into de room, and he jumped up and chucked her under de chin and tried to kiss her. Poor old Hannah nearly fainted, for she neber saw de Doctor act dat way afore; and I was more and more sure he's dead crazy. And den he wanted to know what he done himself ebery mornin', and I told him he went into de library and read in books and wrote things. He sat in de library a little while, and den he said ' he guessed he go fishin'.' An' den I saw he was gone clean, plumb crazy, for I'd often heard him tell about 'a pole and string, with a worm at one end and a fool at de odder end.' An' so he's off. But I saw him stop and talk to Mis Jones' yalla gal, Susan, on de way to de river, and he chucked her under de chin, too, and laughed; and I could see he was trying to get her to go fishin' with him, but she held back and wouldn't go, and he pulled at her, until Mis Jones stuck her head out ob de window and hollered at him to let dat gal go; and then he run off, just like a scar't nigger. I tell you, the naburs is awful stirred up about it, and Susan says he was drunk; but I know he wasn't."

I felt the blood rushing to my head, and I blushed intensely to think of the destruction of my good name which this scoundrel would effect in a few hours. And yet there was some comfort in the thought that a man whose base appetites led him in such low directions would not be likely to aspire to the hand of Mary Ruddiman; he would rather spend my money in the most degrading debaucheries. If he came in contact with Mary, her keen perception would show her at once that he was only the body of Doctor Huguet; that the soul which had held communion with her own had gone out of him. There was nothing to fear, therefore, in that direction, from such a sensual and ignorant barbarian. But the question was, how should I displace him? How should I get back my own body? I stood there, a stranger in my own home. Everything around me was as familiar as my daily life, and yet I could claim nothing. Was it possible to convert Ben to a belief that I was his master? Nothing seemed easier. I thought as Doctor Huguet. I *was* Doctor Huguet. The mind moved without the body. It forgot the body. What more natural than for me, Doctor Huguet, with all my consciousness, memory, knowledge, to assert myself? But then came back to me the dreadful memory of the police cell and the court-room. I could hear again the tremendous bursts of laughter that followed my declaration that I was myself. I realized that no man could see the soul, the real man, but only the shell which his vitality, by the great occult processes of nature, had gathered around him from the material world. We thought as souls; we met as bodies. " The muddy vesture of decay" did indeed " grossly hem us in," as the great poet has said.

In the meantime, Ben was scanning me very closely. I suppose my very bearing and my silence had a dignity which even my gross appearance could not quite overcome. Ben was keen enough to perceive I was something more than the wretched, half-clad creature I looked. When he spoke there was deference in his voice.

" What had I better do, sah?" he asked.

" At present do nothing," I replied; "let him take his own course. You cannot stop him."

" Do you think he's done gone crazy?" he asked.

" No," I replied; " he is bewitched. His soul has

been taken out of his body, and the soul of a black man put in its place."

" Gor-a'mighty," said Ben, with uplifted hands, his eyes dilated and his dark face mottled and faded with terror, for my declaration was in strict accordance with the superstitions which he had been taught from childhood. " Gor-a'mighty! a nigger got into Mars Anthony?"

" Yes," I replied; " when he kicked at Emeline, as he wakened, he was kicking at his wife. His astonishment was unbounded when he saw around him, not the walls of his rude cabin, but the splendors of that bed-chamber. He bit his finger to see if he was not dreaming. He stole that watch when your back was turned, and hid it under the pillow. He filled his pockets, also, from the instincts of a thief ; and he ran after the women from other base instincts."

As I spoke, Ben recoiled from me, the whites of his eyes growing bigger and bigger, his mouth standing wide open, his very flesh trembling with terror.

" Gor-a'mighty," he kept repeating under his breath. He looked as if about to run away.

" Ben," I said, " don't you know me? *I* am Doctor Huguet! I have been bewitched. My soul passed last night into the body of Sam Johnsing, and his soul has taken possession of my body. You listen to me, a black man, talking with a white man's words; you saw him, Doctor Huguet, playing the thief and acting like a low-down negro."

Ben cried: " O Lord ! O Lord ! " and fell on his knees, his eyes rolling wildly. I began to fear that the astounding problem would be too much for the poor fellow's sanity.

"Come, Ben," I said, lifting him up, "follow me to the library, and I will prove to you the truth of what I say."

He followed me humbly, watchful, like a dog.

I entered the large hall and walked straight to the library door. Ben showed increased astonishment. I took from the shelf two or three of my favorite books.

"Now, listen, Ben," I said, "and I will read to you in English, French and Latin. Surely a bare-footed negro could not naturally do that. You will see that the present Doctor Huguet cannot read at all. Hand him one of these books upside down and he will not know the difference. Here is my file of receipts," I said, going to a cabinet, "and there," pointing it out, "is the receipt for $150.80 which you paid for me, last week, for taxes. You remember that there was a mistake the first time, and you had to go back the second time with my check. And there, in yonder drawer, I keep my check-book, and there, on yonder table, is the package of new books which I received yesterday, by express, from New York. You placed them there yourself."

"Yes, yes," said Ben, "dat is all so." And then his look of wonder and terror gave way to an expression of great pity — for he was an affectionate fellow — and he said:

"Poor Mars Anthony! And is you turned into a nigger?"

" Yes, Ben; in a moment I lost my home, my fortune and myself."

" And Miss Mary!" said Ben, and the tears ran down his black face.

" Yes, Ben; that is the sorest loss of all."

" She can never love a nigger, massa," he said.

" I know that; but we must get clear of this bewitchment, and everything may yet come right. And you must help me, Ben."

" Yes, yes; ob course I will," responded the faithful creature. "But how? Does you know who put dis hoodoo on you?"

" Yes, Ben; it was God."

" God!" echoed Ben, and his eyes grew larger and whiter than ever. " What did you do, massa?"

" I did nothing but think," I replied. "I thought thoughts that were false to my higher nature. It is what is done in the inner sanctuary of the temple that defiles the temple. The sun may shine and the flowers bloom on pillar and architrave, but if the priest of God is false at the altar of his soul the light of the building is dead forever. We are what we are in our dealings with our inner conscience."

Ben shook his head; he could not understand this.

" You must pray to God for me, Ben, and ask him to lift this living curse off my soul," I said, " and you must give me some clothes, for I must go to Mary and talk with her. Bring me a suit of clothes to the bathroom, and I will wash and dress myself. First measure me and take money, go to the store and get me some clothes that will fit me; for, now I think of it, my own are too small for this wretched carcass."

In an hour I had given the body of Sam Johnsing the most complete scrubbing it had ever received since it was born into the world; and I was equipped in a suit of ready-made clothes that approximately fitted me. Ben had purchased shoes and stockings and underwear, but he had forgotten to procure one very essential article of apparel — a hat. He, however, bought me a new soft felt hat of my own, in which the hatter had placed my name, and I found I could force it onto my head, despite my thick shock of wool. Thus equipped, with a few dollars in my pocket, I bade Ben farewell, and started forth.

CHAPTER XVI.

AN INTERVIEW.

"Pray thee, sweet mistress Margaret, deserve well at my hands by help-
ing me to the speech of Beatrice."

— *Much Ado, v. 2.*

I WALKED soberly enough as long as I was within
the city limits, for I had no desire to attract espe-
cial attention; but as soon as I came into the region of
fenced fields and country roads the ferment within me
hastened my steps. It seemed to me I would never get
over those ten miles. Fortunately for me, the legs I
had borrowed from Sam Johnsing were big and long
and strong; and, driven by the impetuosity of my passionate soul, they fairly flew over the ground. But
even the limitations of very rapid walking were not
enough for me; occasionally on a lonely road I would
start and run. Now and then I passed gentlemen and
ladies of my acquaintance on horseback or in car-
riages. I instinctively spoke to them, to be rewarded
by an indignant stare that brought me back to a remembrance of my condition.

And all this time my brain throbbed and worked,
and my heart beat violently. I would see Mary. I
would explain everything. *She* would believe me.
She would pity me. We would wait until this awful
visitation had passed from me. There was hope yet
for me. Far ahead I could see the bright light of

joy.   Visions of love and happiness, in my dear home, with Mary beside me, once more a white man, came before me as the woods moved by me in my rapid advance.

The day was hot.   I grew thirsty.   I remembered that by the roadside, a short distance ahead, there was a woodland spring trickling out of the rocks, and falling into a pool of crystal clearness and beauty.   Many a time, when a boy, hunting through these forests, had I plunged my face, rosy with youth and health, into the fountain, and drunk my full of the delightful liquid. Later in life I had rested by the refreshing pool, and philosophized upon the goodness of God, whose hand had fashioned these threads of living water, creeping among the close-packed rocks, and through earth and gravel, and bursting forth at last, pellucid and beautiful, for the good of His creatures.   And I could not help but compare it to a pure human soul passing through all the pressing insistance of multitudinous sins, and coming forth at last without a stain or discoloration upon its bright surface,— a thing of the earth, yet earthless.

I hastened my rapid steps.   I knelt down upon the mossy earth.   My beating mind was still full of my fair-faced love and hope and joy.   I leaned forward. My lips approached the glassy mirror.   Horror of horrors!   I started back.   There was the brutalized face I had for a brief space forgotten!   The low brow, the shock of crinkled hair, the ebony skin, the yellow eyes, the tumid, protuberant lips, the whole animal-like face of the chicken-thief.

I fell back on my knees. I tore at my close-packed wool. I called on God. I shrieked out aloud in the solitude. I realized the awful, immeasurable, unfathomable, unbridgable gulf which separated me from Mary Ruddiman. It seemed to me a profanation to utter her blessed name with those shapeless, swollen lips; and yet I cried out aloud to the forest and the fountain, and the listening squirrels and the attentive birds: " Mary! Mary! Mary!"—I prayed to her to help me, and then I thought of those reproachful eyes that looked out at me from the fading light of my bed-chamber, and threatened me even while they pitied me.

I forgot my thirst. I sat down upon a rock and thought. Should I turn back? Should I intrude in this dreadful form upon the presence of that refined and cultured spirit? And then the thought of self-destruction recurred to me. Was there any escape from this dark valley of desolation save by the darker gates of death? And the hereafter? Might not the philosophers I had despised be right after all? Were not God and the world beyond the grave the dreams of enthusiasts, and reminiscences of the credulous youth of the human race? Was there anything in nature more than we could see? My brain was whirling; for, on the instant, like a revolving panorama, it seemed to me that all space flashed, circling around me, densely packed with unknown creatures, with indescribable forms that flowed into each other, and the universe was full of faces and eyes, all centered upon me; faces misty and shadowy through which other eyes looked; faces behind faces, mingling with each other, as if the illim-

itable void had not room enough for the intelligences
with which God had packed and crowded it. And
something within me seemed to cry out: " Fool! fool!
thinkest thou that thy capacity for thought is but an
orphan accident in the midst of a barren universe?
No, no, the universe is *thought*. Thy mind is but a
fragment, chipped off and dropped to earth, from the
illimitable Soul of Things, bearing upon it the stamp of
its divinity in its sense of right, its imperial conscience.
Death is but the opening of a door. The room is
empty, but the tenant has wandered elsewhere."

"And, after all,"— I said to myself,—" measured by
the line of immortality, this little life is nothing. I may
be cast down, outraged, humiliated, degraded, robbed
of home and love; but in a little while all this will
pass away. All things will pass away. Ages are but
seconds on the dial of eternity. One thing remains
even to the most wretched—to do his duty. Duty is
the obligation he owes to the Creator. It ties him to
the scheme of the universe, and makes him a partici-
pator in the work of the angels."

Strengthened and chastened by these thoughts, I
rose and proceeded slowly on my way.

I approached the home of her who was dearer to me
than life. I feared to meet her. I skirted the woods
until I came where I could see the house. How different from that recent visit, when I rode to the front
door of the mansion, and was received by the whole
hospitable family with open arms, as the honored and
accepted lover of the daughter of the house. Now I
sneaked in the shadows like a thief. I feared the sun-

shine. I opened the bushes with my huge black hands and peered through. I started at every sound like a guilty thing. I could see the porch, the windows, the garden. She was not there. I longed for her, and yet I shuddered and trembled at the thought of meeting her. I looked behind me. I meditated flight. Hah! What is that white object slowly advancing toward the house, along the road, near which I stand, revealed in sudden glimpses through the shrubbery? The descending sun cast long shadows. There it is again! It may be she. It comes nearer. Yes; it is a woman's form, dressed in white. It comes near me. I tremble as if I had an ague fit. My lips are parched, and my tongue and throat dry and dusty. What shall I do? I look again. Thank God, it is Abigail!

I advanced into the road. She started back from the black apparition suddenly confronting her, but with a resolute look on her handsome face.

"Abigail," I said, and I lifted up my hat with all courtesy, " you do not know me, but I know you, and I know the kindness of your heart; and I would ask permission to have a few words of conversation with you."

She seemed surprised at such language issuing from such a repellant face; but the tie of blood had brought her into much unwelcome contact with the negroes around her, all of whom recognized her as one of their own race, and she replied:

" What have you to say? Be as brief as possible."

"Abigail," I began, " you see before you the most wretched creature in all this fair world. My language tells you that there is some incompatibility between my education and my appearance, and yet I fear to tell you my secret because I know you will treat it with scorn and mockery."

. She had listened to me attentively, her interest deepening as I proceeded.

"Go on," she said; "Heaven forbid that I should mock anything you may tell me. I have my own sorrows; and the wretched always sympathize with the wretched."

"Thank you, Abigail," I replied, "for your words of comfort. Do you remember a day, not long since, when I — I mean Doctor Huguet — sat on yonder porch with Colonel Ruddiman and his friends, and you sat at an upper window, and we — they — talked about the negroes, and I — I mean Doctor Huguet — argued in their defense, and claimed that the white people might have derived their long skulls, in some remote age, from a negro tribe dwelling in southern Europe; and that they were afterward bleached white in the lands of ice and snow and caves and clouds?"

"Yes," she replied, looking very much astonished, "but who are you? And how did you know I listened at an upper window to the conversation? I never saw you before, and you were certainly not there."

"Abigail," I replied, "if I tell you something terrible and extraordinary, you will not think me crazy or an impostor?"

She recoiled a step, still watching me intently, but made no reply.

"Abigail," I said, "I am Doctor Huguet!"

She threw up her hands in alarm and horror. Then, as the impossibility of such a thing dawned upon her, she began to smile.

" Why, that is absurd !" she said, and her face almost broke into a laugh. " You Doctor Huguet! Why, Doctor Huguet is a small, aristocratic-looking, white gentleman of family and position, and you "——

" Yes," I added, " and I am a great, ugly negro — one of the ugliest of that wretched race — a poor, homeless wanderer, belonging to a despised, Pariah caste. But you can see, Abigail, that I speak with all the culture and correctness of Doctor Huguet himself, and that I tell you things which no stranger could know."

Her face grew perplexed, and the great black eyes glowed intensely at me.

" But how," said she, " could you be Doctor Huguet? Are you not some educated negro from the North, who has wandered here and become demented?"

" No, no, Abigail," I replied. " How would I know your name if I was a stranger here? How could I tell you the subject of that conversation? How could I have known that you listened in hiding at an upper window, because the conversation had a special interest for you? No one but Doctor Huguet noticed you, for he was lying in the hammock, looking upward, while the others — Colonel Ruddiman, Major McFettridge, Major Berrisford, Attorney Buryhill, and the rest, occupied chairs."

She stopped and thought, and still the great black eyes, in which you could see no pupil, blazed at me.

"But how could one man be two men?" she said; "how could you be, at the same time, Doctor Huguet and "——

"Sam Johnsing, of Nigger Hollow, the most notorious chicken-thief in this county," I added. "No, Abigail," I continued, "I am not two men. I am the soul, the thinking-principle, of Doctor Anthony Huguet, imprisoned in this shameful confinement. Sam, the thief, and I have changed tenements. I am now in his carcass, and he is masquerading in mine. You will see him and you will see the change."

"What caused it?" she asked, and in her face awe and incredulity contended.

"Abigail," I replied, "you remember that that afternoon I defended the negro race against the prejudices of those white gentlemen. I did so partly because I believed what I said, partly out of the wantonness of idleness and the spirit of controversy. And you remember that those who heard me took offense at the freedom of my speech and avoided the house thereafter."

"Yes, yes," she said, "I remember all that. As I listen to you I believe — when I look at you I cannot believe. Go on."

"I asked Miss Mary"—this was the first time I had mentioned her name, and I did it with a pang and an effort—"I asked Miss Mary why the neighbors staid away from the house; and she told me that the views I had expressed had given them mortal offense, and that I could not rise in the political world if I continued to profess them. We had a long discussion, and I — I

shame to say it, Abigail — I made up my mind to suppress the utterance of my honest convictions for the
sake of the triumphs and glories of life. It is true I
had a mental reservation that if I attained place and
power I would use both for the lifting-up of all men,
including the poor, despised negroes. But for success
I trampled upon my conscience. I crushed under my
feet the bright lamp of the soul. And, Abigail, there
are threads that connect the conscience of the humblest
with the great White Throne of heaven; and when any
man murders his sense of right all the legions of angels
are disturbed in their serenity. That night, in my own
chamber, I was visited, not sleeping, but awake, by the
most wonderful and terrible vision that ever blessed
and cursed the eyes of man. Abigail, I saw — *The
Christ !*"

My voice fell to a whisper, and Abigail's face grew
pale.

"Yes; He came to me as He had lived — with a marvelous human countenance, with radiant hair — self-
luminous — and unutterable eyes, and an aspect of such
pity and sorrow that my very soul was shaken to its
innermost depths. And around him, like a living
frame-work, were the hands of millions of negroes,
many of inky blackness, some brown, and some as fair
as your own, all directed toward him in the attitude of
prayer; — millions of sufferers, — millions of the proscribed of humanity, — millions on whom the whole
weight of the world presses with crushing force. And
he spake. Yea, the very voice that said, 'Suffer little
children to come unto me and forbid them not, for of

9

such is the kingdom of heaven,' rang in my chamber, sanctifying it forever, and he said, glancing around that interminable circle, with a look of infinite compassion :

" ' *These, too, are my children.   For them, also, I died on the cross !* '

" As the vision passed away the merciful eyes reproached me.   They seemed to say, ' I had hoped you would have done my work on earth.   I gave you wealth, station, ability, all the good gifts of life.   I gave you a heart to feel for the sorrows of your kind; but you closed up the avenues of your soul with filthy, little ambitions, with the small hopes of small preferments, for a little mouth-honor and lip-glory which pass away like the mist of the morning.' "

The transformation of the face of my listener was something wonderful.   The doubt, the incredulity were all gone; the attention was intense.

" I fell asleep again, Abigail," I continued; " I woke up in a wretched cabin; I found myself within the body of a negro.   This is my punishment.   This is my living death.   I sit in the midst of my sorrows as in a tomb. I cannot die.   I cannot fly into the unknown world out of which can come such visions.   I know nothing, I can surmise nothing of the much that must be there. That is what terrifies me — the unknown, the immeasurable!   I have no fear of hell.   *This* is hell.   The proud mind that dwells in a proscribed body lives in hell.   Coals and flames are nothing to the anguish of a tortured spirit.   It is the soul that feels the burning, not the dead matter of the body."

At the last words Abigail's face softened, and the tears rolled slowly down her cheeks. I had touched upon the secret passion of her life. Hers, too, was the proud mind in the proscribed body; she, too, had endured the flames of hell. Her imprisoned soul, like a bird, had beaten its wings against the roof of her gilded cage, only a few thin lines of prejudice separating her from the heaven she would aspire to. All the warm, hot love of her passionate nature was hurled down from the towers of caste, like the angels of Lucifer, reeling backward from the battlements of heaven, and falling, falling into the nethermost pit.

"Poor Abigail," I said, and I took her fair small hand in my great black paw, "you believe my story?"

"Why not?" she said. "God puts our souls where he pleases, and there is oftentimes no compatibility between the spirit and its tenement. How often have I prayed and wept for death to come, and death would not come. That which happened to you the other day happened to me at my birth: a white soul was placed in one socially a negro. The charm may be removed from you in a few days or months, but I must carry my curse to the grave. The whole world moves upward and forward, but I must go downward or backward — despair or destruction are my only alternatives. My case is greatly worse than yours."

"That is true, Abigail; but let our fates be a bond of union between us," I replied. "If I ever recover my lost condition I promise you I shall toil and scheme to lift you out of your destiny. With my money and your fair beauty I shall establish you in some far

Northern city, or in Europe, where the cruel prejudices of blood shall fall away from you, and you may love and marry where honor points the way, and the barriers of caste shall disappear from around you forever."

She thanked me warmly, with eyes glowing.

"And now, Abigail," I said, "I want you to bring all this to the knowledge of Miss Mary. You know we were to have been married. That, of course, is all past, it may be, forever. But I desire one last interview with her, and then I shall go out into the world alone, to fulfill the destiny, whatever it is, for which I have been appointed. Can you tell my story to her and bring her here? Can you persuade her to believe in the truth of the improbable narrative I have communicated to you? I dread to meet her, and yet I must do so."

She promised to do as I had requested, and left me, walking slowly along the road to the house. I retreated into the woods by the roadside. It was then about one hour before sunset.

CHAPTER XVII.

THE LADY OF MY LOVE.

" Had we never loved so kindly,
Had we never loved so blindly,
Never met, nor never parted,
We had ne'er been broken-hearted."
— *Burns*.

THROUGH the trees I watched the slowly receding figure, with the thoughtful pose of the head, thinking, thinking of my dreadful story, and a great pity went out from my heart toward that fair sufferer; — fair and beautiful and yet proscribed; — alone, facing a hostile world. And yet, so strong is the power of prejudice, I felt, even while I pitied her, that I could not have married her — no, not if Mary did not exist. Beauty of mind, beauty of soul, exquisite beauty of body, such as fires the hearts of men and sets their brains throbbing passionately, all this she had; everything to make the life of man sunshine and his home paradise, and yet, across the golden image of all this perfection ran diagonally that thin, dark *bar sinister;* and prejudice stood up and pointed at it, and hissed its scorn, and all the furies of society with blazing eyes denounced it. Oh, strange, sad world, where a thought of the mind has such power to undo all the works and merits of nature!

So thinking, I saw her enter the door of the mansion.

I waited; I knew she was telling my awful story to Mary. How would she receive it? With incredulity? With sorrow? Would love for me die out of her heart in the presence of the great calamity which had overwhelmed me? Ah! there was the dread.

And still I waited. The tree-trunks cast long shadows. Now and then a lizard gleamed like a line of rapid light. A squirrel sat above me and chattered and scolded me. And glittering insects rejoiced in their brief hour of life won out of the eternity of nothingness. An hour passed.

And then, through the last light of the sinking sun, I saw two figures advancing along the solitary road, toward my hiding-place. They were the figures of women. As they drew near I recognized Mary and Abigail. A short distance from me Abigail paused, and Mary advanced alone, slowly, and looking from right to left. There was only curiosity upon her face.

I stepped forward into the road. I could not speak. She looked at me intently and fearlessly; then she spoke:

" Abigail," she said, " has been telling me a ridiculous story that you are Doctor Huguet. How have you imposed on the poor girl's credulity? Who are you?"

" Mary," I replied, " Abigail has told you the truth. Incredible as it may appear, the soul of your affianced lover, Doctor Anthony Huguet, dwells in this hideous carcass. A visitation of God has fallen upon me."

I repeated to her the story I had told Abigail.

"And do you expect me," she said, "to believe such a statement as that—such an incredible, absurd story. You slander Doctor Huguet in telling it. You are some cunning impostor who has made himself familiar with the circumstances of my family and my relations to Doctor Huguet, and you have sought me for some mercenary purpose."

"O Mary, Mary," I cried, "do not add to my unutterable miseries. Do you want proof of the truth of my story? Wait until you meet that wretched negro, concealed in my body; you will see at once that it is not I. The mind, the soul is wanting. Do you ask for further proof? Do you remember the first time we ever met in my library? Will I tell you what we were discussing—and there was no one there but you and I? You had been reading Ben Jonson's *Sejanus*, and we talked about the resemblance of Jonson's prose writings to Bacon's works, and you claimed that there were passages in *Sejanus* equal to anything in the Shakespeare plays. And you quoted from Ben Jonson: 'Language most shows a man. Speak that I may see thee.' Alas! I speak as Doctor Huguet, and you cannot see me in this mean habiliment. And you remember:

"''Tis place,
Not blood, discerns the noble and the base.'

And do you remember how aptly you quoted that expression in our discussion as to my future political career?"

The astonishment revealed in her face was unbounded — to not only hear such discourse proceeding from such a rude and brutal countenance, but to have the details of our most intimate conversations thus repeated by one of such utterly ignorant appearance.

" This is all very strange," she said, thoughtfully, " but I refuse to believe the impossible. There is no precedent in all the world for such a story. I cannot explain your learning, or your acquaintance with my conversations with Doctor Huguet ; but the most superstitious explanation of such facts would be more reasonable than to believe that Doctor Anthony Huguet has exchanged souls with a negro. I shall have to ask you to pardon me; I must return to the house."

She turned away. My whole soul seemed to pour out of me. I fell upon my knees and grasped her hand.

" O Mary, Mary," I cried, " do not leave me. You carry the world with you. You are my only hope. There is nothing but death for me."

The blood suffused her face for an instant. I can remember how she then drew back; — I can never forget the pale horror of her countenance — the nostrils dilated with indignation — the crescent eye-brows lifted with astonishment.

" Let go of my hand," she said, looking at me with loathing.

But I clung to it as the drowning mariner clings to the last plank. The ocean of desolation roared around me.

" O Mary! Mary! " I cried, " believe me; have pity on me. My love! — my hope! — my life! "

She screamed for Abigail, who came running. Some negroes who had been working in a field, near at hand, but were about going home to supper, started hurriedly toward us. She made one supreme effort and dragged her hand from my grasp, and fled with Abigail toward the house. I fell forward on my face in the dust, the most utterly wretched creature then drawing the breath of life in all the world. I wished for death; I prayed for it.

Then I heard the sound of a horse's feet and the rumbling of cart-wheels. I looked up. It was a negro, one of the Ruddiman household, returning from the nearest village. I rose to my feet. Then I saw the negroes, from the field, rapidly approaching me — nearing the fence that bounded the road. Their manner was fierce; they were running fast. I was not conscious of any wrongdoing, but I did not want to encounter them; and I instinctively darted into the woods. Life is a matter of habit. I had prayed for death — I fled from an unknown danger.

CHAPTER XVIII.

HUNTED TO THE DEATH.

"Nay, Warwick, single out some other chase;
For I myself will hunt this wolf to death."
— *3 Henry VI, iv, 14.*

I HEARD their outcries; they were searching for me. I buried myself deeper in the forest. The sounds ceased. In a little while, drawn by an irresistible impulse, I approached the road, that I might look once more upon the house where she dwelt. I reached a point where I could command a view of the highway. What was my astonishment to find it full of life and bustle! There were Colonel Ruddiman and his sons, with several of their neighbors, all on horseback, and all armed, while behind them came negroes on foot, with hunting-dogs. I could hear their voices, full of animation and excitement.

The Colonel was talking loudly to a barefooted, hatless negro, who ran by his side, and I heard him say:

"Where did the d —— d rascal go?"

And the negro pointed down the road, toward the place where I had entered the forest, and the whole crowd rushed rapidly in that direction.

What did it all mean? Could they be searching for me?

And then a sudden light dawned upon me, and I saw the terrible position in which I stood.

I had been seen — I, a negro — grasping the hand of a white lady, on a public road, and holding on to it, until she screamed and tore herself loose and ran away.

A horror took possession of me. I grew faint. I knew the vast abyss between the races. I knew the terrible wrath of the white man against the negro who insulted or assaulted a white woman; the deep, the ineradicable, the awful wrath, which nothing but the life-blood of the offender could satisfy. It was a race instinct — natural, tremendous, inappeasable. For *that* crime there was no mercy. I should be hanged, shot, torn limb from limb, perchance burned alive. But a moment ago I had prayed for death; now I bounded like a deer into the depths of the woods and ran, ran, ran, until the increasing vistas of sky and cloud, through the trees, told me I was approaching the edge of the forest. I turned and ran back into the thick gloom. I came to a sparkling rivulet, singing its happy way along the greensward. I knelt down and drank. I was very thirsty. This time I forgot the reflection of my dark face in the water. Then a thought came to me. I remembered the dogs which the negroes led. They might be bloodhounds. If so, they were upon my track. My mind ran back over many stories of woodcraft. I rose and walked up the sparkling stream, careful not to break the overhanging boughs; stooping ever and anon to crouch and listen. After I had proceeded about a mile I saw the kind of tree I had been looking for; it was a venerable forest mon-

arch, of great height and dense foliage, and one giant
arm reached down so near the water that by a great
spring I was able to clutch it. I crawled along the
branch to the main trunk, and then up and up I climbed
until I was lost in the great mass of greenery, one hundred feet from the ground. I found a cross-branch
where I could stretch myself out, and there I lay, pant-
ing, while the shadows crawled deeper and deeper over
the forest. But, hark! what is that? There was a confused noise in the direction from which I had come. It
grew louder. I could distinguish a multitude of voices
and the baying of dogs. Nearer and nearer it came.
The wood was full of people. Some bore lanterns, and
others carried hurriedly-extemporized torches, made
from fat pine splinters. I peered through the foliage.
It was a wild, weird scene. On both sides of the
stream came the mob of dogs and men; the former
snuffling everywhere to recover the lost trail; the latter
inspecting the soft sides of the stream and every bush
and tree. The fading light contended weirdly with the
red glare of the torches. They came directly under
the tree. I heard the Colonel's voice commanding,
" Halt!"

" Jim," he said, to a neighbor, " a smart darkey
might have jumped to that hanging limb."

" Yes, Colonel," was the reply; " it is considerable
of a jump, but it might be done."

" Boys," said the Colonel, " give us a volley into that
tree-top — there where the leaves are thickest."

And before I could realize my danger there was a
roar of guns, and the bullets were whizzing and hum-

ming all around me, and the leaves fell upon me in a shower.

" Give 'em another one," cried the Colonel, and I crouched together into the smallest compass, and muttered a prayer of my childhood, when again the guns roared and the foliage around me was full of sounds and flying leaves.

" I don't think any living thing is up there, Colonel," said one of the men, " or he would have dropped."

" I guess that's so," said the Colonel; " you might as well move on, boys. And, Major Berrisford, will you be kind enough to send one of your men to the nearest farm-house, for some more torches? We will be in the dark soon."

And so the dreadful procession moved up the little stream, giving out great red lines of light that flashed and penetrated far into the depths of the forest, while the not unmusical tumult of mingling voices, human and animal, rang far and wide.

" Hunted like a wild beast!" I said to myself. " I, Doctor Anthony Huguet — the peaceful current of whose happy life was, but yesterday, the envy of all beholders; I, the cultured and scholarly denizen of the world; the exemplar and pattern of the community; rich, prosperous, respected, honored — all all this but yesterday;— now I am a black man, a great, hulking, hideous black man, hidden in the top of a high tree, while those who were my dearest friends are hunting for me to murder me ! My God ! " I said, " could the whole varied panorama of human fortune afford another such spectacle ? "

I was safe for a little time, but what of the future? I knew enough of the practices of the people in such cases. The wood I was in was part of the primeval forest — of considerable size — left undisturbed in the settlement of the country, but surrounded on all sides by plantations. I knew that my pursuers, for the whole country-side had evidently turned out for the exciting man-hunt, would place a cordon of guards around the forest, and to-morrow they would advance steadily, from all directions, toward the center, examining every tree that could shelter me. And if they failed to find me in that way, they would keep up the blockade until hunger forced me out into the open fields, where I would be seized upon at the first house I approached for food. There was but one course left for me to take. That was to get my bearings, by the glow which yet lingered in the western sky, and if possible find the north star, and then take advantage of the darkness of the night, to reach that part of the forest nearest my home, and run the risk of getting past the line of sentinels posted in the highway. If I succeeded I would be back in C—— before daylight. If I was caught — well, that would be the end of me and my troubles.

I climbed still higher until through the parted leaves I could see the stars. It was not long until I had found the north star — that kindly guide of mariner and wanderer for ages before the discovery of the magnetic needle, whose " true, fixed quality " has been the theme of the poet in all languages. By the dim light I determined the north direction from the tree, fixing it by an ancient walnut at some little distance. I trusted to occasional glimpses of the heavens for my future guidance. I waited until I thought it was about ten or eleven o'clock, when I began to descend the tree quietly, and reached the ground at last, my clothes somewhat damaged by spurs and branches. Then I found the walnut tree, and from the line between the two I advanced at a right angle, to the east, the direction I was to take. I proceeded slowly, listening, and starting at every sound, bumping against tree-trunks and falling over rotten logs. Occasionally I caught glimpses of the sky, and corrected my direction. Finally, after about two hours of walking, I perceived that I was getting to the end of the forest, and proceeded with increased caution. Stepping with cat-like tread, and peering into the darkness, I reached at length the wagon-road which skirted the wood. If I could pass this I would be comparatively safe. I could not help but think that this body I bore had been trained in many such midnight exercises, under the direction of its former owner, and that every faculty and movement seemed to be perfectly adapted to the work.

I scanned the road, right and left, as far as my keen eyes could penetrate; and I listened carefully for the slightest sound. The silence was profound, save for that thin undertone of insect life, which seems to be the breathing of great Nature when she sleeps her profoundest sleep.

I crept slowly down the bank; I crossed the little ditch made by the road-builders; I stepped hurriedly across the wide, beaten highway; I descended into the other ditch; I crossed it; my heart rose; I would be in the fields in another moment and far away; I climbed the little ascent to a snake-fence; I leaned my whole weight upon the top rail to spring over, when, with a loud snap, it broke, and the fence crumbled under me. My cursed fate was still pursuing me.

A quick, fierce voice cried out:

" Who goes there? "

The next instant a bright flash filled the road, and there was the loud explosion of a gun. And then bang, bang, came the reports of two other guns. I had fallen with the rotten fence; before I could rise the whole road was alive; I felt a sharp pain in my shoulder; a large dog had seized me. I struggled to rise, but before I could regain my feet a dozen hands had clutched me, and a dozen rifles and revolvers were pointed at my face.

" Quick here, bring a light! "

A farmer's boy came running, bearing a flaming pine torch. A great crowd had gathered, for the alarm had passed along the line. They thrust the light into my face.

Doctor Magruder seemed in command.

" Who knows him? " asked the Doctor. A score of voices cried, " That's him! " More than half the crowd were negroes — and they seemed more zealous in the hunt than the whites.

" Which one of you can identify him? " asked the Doctor. There was great commotion, but no one answered.

But one burly fellow, a white man, did not intend to be deprived of the sacrifice he had expected.

" Why, Doctor," said he, " this must be the scoundrel. He is a stranger here. Nobody knows him. And we find him stealing out of the timber at midnight, sneaking away. Let's hang him anyhow!"

And still from up and down the road the crowd gathered, the torches and lanterns flickering in every direction, and the cry was out everywhere, " He is caught!" " He is caught!" And every accession to the crowd increased its ferocity. I gave myself up for lost. They glared upon me like wild beasts. It was a sea of enraged faces. Doctor Magruder, in the center, held me by the collar. He was a just man and loved fair play, but there was no kindness in the way in which he shook me, and roared:

" You d——d rascal, are you the man that assaulted Miss Ruddiman?"

" Doctor," I replied, " I never assaulted or insulted Miss Ruddiman, or any other woman."

Here a negro appeared with a rope, and the excitement of the crowd became intense. They swayed and pushed me back and forth, and a dozen brawny hands clutched me to drag me to my doom. I felt something around my neck. The negro had flung a slip-knot over my head, but before the crowd could pull it tight Doctor Magruder threw it off. I shall never forget, to my dying day, that dreadful array of furious eyes, each one fastened on my own, as if they would strike me dead with their burning, basilisk looks, and every man pressing to seize me. Only Doctor Magruder stood firm.

"Boys," he said, "let us have fair play. It is true he is a nigger, and a d——d mean-looking one at that, but we haven't a particle of evidence that he is the man who assaulted Miss Ruddiman. We don't want to kill an innocent man. It wouldn't be a nice thing to think of when we come to die ourselves."

The crowd grew quieter.

"I'll tell you what we'll do, boys," the Doctor continued. "It isn't very far to Colonel Ruddiman's. Let us go there, and get Miss Mary to identify him. If she says he's the man, you may make a bonfire of him, for all I care. But you remember what Colonel Crockett used to say: 'Be sure you're right, *then* go ahead!'"

This proposition was accepted with cheers. Its logic was unanswerable. And so the procession moved up the road, I in the center, with a dozen hands grasping me. The negro with the rope close behind me. The whole swarming, turbulent mass of blacks and whites around me. The glare of the torches lit up the sky, and from every house and cabin additions flocked to swell the mighty mass. Long before we reached the Ruddiman mansion runners had gone ahead to waken the family with the startling news that the criminal had been caught, and that they were bringing him to be identified and punished.

My God! Who is this comes running to meet us? I saw the white-clad figure of a woman; she flew over the ground; negroes and whites parted before her; her dress was **disarranged,** her great eyes blazing. It was Abigail.

She rushed **forward,** placed her hand on my arm, and cried out, in a voice of command:

" Let him go ! Take your hands off ! This man never harmed any one ! "

Lord ! how my heart rose with a great heave in my breast. The whole world was black as Erebus but a moment before. Yes; in the whole world there was no creature loved me. Death encircled me; the rope dangled behind me; all nature hated me. And here was this splendid, this magnificent woman, forgetting in an instant her natural modesty, and all the social limitations of her sex, and rushing to my rescue, as the tigress leaps through the hunters to the protection of her young.

" God bless you, Abigail," I said, and the great tears ran down my face in streams. " God bless you and love you forever ! "

" Doctor Magruder," she said, to the Doctor, who had come forward, " I was at the interview out of which all this miserable trouble arose. It is a great mistake. This man is innocent."

" Well," said the Doctor, " I am glad to hear you say so, Abigail; but here comes Miss Mary, and we have agreed to leave the whole matter to her decision."

Quick as a flash Abigail turned and darted through the crowd in the direction of Col. Ruddiman and his daughter, who were advancing toward us, and I could see her gesticulating and talking with fierce earnestness **to her cousin.**

The crowd parted as the Colonel advanced with Mary on his arm. I watched her face, and she scanned mine with keen interest. Abigail followed her.

Doctor Magruder lifted his hat courteously, and said:

" Miss Ruddiman, we have captured a negro who is believed to be the man who insulted you this afternoon on the public road; but before punishing him we thought it but just that he should be identified by you. Is this the man? "

" Yes," she replied, " that is the man."

In an instant the negro behind me slipped the rope over my head, and the crowd swayed to and fro, murmuring, and deeply excited.

" But," she added, " he did not assault or insult me. He simply knelt on the ground and begged a favor of me. His manner toward me was perfectly respectful, and his speech far beyond his apparent station in life."

Doctor Magruder quietly lifted the rope from around my neck, and said:

" Then you do not desire him punished? "

" Oh, no! not at all. He did nothing to deserve punishment."

" Well, boys," said the Doctor, " you'll have to give up your bonfire this time. I guess we will have to let the fellow go."

Their hands released me, and I stood in the middle of the road, once more a free man.

But my troubles were not yet over.

" Miss Ruddiman," said the Doctor, again with uplifted hat, " do you know anything about this fellow? "

" No," she replied; " I never saw him before this afternoon."

" Have you any objection, then, to our arresting him and finding out something about him? He is a stranger here to everybody, and seems to be a kind of vagrant."

" I have no objection whatever," said Miss Mary, affecting, as I thought, an indifference which she did not feel really; for while she had not, for one instant, believed that I was Doctor Huguet, there was enough about the conversation I had held with her to perplex and interest her.

" See here, my man," said Doctor Magruder to me, " where do you belong? "

" I live in C —— ," I replied.

" What is your name? " he asked.

I did not at once answer. I looked into the faces of Abigail and Mary:—the first regarded me with pity, the last with curiosity.

" Come, answer," said the Doctor; " what is your name? "

Should I lie and deny myself? Or should I speak the truth and be laughed at? But what did I care for laughter? Low as I had fallen, I would not acknowledge the name of the wretched chicken-thief. It stuck in my throat like Macbeth's " Amen." I could not pronounce it. I lifted my head boldly and said in a clear, loud voice:

" My name is Doctor Anthony Huguet! "

Abigail smiled a smile of approval. Mary looked astonished. There was silence for a time. It took a little while for the prodigious statement to work its way through the understandings of my hearers. The white men grasped the conception first; they smiled; then they laughed; the negroes took it up; there was a roar and burst of apparently inextinguishable laughter. Now and then would come a lull, and it would break out, and rise and fall again and again, like a storm. The white men held their sides and laughed; the negroes cracked their thighs and danced and shouted.

"Why," said Doctor Magruder, "the man's crazy."

And the mob roared louder than ever. The idea of a crazy negro, who thought himself a white man, and such a white man! was too ridiculous; laughter gave but a feeble expression of their immense internal merriment. They grew helpless with jocularity. I could have tied all my recent captors with wisps of straw.

But through all this tempest and uproar I stood like an ugly statue of Hercules,— carved out of ebony,— grim and smileless.

"O fools!" I said at last, "that cannot see the immortal spirit of the man through the cloudy covering of the flesh. You read no further than this mask-like face; you cannot see the mind that glows and burns within. To you the lamp is more than the light."

There was dead silence. Never before, in South Carolina, had such a speech been heard to issue from a black man's lips. The sheer force of my outraged intellect had risen to a certain level of stern dignity, in spite of all the rude assaults and injustices of fortune.

I forgot my love and my sorrows. I was a man again, commanding men by the power of my soul.

" If you have no further business with me," I said, raising my hat courteously to the ladies, " and if I have already contributed sufficiently to your amusement, you will pardon me for withdrawing."

And I turned my back upon them and strode away.

" By the Lord Harry," said Doctor Magruder, " that's the most wonderful nigger I ever met. He talks with the eloquence of a Calhoun, and marches off, in his rags, with the dignity of a Chesterfield. Look at him! You would think he owned the highway. Well! I'll be d——d! "

But what a sense of exaltation came over me! Out of the very wells and caverns of humiliation I had climbed to the light. I had risen upon the wings of my own soul. I had found that there is that in the mind of man that can survive " the wreck of matter and the crash of worlds." Only the cowardly fall. The brave man dares all the bolts of fate. Death simply releases him from unfortunate conditions. The mind is god-like — it is God. I would make this black hide as glorious as the crippled figure of the slave Æsop, or the satyr-like features of the persecuted Socrates.

And, so thinking, even the image of Mary grew dim for a time, and, full of high resolves, and with head erect, I marched back to C——. There Ben sheltered me, and, after listening, with distended mouth and eyes, to my wonderful story, gave me food and a bed in one of the garrets. He told me, before leaving me, that Doctor Huguet — the new Doctor Huguet — had been carried home at midnight, dead drunk, and in that condition he had put him to bed, where he now lay snoring.

CHAPTER XIX.

IN THE COURT-ROOM AGAIN.

"If you be ta'en, we then should see the bottom
Of all our fortunes."
—*2 Henry VI., v. 2.*

IT WAS the afternoon of the second day of my imprisonment in Sam Johnsing's body. Tired and worn out, I had slept through the morning. After dinner I set out for a walk, and to think over my plans for the future.

How could I rise above my condition? I had intellect, education, eloquence, energy. Surely a black skin could be no impediment to all these powers of the soul. "It is the mind," the great poet says, "that makes the body rich." Yes; I remembered the passage:

"For 'tis the mind that makes the body rich;
And, as the sun breaks through the darkest clouds,
So honor peereth through the meanest habit.
What! is the jay more precious than the lark,
Because his feathers are more beautiful?
Or is the adder better than the eel,
Because his painted skin contents the eye?"

This terrible race-prejudice, I said to myself, has continued to exist because there are no great scholars, thinkers and speakers, of the negro race, to challenge and overcome it. White men could not have been suppressed in that fashion! I will lead the way! That may have been the purpose for which this ghastly transformation has been inflicted upon me. And I swelled with pride in anticipation of my triumphs, close at hand.

I walked on, full of these high thoughts, muttering to myself, when a heavy hand was laid upon my shoulder. I turned and found myself confronted by a policeman. I knew him well — an honest, over-officious fellow.

" See here, nig," he said, " where you goin'?"

This was a rude awakening from my reverie, and I made no answer. The policeman spoke again:

" I see you comin' out of Doctor Huguet's house. What was you a-doin' there?"

" I was visiting Ben," I replied; " he is an old friend of mine."

" An old friend of yours!" was the answer. " Do you think I don't know you, Sam? You hadn't clothes enough to cover you yesterday, and now you are tifficked out grand. Where did you get that five-dollar hat?"

And with this he rudely grabbed the hat from my head, and looked into it.

" Whew!" he said; " Doctor Huguet's hat! Is that your lay, you black rascal? Got above chickens this time, and taken to high-priced clothes, hey? Kind o' risin' in the world, Sam. Shouldn't wonder if ye'd try burglary next, and become respectable. Come along, Sam. I knows a gentleman down street that wants to have a talk with you very bad. A very friendly, pleasant gentleman he is, too. I guess you know him,

Sam; visited him several times afore in his private parlor."

I thought of resisting, but the formidable club came out, and I saw that it would be useless to struggle; and with a heavy heart I walked beside my captor to the station-house. I heard the heavy door clank behind me, and I sat down upon the rude bed, utterly dejected and hopeless. My philosophy was all gone. Honor did *not* peer through the meanest habit. The mind did *not* make the body rich. All that was fiction, not fact. I thought of Mary's favorite quotation:

> "'Tis place,
> Not blood, discerns the noble from the base."

And it seemed to me that Ben Jonson had come nearer to the truth than Shakespeare.

"What, Sam!" said the judge, as I rose, at the call of my new name; "here again? What have you been a-doing this time?"

I did not speak.

"Stealing, your honor," replied the clerk.

"The same old story," said the judge. "What did he steal?"

"Doctor Huguet's hat," said the constable. "I saw him comin' out of Doctor Huguet's house yesterday, and, knowin' his character, I arrested him, and found him wearin' this hat."

And the constable handed up the hat to the judge.

"Clear case, Sam," said the judge, after reading the

inscription inside the hat. " How did you get this hat ?"

I hesitated before answering. I knew that if I stated that Ben had given it to me, the faithful fellow might get into trouble, and might even lose his place. And so I replied:

" It is my hat. I am Doctor Huguet."

" Come, come," said the judge, frowning, " that joke is played out. It was well enough for one occasion, but it is monotonous when repeated. Is Doctor Huguet here? "

" Yes, your honor," replied the constable; " I sent for him this morning. Here he comes."

I turned, and saw myself advancing through the door of the court-room — myself, but badly changed by drink and dissipation. The face was pale, the eyes watery, the hands trembled. He advanced timidly, glancing from right to left round the room, which was only too familiar to him.

" Doctor Huguet," said the judge, courteously, " I am sorry to have troubled you, but we have a negro here who has been arrested with a hat in his possession, with your name written in it, and you have been sent for to identify it as your property. The most amusing part of the matter is that he says he is himself Doctor Huguet ! "

Sam's face grew pallid at these last words, and he turned round until his eyes encountered mine. He saw his old self standing before him, and he shook like an aspen leaf. He fell back as if he would retreat from the room. Every one observed his terror.

" Hold on, Doctor," said the judge; " your testimony is absolutely necessary."

I could see Sam bracing himself and rallying his faculties, while he looked at me vindictively.

" Swear Doctor Huguet," said the judge. The oath was administered by the clerk.

" Doctor," said the judge, " examine that hat and say whether or not it is yours."

Sam scarcely took his eyes off my face, or looked at the hat, while he replied:

" Yes, sah."

" Did you give it to the prisoner ? "

" No, sah."

" You didn't sell it or give it to any one ? "

" No, sah."

" That is sufficient, Doctor."

At this I cried out in thunder tones :

" Sam Johnsing, you d——d chicken-thief, drop that hat ! "

The hat dropped instantly, and Sam reeled under the words as if he had been struck a heavy blow. He glared wildly around him.

" How dare you address a white man in that way, you miserable nigger?" exclaimed the constable.

" He a white man !" I cried. " He is the soul of Sam Johnsing, the chicken-thief, in the body of Doctor Huguet. *I* am Doctor Huguet !"

" Crazy again," said the judge.

" No, Judge, not crazy," I replied. " Ask that man to spell out his own name in that hat. He cannot do it. He does not know the first letter of the alphabet.

Hand me yonder copy of the statutes, and I will read it for you, Latin phrases and all."

There was a great sensation in the court-room. The judge looked curiously at me and at Sam. That worthy clung to the sides of the witness-box for support. It seemed to me that the judge thought for a moment of applying the test I had proposed. But no evidence could overcome the evidence of his own senses. There stood the white man, Doctor Huguet, and there the black man, Sam Johnsing. How could the one be the other? It was absurd. And so he said, politely, to the Doctor:

"Doctor Huguet, the court will excuse you."

Sam looked at him vacantly.

"You can go."

Sam rushed for the door.

"Sam Johnsing," he said roughly to me, "I did intend to send you to jail for three months for insulting a white man, as well as for larceny. But I don't think it right to burden the county with the expense of supporting such a miserable wretch for so long a time. You will, therefore, stand committed for thirty days. Jones" (to the constable), "take him to jail."

"May it please your honor," I said, "you are sending me to prison for stealing my own hat. I told you the truth. I am Doctor Huguet. By a dreadful visitation of Providence I have been forced to exchange bodies with that miserable wretch, Sam Johnsing, and he is now masquerading in my body. You think this is impossible. The possible and the impossible simply represent the limits of our experience. Who can say what is possible or impossible in a universe of which we know so little? A miracle may be simply an extension of our experience. I have offered to submit to a test. I will submit to any test you may apply. You know that Sam Johnsing was an ignorant, a most ignorant, degraded fellow. Bring me your Greek, Latin, French and German books, and I will translate them for you. Send for one of your physicians, and let him examine me in the most recondite studies of his profession. Call in your college professors, and I will challenge them to a discussion of the literatures of the world. Give me an opportunity to defend my right to be what I am. Summon the scientists of the world to examine my case. Do not treat me as a criminal and send me to prison."

The judge sat with open-eyed astonishment as these cultured and elevated sentences poured from my thick lips. He was lost in wonder at the contrast between what I appeared to be and that which I said — between what he knew of Sam's past career and that which came out of my mouth. But it was plain that, great as was his surprise, he did not for one instant entertain the slightest belief that I was really Doctor Huguet, or that such an exchange of bodies, as I had asserted, could be possible. He was simply overwhelmed with surprise and perplexity.

There was dead silence in the court-room for a minute or two. At last the constable who had arrested me, and who now had his hand upon the collar of my coat, cried out:

" Why, the nigger's bewitched ! "

This explanation seemed very reasonable to court and spectators; and the constable, with the air of a man who has successfully solved a puzzling conundrum, marched me off, bare-headed, to the county jail.

CHAPTER XX.

IN JAIL.

"I have been studying how I may compare
This prison, where I live, unto the world."
—*Richard II., v. 5.*

"ROBBED of my fortune and convicted of stealing my own hat!"

I smiled a grim, bitter smile as I sat upon the side of the iron cot and looked at the bare walls and the high barred window, through which a gush of sunshine fell and blazed upon the stone floor.

Was ever any other poor wretch on earth punished by such violent contrasts of fate? My own hat, which I had bought and paid for with my own money, handed me by my own servant, employed and paid by me,— and here I am in prison for having purloined it! Here I am, with all the education possessed by any man in the commonwealth, and I can get no one to believe that I am anything but a wretched, illiterate negro; a sneak-thief, a marauder of chicken-coops and hen-roosts and clothes-lines! It is horrible! Even when I stood up there in the court-room, and, in choice and even eloquent language, demanded that I be put to the test of scholarship with the wretch who bore my person about with him, I could not get a hearing. Oh, the brutal impassiveness of public opinion under the domination of prejudice! It is stolid. It is colossal.

The noise in the court-room was gone.   I was alone.
I would think.

"Had I left anything undone that it was in my power
to do, to prevent or avert these misfortunes?"

I thought back all along the line of events since I
had wakened in the stifling air of the negro hut, and I
tried to find a flaw, a point where I might have acted
differently.   There was not one.   I was simply powerless.   My mind was as bright and active, my knowledge as great, as it was before this great calamity fell
upon me.   And I had acted wisely, under all the circumstances.

Why, then, had I failed?

Failed?   How could I help but fail?   It was this
dreadful black skin that dragged me down.   This it
was that had rendered education, knowledge, wisdom,
energy, of no avail.   This was the impassable wall
against which I might plunge in vain.   It rose up, up,
all around me, until it hid the very face of heaven
from my gaze; it closed me in more completely than
the walls of the cell; and there was no window of hope
in it through which the bright sunshine could stream
to illumine my gloom.

Ay, there was the rub.   The utter hopelessness of
my condition!   When that mighty Spirit, in some
divine freak of thought or purpose, put forth His
terrible power, and plunged me into this dreadful
abyss, He intended to punish me for having been false
to my own conscience.   And how long did He intend
that this punishment should endure?   That was the
question.   Would I carry this horror to the grave?

Would I rot in the carcass of Sam Johnsing? Would the worms riot under this black skin? And would even the grave — dreadful thought! — terminate my sufferings? Should I not go into other regions of life disqualified and degraded? Should I float from sphere to sphere in some lost caste of spirit-life? Or should I return to earth, and, conscious of the past, repeat my dreadful career, age after age, over and over again, horrors multiplied by horrors!

The day darkened as I sat and thought, but it was nothing to the profound darkness that settled on my soul. My head sank into my chest; my shoulders drooped. I seemed to cringe into myself, as if the very props of life had been withdrawn from within me. Night came, but, with its stars, it was as daybreak to the moonless and starless night that reigned within me. Never before had I realized the glory of my *white life*. Never before had I understood what " honor, love, obedience, troops of friends," meant. Never before had I comprehended the dreadful burden of disqualification and disability borne by the colored people of America.

With one fell blow everything had been shattered but my intellect. The man who is suddenly deprived of sight knows that all things are as they have been, though he can see them not; but he can grope around him and find the outstretched hands of love and pity. But I was like one who still retains sight, but knows that the light has gone out of the universe forever, even to the farthest reaches of the remotest stars. For me there were no loving hearts and hands. Those I worshiped fled from me, as if I bore about me the contagion of the pest-house. My soul might be as beautiful as the night " clad in the glory of a thousand stars," but there was no heart in all this world that could pierce the thick iron armor of race-prejudice to hold loving communion with my spirit.

I was utterly alone! A lost soul in the universe! True, I might descend the slimy steps of destiny and merge myself in the despised caste, and be lost forever beneath the contempt of my race. There my animal-like cravings for companionship might be satisfied; and I might make new ties and perpetuate my loathly features. I might become one of the pariahs,—one of the outlaws,—and share with the poor wretches their abject miseries. But that doom was, to one of my training, worse than death and the grave. For in death all are equal; and the grave turns us at last into flowers, —bright flowers,—things of beauty, that fill the air with perfume. In the dust of the grave there are no stirrings of ambition; no unsatisfied longings; no jealousies; no pride; no wounded sensibilities; no great passionate bursts of hearts that are trampled under the feet of men; nothing but peace and sleep. Ay, profound and dreamless sleep — sleep that takes no note of night or day, or time or season; of the wind's scream or the song-bird's melody; of the growing grass or the falling leaves; of sunshine or rain;— sleep that merges the individual into the universal nature, as a drop of water is lost in the interminable ocean. And if from this dissolving clod the extricated spirit is carried by the great Purpose into other realms of being, will not God be there too ? Will not that region be part of God's world, wherever it may be ? Can not the soul trust itself with safety to Him who made it ? Will the Creator, Saturn-like, devour his children? It cannot be.

And why should I live to be the butt and scorn and foot-ball of fate ? Why should I believe that that which I have seen was, in truth, the Man of Nazareth ? What hold have we upon the veracity of a spirit-world of whose conditions and limitations we know nothing ? Why may not that have been an infinite devil that I met, for —

> " The devil hath power
> To assume a pleasing shape. "

Who can talk through the veil that hangs around the visible world, and have any assurance that the voices which come back to him are of angels or demons ? And if some arch-fiend, making mankind his sport and jest (and we have many facts wich lead to the possibility of that conclusion), has picked me up, out of my serene happiness, loving and beloved, at the very acme of human fortune, and dropped me into this dark, loathsome and unscalable well, what assurance have I that he does not sit upon the curb-stone to grin down upon me forever ? Is he not chuckling over his work, even here and now ? Is he not holding his sides as he contemplates my unutterable miseries?

Why should I not die ? Has life any hold upon me ? Without love there is no life — but the mere hanging-together of physical shreds of being. And that fair creature, whose gentle nature and noble soul pervade

me like a new existence, she is gone from me forever!
Never, at the farthest reach of my imagination, can I
hope for anything from her but her pity.   Shall I live
to see her wedded to another ?   Shall I live to see her
beloved features reappearing, like light through a vase,
in the pledges of another man's honorable love ?   Shall
I follow her, groaning, like a lost soul cast out of Paradise — a black, bitter shadow, trailing behind her
happiness and glory ?

Why should I live?   God, it is true, has implanted
in us all an instinct of self-preservation, so that in the
most loathful conditions we cling to existence.   But
could the universal plan have contemplated such a state
of abasement as that into which I had fallen?   When I
leave these walls what manner of world do I enter?
A world where contempt encompasses me.   A world
without opportunity.   A world without hope.   A world
without joy.   I cannot move my eyes but I behold
something to remind me of my misfortunes.   The evil
reputation of the man whose carcass I drag around with
me I might overcome in time, by an honest life; but
what honesty, what well-doing, what intelligence can
surmount the dreadful prejudices which accompany my
complexion?

And I cried out aloud:

" Oh, my white brethren!   Little do you appreciate
what a glory it is to belong to the dominant caste;
what a hell it is to fall into the subject caste!   Little
do you appreciate your race-advantages, to be ' the
beauty of the world, the paragon of animals,' the perfection of your species.   Little do you think what a

boundless debt of gratitude you owe to the good God, for his mercies, to be expressed in boundless tenderness and generosity to your unfortunate brethren."

And I felt like Lear:

> " Oh, I have ta'en
> Too little care of this. Take physic, pomp,
> Expose thyself to feel what wretches feel,
> That thou mayst shake the superflux to them,
> And show the heavens more just."

Why should I live ? Would it not be better to end it all in death ? Thus would I escape the grasp of that spiritual power, whatever it might be, which had placed this horrible doom upon me. Yes, I would shake myself clear of this loathsome carcass. There was one gate of escape yet open — death. And so my soul would be liberated from the accidents of time.

But how ?

I searched my pockets for a knife, for anything with which I might inflict a wound, and drain Sam Johnsing's blood out of his wretched body. But, with the exception of a few coins, there was nothing in my pockets.

Could I hang myself ? Yes. I might tear up the vermin-infested bed-clothes, twist them into a rope, and tie it to the cross-bars of the window. But there was no chair or stool that I could stand upon and kick away and leave myself suspended.

Fate ! Fate ! Am I denied even the poor privilege of death ?

No; there is one resource left ! I had heard of men killing themselves by butting out their brains against a wall.   It is hard to keep a man within the boundaries of life if he is determined to escape beyond them.   I would open the gate of death in that way.

I selected a spot where I could have the longest run. I stooped my head for the start.   I shuddered.   My life within me revolted against hurting itself.   Existence pleaded for continuance.   But then I caught a glimpse of my great, black hands, and the horrors of my condition came back upon me in an avalanche of woe, and I sprang forward like a race-horse that has been struck a keen blow.   I remember nothing more.

It was morning.   My first consciousness was a slant glory of light on the cell wall facing me; the next was a great racking pain in my head and the back of my neck.   Where was I?   It took me some time to recall it all.   The jailer stood beside me.   I tried to move.   I was very stiff.   Then I observed that my feet were tied together.

" See here, you darned fool," said the man roughly, " what did you mean trying to butt your brains out?"

I looked at him intently.

" I want to die," I said.

" That's a mighty queer thing," he said.   " I never knew a nigger before that wanted to kill hisself.   If your skull hadn't been an inch thick you would have smashed it.   I heard the noise out in the hall.   It sounded like a gun.   No egg-shell about that conk of yours, Sam.   I thought you were gone up sure, when I came in and found you layin' there, bleedin' like a stuck pig. You mustn't try no sich foolishness ag'in. What do you want to die for?"

" I am the most wretched creature alive in this world to-day," I replied.

The man looked at me with astonishment.

" See here, Sam," he said, " what's come over you? You don't act like yourself and you don't talk like yourself. You used to sing and dance juba when you were here before, instead of rammin' your head agin a stone wall. What's the matter with you?"

" It would be useless," I said, " to talk to you. You would not believe me, and you could not understand me. But can you not see that my conversation is utterly unlike anything Sam Johnsing was ever capable of? To all appearances I am Sam Johnsing. And yet I am not Sam Johnsing, but Doctor Anthony Huguet. And neither you nor any one else — except two persons — will believe it. Here is some money. Take it all, and go out and buy me ten grains of morphine."

The jailer started back.

" Why," said he, " you are a darned fool. Do you want to kill yourself? Sit up and eat your breakfast."

" No, no," I replied; " place it on the floor. I cannot eat it now."

The jailer withdrew with an utterly puzzled expression on his countenance. Surely something was the matter with Sam Johnsing, when he wouldn't eat! He confided his bewilderment to his wife and his assistant; but they could make nothing of it.

For hours I lay there thinking. My last hope was

gone.   I could not even die!   The big tears ran down
my face, mingling with the dry cakes of blood and soft-
ening them.   And then I cried out aloud:

"Oh, my God! Have mercy on me.   Christ Jesus,
have mercy on me!"

And on the moment it seemed to me that a voice
spoke somewhere within my mind, and said:

"Shame on you!   A scholar and philosopher!   To
be so cast down by the accidents of fortune.   Is there
nothing to work for in all this great round world but
your own miserable self?   Think of the millions who,
from the cradle to the grave, are enfolded in the horrors of injustice and oppression from which you would
escape by death.   Coward — thrice coward! When God
is trying to lift up the world, wouldst thou fly from the
responsibilities of existence into the dust of nothingness?   Up!—up!   Rouse thyself, and do thy duty!
Make thy cause the cause of the afflicted.   Live to
preach courage to one race and charity to another.
Live to extend the hand of pity to the downtrodden
and the hopeless.   Live to rebuke the indifference of
the prosperous and the cruelty of the heartless.   Live
to exemplify the spirit of Christ on earth — that spirit
which walks abroad among men, linking the hands of
enemies together as brethren, and lifting up their faces
in joy and gratitude to Heaven."

And there was a great silence in my soul after these
words were spoken.   And I marveled, and I said to
myself:

"What is the mind of man?   Who is it that thinks
because he intends to think?   Who is it can anticipate

his own thoughts? Where do they come from? Where did this voice come from? The mind is like a great, shoreless pool, and thoughts arise to its surface as mermaids project their shining shoulders above the silent sea. But from what unsoundable depths do they arise? How far down, toward the central ever-lasting purposes, do those waters reach? Do they not rest upon the Will of the universe? And are not these apparently self-acting intellects of ours part of the great automatic mechanism we call Nature? Is there not a rhythm in the music of the spheres? Are not all things weighed, measured and counted? Can there be an accident in a world that is full of God? And if this be so, are not my sufferings foredoomed and necessary? Are they not part of the universal scheme? And, if this be so, are not my very miseries Heaven-inflicted dignities?"

I had violated my conscience. Yes, that alone was divine. Flesh is matter — stuff. Life is but a cleavage from the all-pervading life. But the sense of truth and right in the individual is part of the Godhead. He who deceives or misleads it, in himself or others, trifles with and insults God. He commits the highest sacri-lege. He befouls the innermost altar of the tabernacle. He turns the Creator out of His dwelling-place.

With these thoughts I was greatly cheered. My punishment was just. Then I might atone for my wrong-doing! There was still work for me to do in the world. My inmost monitor had spoken, even as the *dæmon* spoke to Socrates.

I called the jailer. I told him to take the bandages

from my limbs.   I assured him that I would not again attempt suicide.   I asked for water and washed myself. I ate my breakfast.

I would patiently wait until the end of my imprisonment and then go out into the world and do my duty.

CHAPTER XXI.

MY FAITHFUL FRIEND.

"Soft! who comes here ?
A friend of Antony's."

—*Julius Cæsar, iii. 1.*

EARLY next day Ben came to see me. He had just heard of my imprisonment. He brought me money, clean clothes, and breakfast from a neighboring restaurant. I was deeply moved and gratified. The poor fellow was all kindness and attention, respect and pity. I sent him out to buy me a new bedstead and bedding, all fresh and clean, and a table to write upon, with pen, ink and stationery, and a comfortable chair or two. Ben carried the filthy thing I had been sleeping on out into the prison yard, and then proceeded to scrub and whitewash the cell. The jailer, his wife and assistants looked on with unbounded astonishment. In answer to their questions, Ben told them that I was really Doctor Huguet, and that I had been *hoodooed* and bewitched, and turned into Sam Johnsing. These poor whites are many of them almost as superstitious as the negroes, and they listened to Ben's statements with open-eyed wonder and more than half credence. Their treatment of me became much more kind and respectful.

Ben made arrangements that my meals were to be

served to me from the neighboring restaurant. I requested him to bring me, the next day, a number of books, of which I furnished him a list.

Ben gave me some interesting news about the real Sam Johnsing. He had been spending most of his time at " Mother Bindell's," a notorious place, where all the depraved white men and dissolute colored women of the neighborhood congregated; and there he had been disbursing his (my) money lavishly, in a continued royal state of drunkenness and uproar, and was winning golden opinions from all the ruffianry of the neighborhood. The malignant hatred he manifested toward all negro men (not women) endeared him to the hearts of the youthful Caucasian chivalry; and they had taken up the movement which Colonel Ruddiman had inaugurated in my behalf, and it was very probable that he would be elected to Congress! What a mockery of fate was this!

There was, however, one dark cloud upon the horizon of Sam's delightful existence. Colonel Ruddiman and his gallant sons had heard, with astonishment and rage, of the conduct of Miss Mary's affianced lover, and they swore vengeance upon him. He was disgracing her and them, they said, as well as himself, by his foul, vile life and his degrading associations, and they proposed to call him to account. In fact, Colonel Ruddiman had already visited my house to interview him, but had not found him. Miss Mary had heard nothing of all these reports; they had, indeed, been carefully kept from her; but she was surprised that her lover had not written to her or called upon her, for it had been my habit to write to her at least once a day, when we were separated from each other.

I penned a note to Abigail, telling her of my misfortunes, of my conviction for stealing my own hat, and of my present habitation, and gave it to Ben to forward to her, for I desired to learn in this way all I could about Mary.

With my clean, comfortable cell, my books and newspapers, and my easy-chair, I began to forget, for a time, many of my sorrows. The conviction grew upon me, also, that the spell under which I suffered would pass away and that in the meantime I must bear with stoicism and philosophy the extremest blows of fortune.

CHAPTER XXII.

A VISIT.

"How now! What news?"
—*Merchant of Venice, i. 2.*

THE third day of my imprisonment Abigail came.
She had received my letter.

She looked at me most pitifully as she took my hand.
I had many questions to ask her.

She had had, she said, numerous discussions with Mary about myself; but that strong-minded young lady utterly refused to believe in the possibility of the great transformation which had overtaken me. She loved me profoundly, but she had little belief in the supernatural; and, so long as she had not beheld any change in Doctor Huguet himself, it was impossible to convince her that her lover was not still himself. Like most persons of strong and resolute mind, she abided much by precedent, and in all her reading she could remember nothing like the calamity which Abigail insisted had befallen me. She was annoyed that she had not received a visit or letter from her affianced lover for several days. She fell back, however, upon her usual resource, reading, and buried herself in the library.

Abigail had noticed also a change in the manner of Colonel Ruddiman and his sons. They appeared uneasy and irritated, and had little to say. Indeed, she had one day entered the Colonel's bed-room, unexpectedly, and found him cleaning his dueling-pistols. The neighbors no longer called, and the house was gloomy and silent.

Abigail offered me some money out of her little hoard; but I declined it, thanking her, and assuring her that I was abundantly supplied by Ben.

As she was leaving she told me that Buryhill had paid two visits to the house, and had been closeted with the Colonel for an hour or more each time. After these visits the Colonel's gloom seemed to increase, and she fancied he looked very dejected.

I could not penetrate to the central meaning of all these conflicting details, but I fancied the clouds were gathering thickly around those I loved; and I cursed the hard fate which had shut me up in prison at such a time. And yet, shut up as I was in the dark cell of my loathsome body, I doubted if I could be of much use to them if I had been free.

And so the days sped. Ben called often, and Abigail at least once a week.

The news began to thicken.

Ben told me that the Colonel had been at my house twice to see Doctor Huguet, but the wretch who bore that name was seldom at home, except when he was brought there in a state of helpless intoxication, accompanied by pale, haggard, prematurely-aged young men —armed roysterers, in top-boots, with riding-whips and spurs; noisy, insolent, ignorant, arrogant creatures — who took possession of the house and defaced it with tobacco-spit, empty bottles and broken furniture. Ben was powerless, for these creatures were his master's friends; and if he had attempted to stop them they would have proved their white manhood by shooting him down, with as little compunction as they would a dog. He did the best he could : he secreted all the portable valuables, such as the plate, jewelry, etc.; locked up the book-cases and all my private papers, and closed half the rooms in the house against them. Fortunately, they did not stay long at any time. There were other places more attractive to them.

There is a sort of freemasonry among the negroes, whereby the servants of one house communicate the occurrences which happen in it to the servants of all the other houses ; and thus the news will spread, with almost telegraphic rapidity, throughout a whole neighborhood. It is said that the Indians have the same system. We are told, for instance, that the massacre of General Custer and his troops was known to the red men, five hundred miles from the scene of the disaster, long before the whites had heard of it by the electric wires. I suppose that our own race, before the days of newspapers, used the same means of disseminating information, and any startling news passed from mouth to mouth with wonderful rapidity.

And so the facts which I am about to relate reached Ben and were by him communicated to me.

CHAPTER XXIII.

" MOTHER BINDELL'S. "

"There's no more faith in thee than in a stewed prune; nor no more truth in thee than in a drawn fox; and for womanhood, Maid Marian may be the deputy's wife of the ward to thee."

— 1 Henry IV., iii. 3.

AT a cross-road, on the highway between C——
and Colonel Ruddiman's residence, stood, until recently, a dilapidated frame house. It had once been a prosperous wayside inn, but its glory had long since departed. Everything about it indicated decay and neglect. The rain and sun had long since removed, except in a few sheltered places, the paint which had formerly adorned its clap-boards; the shingles were mossy and rotten with age, and lacking in places; the shutters — what was left of them — hung loose, often depending from a single hinge ; many of the sashes were innocent of glass. The dilapidated fence inclosed a broken-down barn, and an inclosure over which tin cans, beef-bones and fragments of skirt-hoops, with other rubbish, were scattered.

The doors were black with handling, and here and there a panel was cracked or altogether missing. Filth, nastiness, demoralization were everywhere.

In day-time the place seemed desolate and deserted, but toward evening signs of life began to manifest

themselves.   Smoke ascended from the kitchen chim-
ney, and a gray-haired, haggard, suspicious-looking,
evil-featured old white woman went in and out — the
proprietress of the mansion.   Mother Bindell had a
dreadful history.   Her husband had been hanged for a
murder which it was shrewdly suspected she had herself perpetrated ; two of her sons were in prison for
burglary, and her three daughters flaunted their shame
in distant cities.   Her house was a haunt for criminals,
black and white.   The neighbors had often threatened
to have it suppressed by law or force, but the influence
of a certain class of degraded young white men had so
far shielded her from justice.

As the shades of twilight gathered, the other inhabitants of the house, who had slept throughout the day,
began to show themselves at doors and windows.
They were all mulattoes, of varying shades of darkness, from the pale octoroon to the coffee-colored half-
blood ; — slatternly, sluttish, full-breasted wenches,
with all the marks of dissipation, licentiousness, and
even disease, upon their persons — lazy, sensual, brutal,
ignorant, high-voiced, profane creatures ; bare-footed,
bare-legged, or slip-shod ; their gaily-colored, cheap
dresses little more than covering their bodies.   They
were ready for another night of drunken revel and
debauchery with the young white men who frequented
the place, chief among whom was now Doctor Anthony
Huguet — the scholar and gentleman, and prospective
Congressman !

It was nine o'clock at night.   The uproar was great.   A

crowd of men and women, black and white, were drinking or looking on, while four young white men, their faces inflamed with liquor and their eyes wild with the excitement of the game, were playing cards, when, above all the tumult of rattling glasses, talk, oaths and laughter, a tremendous pounding was heard at the door. Mother Bindell — considerably alarmed, for her regular customers did not make their presence known in that way — with her red weazel-eyes winking with apprehension, and her gnarled, withered old hands, which had never done a good deed since they were made, trembling with nervousness — pushed her way through the now silent crowd to the front door and opened it. A strong, manly voice was heard to ask, out of the darkness :

" Is Doctor Huguet here ? "

The old woman, true to her instincts, began to prevaricate :

" I do not know — he"——

But the visitors pushed past her, and Colonel Ruddiman and two of his sons entered the room, and looked, with scowls on their faces, at the shameful scene.

In a corner, maudlin-drunk, sat the man who bore the name of Doctor Huguet, with a mulatto girl on each knee, their arms twined around his neck, while he alternately bestowed upon them slobbering kisses. They were all so much under the influence of liquor that they were unconscious of the silence that had fallen upon the revelers, or of the large man who stood before them, with his face crimson with rage.

It was but for a moment. Seizing each of the

women, the Colonel flung them right and left, and they
fell in helpless heaps of relaxed flesh and calico upon
the floor. Then he cried out, in a voice of thunder,
which penetrated even to the dim consciousness of
Sam Johnsing:

"Oh, you infernal scoundrel! Is this the way you
prepare yourself to enter a respectable and honorable
family? Is this the way you keep faith with the noblest
woman in the world?"

Sam looked up at him in stupid confusion, winking
his bleared eyes, as he tried to collect his scattered
senses.

"Get up!" cried the Colonel, clutching the small
figure by the throat, and lifting him to his feet. "Get
up! You have insulted me and my family, and I de-
mand satisfaction. Nothing but your life-blood can
wipe out the stain you have put upon me. You have
made my dearest child an object of pity and sympathy
for a whole county. While she believes in you and
waits your coming, you are here reveling in the arms
of these beasts! Select among your friends here some
one to act as your second. I have brought my pistols
with me. As a man of honor you will be glad of this
opportunity to expiate your conduct."

He released his hold of Sam to take from one of his
sons the mahogany box which contained the dueling-
pistols, when the wretched creature collapsed in a heap
on the floor, half-seated, half-kneeling, with uplifted
hands, while he commenced to weep, and cried out, in
a trembling voice:

"Foah God, massa! I haint done nothin'. I don't

want to fight no dooel. I never tetched your chile —
don't know her, s' help me God!"

The Colonel looked at him with unbounded astonishment. While he knew that Doctor Huguet had fallen
suddenly into profligate habits, yet such lapses from
virtue were not unusual among men; but that a Southern *gentleman* would refuse to fight the man he had
wronged, and would fall on his knees and weep, actually
blubber, as the wretch was now blubbering, was something so far beyond the Colonel's experience of Southern
mankind that he stood paralyzed, speechless, looking
down at the abject creature groveling at his feet.

Here one of the young men — Harry Sanders, a tall,
handsome fellow (if a face can be called handsome in
which there is nothing of goodness), who possessed the
manners of a gentleman, without the finer instincts and
characteristics which really constitute one — staggered
forward.

"You see, Colonel," he said, with a lurch and a
hiccough, "the Doctor isn't in a condition to fight to-
night; he couldn't hold a pistol, but he is my friend,
yes, sah, my friend, and a fine, gallant — hic — fellow he
is, and I will promise you, Colonel, on the honah of a
gentleman, sah, that as soon as I can get him sober
enough he shall call at your house, sah, and either
make such apologies as will satisfy you, or give you the
satisfaction — hic — of a gentleman — satisfaction — a
gentleman, sah — by God, sah."

And he thrust his hand out to the Colonel.

"See that he does," said the Colonel, refusing the

outstretched member, " or I shall hunt him up, and shoot him like a dog.

"And you, sir," he continued, to young Sanders, "I am ashamed to see you here. Your father was a gallant gentleman, and my friend, and he died in defense of his country. What would he say if he could look upon you here, in this shameful company? If he knew your mode of life, he would rest uneasy in his bloody grave at Gettysburg. And you, young men —most of you I know—you are all of you of good families. What will become of our unhappy country when you assume the reins of government? Our noble heroes have died in vain if the New South is to be ruled by such as you. Instead of improving your minds by studying the careers of the great men of our country, you spend your nights in this villainous brothel, in the embrace of negroes. Is it any wonder that decent black men, knowing all this, look down upon you with unbounded contempt, and aspire to sway the politics of the land? Are they not better fitted, by lives of virtue and industry, for self-government, than you are? Shame on you! You are the disgrace of a noble race! You, indeed, the representatives of white chivalry! You cannot endure that a black man should come within a hundred feet of you at the ballot-box; but you cannot get close enough to a beastly, diseased black woman! Shame on you. Pah! The very air of this den chokes me. I will see that the next grand jury of the county finds an indictment against this wretched hovel."

As the Colonel proceeded, the young men, scowling

but frightened, had retreated through the open doors, or leaped through the windows, and the negroes had hurried up-stairs to hide themselves, like bats from a light.

"And you," said the Colonel to Mother Bindell, who was about to slip into the cellar, "you! you miserable old haridan! The neighbors ought to turn out and hang you! If they had done so fifty years ago the world would be better off to-day by many thousands of dollars and many valuable lives. Scuttle away into the cellar, like a gray old rat, you old soul-destroyer! You ought to be burned alive in your filthy habitation."

With a parting scowl at Doctor Huguet, who was still on his knees, crying, the Colonel and his sons marched out.

CHAPTER XXIV.

SHE SEES HIM.

> "In thy own chair — thine own place at the banquet —
> I sought thy sweet face in the circle; — but,
> Instead, a gray-haired, withered, bloody-eyed
> And bloody-handed, ghastly, ghostly thing."
> —*Sardanapalus* (*Byron*).

IT was two days before the expiration of my term of imprisonment.

Abigail came to see me. Her face was flushed and her eyes shining. Her first words were:

"She believes in you now! She has seen him!"

My heart beat wildly.

"How was it, Abigail? Tell me all."

"You remember," she said, "that young Sanders promised the Colonel that he would bring Doctor Huguet — or what he takes to be Doctor Huguet — to the house to apologize for his conduct. But there was a good deal of delay in the performance of the promise. The difficulty was that by the time the Doctor became sober Sanders was drunk; and when Sanders had sobered up sufficiently to remember his promise, the Doctor was off again on another spree. And so it went, until at last, by some strange chance, they were both sober, or comparatively so, at the same time; and Sanders brought the miserable wretch to see the Colonel. He marched him along, like a captive, from the horse-block, up the walk, to where the Colonel sat alone, looking very unhappy, on the veranda.

" ' Colonel,' he said raising his hat, ' Doctor Huguet is here, as I promised, to make his apology to you for anything in his conduct which you might take exception to. The Doctor is not much of a talker, but he feels very badly over this whole business, sah. But then you were young once yourself, Colonel, and you know young blood will have its way. And, although the Doctor is not a boy, yet he is a bachelor, sah, and there are excuses, you know, sah.'

" I was in the garden and witnessed the whole scene. The Doctor was very much changed by drink and late hours; his eyes were inflamed and his face red and bloated. He held his hat in his hands and kept turning it round and round as Sanders spoke. There was dead silence for a time, and then Sanders nudged the Doctor with his elbow, and at last he spoke, in low, thick tones.

" ' Yes, sah,' he said, ' I's very sorry; and shan't do it agin.'

" The Colonel looked at him with mingled bewilderment and contempt, for he could not forget their last interview, and the Doctor's manner of speech was so different from what he had expected. He could not quite understand it all. But I think some secret troubles had softened his heart, or diverted the flood of his wrath; or he perhaps remembered that his daughter was in love with this man and unhappy. I saw him pass his hand across his eyes as if to sweep away a mist, and then he said, looking at Sanders;

" 'Well, well, it is bad enough. The Doctor's conduct has been horrible and disgraceful. But many things go wrong in this world, and we are all liable to fall. But I never can feel toward him as I did; he may, however, see my daughter once more, if he desires to.'

" Then he saw me and called to me:

" 'Abigail, come here.'

" I approached the veranda, and, as I did so, both the visitors looked at me. Their dull faces lighted up with curiosity, and the Doctor's eyes fairly blazed upon me with lustful fire. I shuddered.

" 'Abigail," said the Colonel, 'go to Miss Mary and tell her that Doctor Huguet is here. Gentlemen,' he added, turning to his visitors, 'will you enter the parlor?'

" He showed them the way, and then he walked off to the stables, lost in thought, and looking very unhappy.

" I gave Mary the message. She was delighted. She sprang to her feet and began to arrange her hair before a mirror.

" 'Tell him I will be there in a minute,' she said.

" I hurried to the parlor. Sanders was examining the pictures. The Doctor was looking out of a window. I went up to him, and said:

" 'Miss Mary will be here directly, sir.'

" 'And who may you be, honey?' he asked.

" 'I am Abigail,' I replied.

" He approached me, and, before I could anticipate

what he was about to do, he flung his arms around me and began to kiss me.

" I struggled with him, but he held me fast. I was about to cry out, when he relaxed his grasp and looked beyond me, with his eyes full of astonishment, to the door. I tore myself loose and turned around, and there in the doorway, as in a dark frame, clad all in white, was Miss Mary, very pale and her eyes full of a strange light.

" ' I could not help myself,' I said, approaching her; ' he took hold of me.'

" She paid no attention to me, but walked straight past me toward the Doctor. She paused close to him; they looked each other full in the eyes for a moment, and then she gave the most dreadful shriek I ever heard; she clasped her head between her hands and fled from the room, white as a ghost and screaming.

" ' Gor-a'mity!' said the Doctor.

" I ran after her. I found her in her own room, lying at full length upon the bed, with her face in her hands, sobbing as if her heart would break.

" I bathed her face with cold water, and tried to comfort her. She turned and looked at me, with her eyes very wide open.

" ' My God,' she said, ' *that is not Doctor Huguet!* No! no! that is *not* Doctor Huguet! I went to him, Abigail, with my heart full of love; but it was as if I had approached a window where a bright-faced child, in some sportive game, waited to laugh in my face, and the curtain was drawn up, and the devil glared suddenly out at me! O Abigail, it was dreadful. My God! my God! Such eyes! Such a soul! So dark, and base, and despicable, and cruel! The very devil looked out at me. Oh, my God! *where is Doctor Huguet?*'

"And she flung herself upon the bed and sobbed and sobbed. Then she sprang to her feet and cried:

"'Tell him to go! I shudder when I think of that dreadful creature being under the same roof with me.'

"I hurried to the room and dismissed the visitors. They were not loath to go, for the apparition and the scene they had beheld was too much for both of them. They hastened to some more congenial place.

"When I returned to Miss Mary she was sitting up on the side of the bed.

"'Abigail,' she said to me, 'tell me, do you really believe the strange story which that tall, ugly black man told us, that *he* was Doctor Huguet, and that he had exchanged bodies with a vile chicken-thief?

"'Certainly,' I replied, 'I believe it as firmly as I believe in my own existence. Did he not talk like Doctor Huguet? Did he not know all that Doctor Huguet knew? Did he not tell you of your most secret conversations with Doctor Huguet? Had he not all the learning and eloquence of Doctor Huguet? And, now you have seen the other, what is he? Certainly not the Doctor you loved. I have not told you what I knew about his life of late, for the Colonel requested me not to do so, but his conduct has been of the most debased and profligate character. I will not shock you by narrating the stories that are repeated by the servants.'

"'But, Abigail,' she replied, 'no one ever heard of

such a thing as two men exchanging souls and bodies. It seems impossible.'

" 'Who can place limits to the power of God or his angels?' I replied; 'but it is useless to discuss the question; you know that *something* that was in Doctor Huguet has gone out of him; and that *something* was the thing you loved, and that held communion with your spirit. Call it soul, or what you will, Doctor Huguet has lost it.'

" 'But, Abigail,' she said, 'if this be true, how dreadful, how awful must have been the sufferings of the real Doctor Huguet! Not only to lose, in a moment, home and family and wealth and station, but to be spurned by the one woman whom he loved above all else in the world, and who worshiped the very ground he trod on. Oh! it is horrible! And to think that I could treat him so cruelly.'

" And here the sobs and tears broke out afresh, and her frame shook convulsively.

" 'Lost, lost! lost forever!' she cried. 'Poor, unhappy man! Wretched beyond all the children of men!'

" And then she started up excitedly, and said:

" 'Where is he now?'

" 'He is in prison.'

" 'In prison?'

" 'Yes, in prison.'

" And then I told her all your dismal story.

" 'I will go see him,' she cried; 'quick! my hat.'

" And then she grew ghastly pale, and fell back upon the bed, and shuddered, and cried:

" 'But he is a black man!'

" And again she sobbed and called on God, in such a way that I began to be alarmed for her reason, and hurried out and brought the Colonel to her. When she saw him she flung herself upon his breast and wept, and cried out:

" ' O father ! father ! Doctor Huguet is a negro ! '

" The astonishment of the Colonel cannot be described. He thought she had become insane. He petted and soothed her ; but she repeated the dreadful cry over and over again, ' Doctor Huguet is a negro!'

" ' What does she mean, Abigail ? ' he asked.

" She quieted down while I told him the terrible story. He was incredulous — such a thing could not be possible ; — but she joined in, vehemently, in the argument to convince him. All doubt had passed from her mind. Her excitement was intense, and every now and then she would murmur, as if to herself : ' My poor love ! My poor love ! '

" The Colonel was bewildered. The one thing that stood out most vividly before him was the thought that his daughter — *his* daughter — was affianced *to a negro!* Then came another reflection — that this must be kept from the knowledge of the world. Better to break off the match with the drunken wretch, under the plea of his changed habits, than to admit that the man she had loved had been transformed into a black man. That would make them the jest of the world.

" And so, with many terms of endearment and consolation, he impressed these views upon her and upon me likewise. He would see what could be done to help the real Doctor Huguet; for all they could do was, without publicity or exposure, to make his state as comfortable as possible, and wait for the passing away of the dreadful spell which had been cast upon him.

" Mary was but slightly consoled, and when I put her to bed she kissed me, and sobbed herself to sleep."

This was Abigail's story. I had listened to it with the most intense interest and the strongest emotions. It was a joy to know that Mary at last believed in me, and sympathized with me. I gloated over the words which testified to her continued love. They softened the gloom of my miseries. I would treasure them up, to be recalled through all the dark future.

CHAPTER XXV.

FREE AGAIN.

"Where am I now? Feet, find me out a way,
   Without the counsel of my troubled heart :
   I'll follow you boldly about these woods,
   O'er mountains, through brambles, pits and floods.
   Heaven, I hope, will ease me.   I am sick."
                    —*Philaster* (*Beaumont and Fletcher*).

THE day arrived on which my sentence expired.
   I shook hands with the jailer and his assistants.
They regarded me with a species of awe.   I certainly
had not acted like the notorious Sam Johnsing.   I
think they were rather glad to get clear of me : there
was to them something mysterious and uncanny about
the whole business.   They could not understand it.

   Ben was on hand to take charge of me.   He insisted
that I must go to my own house; and there he would
secrete me, and care for me, until the " hoodoo," as he
called it, terminated.   But I declined his kind offer.
I told him that the spell had been placed upon me
because I had not done my duty according to the lights
of my own conscience, my inmost monitor; and that I
could only escape from the curse under which I suffered by going out into the world and laboring for the
welfare of the black race.   If I hid myself, and lived
a life of pampered idleness, the spell would remain
upon me forever.

Then he wanted me to agree that I would receive a certain sum of money from him every week — enough to pay my board and other expenses of living. He would take it out of my own income. But this offer also I declined. I told him that I desired to show the negroes that the fault of their not rising to greater heights of distinction, and so overcoming the cruel prejudices which surrounded them, was because they did not address themselves to the task of success with a white man's brain and energy. I proposed, I said, to throw myself, bare-handed, into the shock and battle of life, and win by sheer force of intellect. In the day of my success it would not do to be subject to the reproach that I was indebted, for my triumph, to the fact that I had been in receipt of an income which placed me above want, and gave me an advantage over other black men. No! I would go into the conflict as a negro, and win as a negro, or fail as a negro; but I had no fear of failure. I felt so confident of the advantages which my thoroughly equipped intelligence gave me that I was sure I should revolutionize the whole social status of the negroes of the entire world. Yes, I said, the new era for the black man of America would date from my going forth from these walls to-day, even as the calendar of the Moslem begins with the Hegira of Mahommed from Mecca to Medina.

And so, shaking hands warmly with my faithful friend, we parted, and I started forth upon my mission.

I had given the subject a good deal of thought, during my imprisonment, and it had seemed to me that, if

I was to teach the colored people, it would be well to seek a place as a professor in some college or university. This would give me a vantage-ground — a standing — from which I could readily move to a higher level of statesmanship and statecraft.

There were two institutions of learning in C——, both of prominence. I would make my first applications there.

I sought out the president of the most important of these first. I found him a pleasant, smiling, affable gentleman, with gray hair, and gold spectacles on nose, an eminently respectable, scholastic-looking personage; a minister of the gospel and a pillar of society. He received me courteously and asked my business. I told him I wanted an opportunity to teach in his college, in however humble a capacity, or for however small a compensation. His face broke into a broad smile, which he politely tried to suppress.

" What can you teach? " he asked, good-naturedly.

" Latin, Greek, French, German, Italian, music, English literature, or medicine," I replied.

He looked surprised and handed me a copy of a Greek work, and requested me to translate a few lines of it into English. I did so readily and correctly.

His astonishment was great, and his manner became more respectful. He asked me several questions as to where I had been educated, all the time studying my rude, black features with a bewildered expression. He offered me a chair. I inquired whether there was any place in his institution I could secure, in which I could make use of my knowledge to earn a living.

He politely told me that he regretted to say there was none; that his institution was purely and solely for the education of white students, and that they would not receive learning from one of my color. He added that such prejudices were foolish, he was ready to acknowledge, but they existed, and as a practical man he had to recognize them; if he employed a single negro tutor in his school he might just as well close up his doors. He said they needed a servant, however, to look after the stables, and ——

But I interrupted him, and replied that I did not want to do menial work; and, thanking him for his courtesy, I bowed myself out.

I was not discouraged; I expected rebuffs. I made my way to the other institution. The head of it was very unlike the gentleman I had just seen. He was beetle-browed, dark — dark as a mulatto — with great quantities of black hair on his hands and arms; in fact, his hands were *furred*, so to speak, except on the palms and knuckles. I could not help but think of Darwin and Evolution and the great apes. His voice was coarse and gruff, and his manner brusque. He had none of the sweetness and suavity of the other gentleman. He roared with laughter, in my very face, when he heard my proposition; and did not even trouble himself to test my attainments, or make any explanations, but rudely ordered me out of the room. He told me he had no time to waste in such nonsense.

Still I was not discouraged. If I could not get employment in any institution of learning, at least the merchants' stores were open to me. I must find a resting-place, a fulcrum, for the Archimedean lever with which I proposed to move the world.

I walked past several stores and scanned the proprietors and the establishments carefully. At last I came to a large dry-goods shop, with many salesmen. A benevolent-looking old gentleman seemed to be in charge of the place. I entered. I think the employer was of Quaker stock, for he used the " thee" and " thou" of that quaint, interesting and admirable people.

I told him I wanted a situation as a salesman; that I would work for the first month for nothing (I had money enough to carry me along for a time); and after that I would ask such small stipend as he thought would be reasonable, sufficient merely to pay my board.

The old gentleman smiled on me blandly and replied:

" Thee cannot belong to this place, friend, or thee would know that people of thy color cannot be employed, side by side, with white people, in such an establishment as this. If I employed thee, and thou wert ready to work for nothing, still it would not do. The mere sight of thy black face (I say it kindly, friend), behind this counter, would drive away every white customer from my store and bring me to bankruptcy."

" Is there no store in which I can get employment ?"

" No," he replied; " not one. The line of color is clearly drawn."

" Are there any negro stores ?" I asked.

" No," he replied; " thy people are generally poor and would scarcely be able to maintain stores; and if they were established the better off among them would probably prefer to patronize the white stores, for they are, naturally enough, ambitious to be something higher than their fellows. The aristocratic distinctions are as clearly defined among thy people as among the whites, as thou art probably aware."

My heart began to sink. What a dreadful and all-pervading thing this race-feeling was. No outlet for a black man among the whites, and none among his own color! No wonder they were forced down into servile places, such as waiters, barbers, etc. But I would not be driven in that direction. I would continue the fight. I thanked the pleasant-looking old gentleman for his courtesy and politeness, and started out again.

I walked for some time before I had the courage to make another attempt. At length I passed a lumber-yard. In the office a fat man sat perched upon a high, three-legged stool, making entries in a book. I bowed politely to him, taking off my hat and stand-ing humbly before him, and asked him if he needed a clerk.

"A clerk!" he replied, in a loud voice, staring at me insolently.

"Yes," I replied; "I am a book-keeper and have a thorough education. I can speak French and German as well as English. If I could make myself useful to you I would work for a very small compensation."

He hopped down off his chair, and, pointing to the door, yelled at me:

"Get out of here! It's a pretty state of things when d—d niggers, like you, can speak French and German and know more than their betters, and ask to be book-keepers! Go down to the levee and yank cotton

bales.   That's the kind of work you are fit for!   Out
of here!"

I retired before this burst of vituperative bigotry,
perfectly overwhelmed.

But why pursue further the wretched narrative of rebuffs
and disappointments?   All day long I passed from place
to place, trying to find employment fit for a gentleman.   Sometimes I was treated civilly, sometimes
insolently, and sometimes canes and yard-sticks were
raised over my head.

I had the money to pay my board in a comfortable
hotel, but all such were shut in my face; and I had to put
up for the night in a low, dirty haunt of men of my
own color.

It was a long time before I could get to sleep.   The
high hopes and aspirations with which I had started
out in the morning were all blasted and withered.   I
began to lose confidence in my own theories.   The
Archimedean lever would not work.   I could not find
a fulcrum for it.   It seemed to me that the eloquence
of Daniel Webster or the learning of William E. Glad-
stone, wrapped up in a black hide, would amount to
nothing.   The saddest part of the business was the
dreadful revelation of the baseness of human nature which I had witnessed; for, during the day,
I had made applications for employment to several
of my intimate friends, whose faces had never before been turned to mine save when wreathed
in obsequious smiles, and I had started back before
the dark and scowling brows with which they
greeted a helpless inferior.   The world is a wretched-

looking object viewed from below, but grand and gaudy as stage scenery to him who can contemplate it from above. The highest test of a true gentleman is gentleness to servants and courtesy to the unfortunate. The man who can address a beggar with the same tones of voice which he will use toward a prince is one of nature's noblemen — yea, a species of demi-god, and fit to be worshiped by common humanity.

I had also found that it was impossible for me to force my way into many of the trades and mechanical pursuits, even as an apprentice. They all had their laws limiting the number who could learn the business.

What was left for me? I must either resort to servile employment or hard physical toil.

What should I do? Should I go back to Ben and avail myself of his offer to support me out of my own funds, while fighting this dreary battle of life? Would the negroes believe in me and follow me if I appeared to be an idle pensioner on some other man's bounty; or if, with the evil reputation of Sam Johnsing, I had no visible means of support? Would not my going to work to earn an honest living, by hard toil, be the very best way to get clear of the evil fame and name of that lazy chicken-thief? If I was to lead the negroes to better things I must first win their confidence. Yes, I had better go to the levee in the morning and seek employment as a stevedore, and pursue it until something better presented itself.

But my heart was furious within me when I thought that, with all my education and ability, there was no

resource for me but the hardest physical toil.   I struck
out in the darkness, as if I would pound down the walls
of caste with my fists, but it was in vain.   I struck only
the invulnerable air, as unassailable as the prejudices
which surrounded me.

CHAPTER XXVI.

THE SCENE SHIFTS.

"My heart is like an anvil unto sorrow,
Which beats upon it like the Cyclops' hammers,
And with the noise turns up my giddy brain."
— *Marlowe.*

WHEN I rose next morning I was half sick. I had a raging pain in my head and a feverish feeling. I attributed both to the ferment of my spirit and my disappointment and rage at the overthrow of my high-seated hopes and plans.

I ate the miserable breakfast placed before me, and at an early hour was on the levee seeking work. Here the huge body and the great limbs, which had been my curse so often, stood me in good stead, and I was accepted and put to work, with a number of other negroes, unloading a ship filled with coal. It was very hard work. The sun was broiling hot, shining down from an unclouded sky, and its rays beat pitilessly upon me, and were reflected with added force from the great sheet of water. And my perturbed soul raged within me at the limitations of my condition. Here was I — Doctor Anthony Huguet — a man completely cultured and profoundly learned, working side by side with a gang of creatures who knew little more than the street-car horses, and had no higher instincts; and all my education was locked up within me perfectly useless. I could not avail myself of it; I could

not even make an exhibition of it, for those around me
would not understand it; Greek and Latin would be no
more to them than the chattering of a chimpanzee —
syllables without meaning.

The sweat rolled from me at every pore; the blood
rushed into my head in torrents, under the force of my
unhappy thoughts; the merciless sun beat down upon
me unceasingly, and the exhausted air seemed dead
and pulseless, when suddenly the ship and masts and
men all began to whirl wildly around me. I staggered,
and felt that I was falling down, down into the black
hold of the ship, and then I knew no more.

This is not the ship's hold — no; I am on a bed; a
soft and comfortable bed. I am not lying on the black
and angular anthracite. How did I come here? Did
I not fall among the coals? But my thoughts grow
dim. I can scarcely hold them. I wander off again.
I dream that I hear once more the voice of the mate giving orders. I would jump to obey him. No; I cannot;
I am weak; oh, so weak; I can scarcely lift my hand
from the bed. Yes, I am in a bed; that is certain. And
some one has lifted up my head and is giving me a drink
— a drink deliciously cool. With an effort I rally my
faculties and open my eyes. A great black face is
close to mine. Who is it? I seem to know it; and yet
I do not. It looks at me with great kindness and pity.
And then, as if out of a dream, it comes, and I remember it. It is the face of the woman I struck that
fateful night when I first entered the loathsome carcass
of Sam Johnsing. Yes; it is Sam Johnsing's wife. It

glared at me then, but how tenderly it looks upon
me now. Again she lifts my head, and places
some pieces of broken ice in my mouth. Consciousness floats away from me for a space. I seem to
drift, drift on a great dark river, with clouded, gloomy
shores. And then I feel that some one is again giving
me a drink — this time a warm and pleasant drink —
and a voice says, soft and low:

"Dar, honey, dat's beef-tea; dat will do you good.
Does you know me, honey?"

With a great effort I replied:

"Yes."

And then something came softly from the other side
of the bed, into the range of my vision. Oh, what a
bright, fair, glowing, beauteous face it was! I knew it
well; it was the face of Abigail. I tried to utter my
joy, but she laid her hand upon my arm and said:

"Do not speak. You have been very sick for more
than a month past; you have had brain fever. But the
crisis is past. You are better now. The doctor says
you are out of danger. Mary and I have been here every
day, and Colonel Ruddiman has supplied all your wants.
But Emeline, here, has been your good angel. Before
we knew you were here (you were recognized on the
levee and carried hither), this poor woman had sold or
pawned all she had, even to the cradle of the baby, to
furnish you with medicines and pay doctors' bills. You
would have died but for her faithful and unremitting
devotion. Don't try to speak! I tell you all this that
you may know you have friends who love you and believe in you, and that you may have a cheerful heart

and become well. But see! here is Mary. She went
to the druggist's for some medicine."

I had taken and pressed the hand of the poor woman
I had once so brutally assailed. I reached my other
hand out to Abigail; and then I was conscious of some
one entering the door, and I heard the rustle of a dress
and Abigail saying, in a whisper:

" The delirium is past, but he is very weak."

My poor, throbbing heart leaped and fluttered in my
breast, like a wounded bird; and the next instant a
great feeling of abasement came over me, as I remembered my condition; and I would have sunk through
the bed — I would have hid my deformed face and
head from the sight of her I loved so profoundly.
Oh, the wretchedness of him who loves and knows
that he cannot be loved again !

And then there came, where my eyes could rest
upon it, the lovely face of Mary Ruddiman. What
a shrinking of her whole being there was when her
eyes encountered my poor countenance; and then what
an infinite pity shone out of every line of her gracious
and dignified face; and what a sorrow trembled and
thrilled in her voice, as she said in low, sweet tones:

" Oh, my poor friend, my poor, poor friend ! God
shield and deliver you !"

" Mary, Mary," I said, but so feebly that she could
scarcely catch my words, " while it delights the very
depths of my soul to see you, and to know that your
pity reaches out to me, like a divine hand, across
the abyss of all my wretchedness, yet do not look
at me. I cannot bear that this miserable carcass

should stand between me and your sympathy; or
that the eyes I love so deeply should rest upon this
face which I abhor with such intensity. Sit, I beg
you, where I can look upon you, but turn your eyes
away from my countenance."

She did so. She was crying softly.

"Doctor Huguet," she said,—"for I firmly believe
you are, indeed, Doctor Huguet — you cannot tell how
I have grieved over your dreadful sorrow ; for I feel
that it was my foolish ambition that caused it. I was
your temptress, your evil genius. I led you away from
your highest instincts. I, who should have encouraged
you in all goodness, degraded you to the low level of
low ambitions — as if there were anything higher or
nobler in all this world than duty faithfully performed.
For me — for my acts — you have suffered. But night
and day I have stormed heaven with my prayers for
your deliverance ; and I feel that the merciful Christ
will not punish you forever for the crime of a silly
woman, and that this dreadful doom will pass away
from you."

I tried to stop her, but she spoke with great rapidity
and earnestness.

"Do not blame yourself," I said. "If you have
sinned it was for love of me. You had no thought of
ambition for yourself; your dreams were all of my
greatness and my glory. Your fault was nobler than
any possible virtue. God will not relentlessly punish
such an act of unselfish devotion. We will yet be
reunited. I feel it in my heart. I have that faith in

the justice of the invisible world that I am sure we will some day be happy together again."

It is marvelous what a physical tonic there is in love and joy. They had lifted me up like wine; but Abigail was wiser than we, as lovers, could possibly be, and stopped our conversation. She laid her finger upon my thin, rapidly beating pulse, and then, with some final directions to Emeline, took Mary away with her.

Oh, how delightful was the sweet sleep as it crept over my senses! The little cabin, with the sunshine flooding in through the open door, faded slowly away, but the face of Mary grew brighter as the shadows of slumber mustered thick around me. And joy sat in my heart; and Hope stood, with fair face and bright torch, the eternal angel of human life, pointing forward to sweet and flowery paths of peace and love; and my poor bruised and battered soul, scarred with wounds and trampled under the feet of Fate, glowed and expanded and shone like a great star — a world of happiness.

Oh Love, thou art the medicine of the soul! Life without love is half-death. Woe unto him whom nothing loves! Better were it for him that he were in his grave.

CHAPTER XXVII.

I FIND MY MISSION.

" And is there care in heaven ?   And is there love
In heavenly spirits to these creatures base,
That may compassion of their evils move ?
There is; else much more wretched were the case
Of men than beasts."
—*The Faerie Queene* (*Spenser*).

IT was but a few days until I was sitting up in an easy-chair, nourished by all sorts of nutritious foods and beverages.   I gained rapidly in strength, for my mind was in a state of comparative peace.

I had fought the good fight.   I had done my best. I had been worsted.   The issue now was with Him who had placed me in this condition.   I could only " suffer and be strong."   My way would be pointed out to me.   But how sweet it was to look out over the fields and gardens, and the humble habitations of men, and remember that I possessed the sympathy and love of the good and noble, and that miles away they were thinking kindly of me.

My friends came often to see me.   Their visits provoked no comment, for there is a great deal of gentle charity in the South from the white people, especially the ladies, to the sick and poor among the negroes. Indeed, strange as it may appear, in view of the political rivalries and hostilities, the strongest bonds of love extend from the one race to the other. I have known a struggling white gentleman, with but a small income, set aside one-fourth of it every month for the support of his " mammy," an ancient and helpless nurse, whose black breasts had fed him in his infancy; and I have known the dark foster-mother to love her white charge more tenderly than her own offspring. It is a great pity that, among such noble and generous natures, political differences should ever arise to array them against each other, when they should all dwell together in peaceful Christian love and charity. But time will sweep away these evils, and leave only good behind; for God rules, and His path is toward the betterment of mankind.

I was a great source of wonderment and speculation to the negroes around me. They had known, and despised, and feared Sam Johnsing, for their little possessions had never been safe from his midnight raids. And they saw that I *was* Sam Johnsing, and, at the same time, that I was *not* Sam Johnsing. It was whispered about among them that something uncanny had happened to Sam. As I sat in the shade of the hut, dozing, one sunny afternoon, I wakened to hear this whispered conversation from the inside of the house:

" I tells you," said the Reverend J. J. Love, a preacher among them, " I tells you dat he is no Sam Johnsing. Didn't he kote de Bible to me yesterday? What did Sam eber know about de Bible? What do you think, Sister Emerline?"

" Well, I don't know for suah," said Emeline; " he is and he isn't. He is Sam and he isn't. He don't act

like Sam. He allays speaks so soft and kind, jist like
a white gem'man. And I tried him yesterday; I left
some money on de table near him, and I watch him.
He never tetched dat money! Sam would a stole it
quicker'n a wink."

" Dat's so," said another voice; " Sam would a stole
anything he could laid his han's on."

" And did you heah," said the preacher, " how pretty
he talked 'bout God; and 'bout de niggers bein' honest
and 'ligious ?"

" Yes," said the third voice, " I tells you Sam is
dead, and de angel Gabriel has done gone and took
'session ob his body. Dat's my 'pinion."

" No," said the Reverend J. J. Love, " not de angel
Gabriel, but Fader Abraham."

" Well, I don't car'," replied the other, " it's eder de
angel Gabriel or Fader Abraham or Moses or John de
Baptis'; no common nigger eber talked like dat.
When he gets strong, bress de Lord, we must make
him preach for us."

This proposition met with general assent; it set me
to thinking.

Why not ? I was a negro, cast among negroes, but
with a white man's education and eloquence. Was this
the path that was marked out for me ? Was this my
avenue to do good? Had I been led, through all my
miseries and misfortunes, to this task ? And why not?
Is it possible that the great and perfect mechanism of the universe, which has endured for so
many billions of years, does not extend to the
details of men's lives? Is not God building up His

splendid civilization, on this planet, with our life-works, even as He fattens the productive soil with the death of plants and animals? Who can ask the purpose of his own being, unless he can comprehend the whole scheme of Divinity, broad enough to inclose the fathomless depths of the stars, and enduring enough to reach throughout eternity? Can the plant-root, as it reaches down into the earth and eliminates organic matter for its sustenance, ask what living thing died, centuries ago, to furnish it with that storehouse of food? Can the artist tell at what point, in the long line of his peasant ancestors, there was imported into their blood that touch of genius which has flowered out in himself, in beauty and glory, for the pleasure of man and the up-building of society? No; as one of the wisest of the wits of America once said, " we cannot control the character of the cards that are dealt to us in the great game of life, but we can at least play them to the very best of our ability." It is the duty of every one to do his utmost in the sphere of action assigned to him. The bricks in the foundation-wall are necessary to the glorious statue which they uphold. They are not the statue, but the statue cannot stand without them. If William Burness, the poor gardener of Ayr, had not done his whole duly, in the midst of grinding poverty and wretchedness, we should have lost the sweetest lyrics in the language, written by his immortal son. It is the black mud that feeds the lily. It is from the refuse that the sweetest odors, freighting the zephyrs, are distilled.

CHAPTER XXVIII.

DOING MY WORK.

" And now such is thy stand, while thou dost deal
  Desired justice to the public weal,
  Like Solon's self, explain'st the knotty laws
  With endless labors, whilst thy learning draws
  No less of praise, than readers, of all kinds
  Of worthiest knowledge that can take men's minds."
                        —*Underwoods* (*Ben Jonson*).

A MILE from my hut, in the outskirts of the city, among fields and orchards, there stood an old barn, dilapidated and deserted. The farm to which it belonged had been sold for debt, and was now owned by a money-lender in an adjacent State. He found it difficult to rent the farm, and the negroes had taken possession of the barn for their Sunday religious exercises. Here, once a week, they assembled in great numbers, and worshiped God in their own emotional and excitable way, with shouting, singing, prayers and exhortations. Here my new friend, the Reverend J. J. Love, officiated with great zeal and unction. He was wholly illiterate, but he had a wonderful memory, and he had picked up many Bible phrases, which he sometimes applied in ludicrous fashion. He was tall, spare, white-headed, with bushy gray eye-brows, a face all seamed with lines and wrinkles, and a certain dignity of manner. There are three things which testify to the inherent civilizability of the negro race: First, their desire for learning; second, their strong religious instincts; and third, their wish to be respectable and to imitate the best examples given them by the whites. It does not seem to me that the red men manifest any of these traits; hence I argue that the negro race will rise upon the breast of the great tide of civilization, while the Indian is very apt to be buried under it.

I came to the conclusion that the negroes needed education even more than exhortation. Their reason required development more than their emotions.

My first step was, as soon as I was able to walk, to go into C—— and find who had charge of this barn. It was my old acquaintance, Buryhill, as affable and as voracious as ever. I soon came to an understanding with him, which I took the precaution to reduce to writing and have him sign. For a small sum paid down (I got the money from Ben), I rented the barn for a year, with the right to repair and improve it. I then purchased shingles to patch the roof, sash for windows, lumber enough to floor it and provide it with a platform, tables, benches, etc. I then laid in a supply of books and other school necessaries. I hired negro carpenters — there were some who had learned their trade in the old slave days — and I soon had a very comfortable and cleanly school-house.

The negroes had watched these proceedings with great interest, and some of them had voluntarily assisted in the work. When all was ready, I gave notice that I proposed to open a school for the colored people, not for the children alone, but for persons of all ages. In the daytime the little ones were to be taught; and at night the men and women, who were busy with their work during the day, could receive the benefits of education free of charge.

It was a motley gathering that met me the first night. The whole country-side had turned out. Old and young, male and female, were there — the little pickaninny and the gray-haired deacon of the church sat side by side. The Reverend J. J. Love was conspicuous in the front of the crowd.

My purpose was to instruct them, and to do so I must get into *rapport* with their minds. I must not shoot above their heads, and I must make knowledge useful and interesting. I must, as far as possible, imitate the example of Christ, and teach in anecdotes, for the " parables " are simply stories, containing, each one, an instructive moral.

I had the school-books piled up on my desk. I first divided my scholars into those who knew the alphabet, those who knew how to read and write, and those who were totally illiterate. The greater part of the audience belonged to the latter class. I distributed the books accordingly. I asked the Reverend J. J. Love what he would study. He replied, pompously, " 'Stronomy." I gave him a text book on that subject. He sat for an hour, holding it upside down, and looking at it intently with a profound aspect. Finally, as nothing came out of this proceeding, he came up to me, rather sheepishly, and said:

" I guess I'll take one of dem ere spellin'-books.
I guess dat's what I wants. "

From my charts on the wall, I first gave an hour's
lesson on the alphabet.   I told the story of its origin,
and stated that for ten thousand years it had been sub-
stantially repeated, from nation to nation, with gradual
changes in the form of the letters.   I suggested that it
came first, in all probability, from the antediluvian
world of Noah and the Flood, of which they had all
heard something.   Then I told them that without education they could not be a free people; for Freedom
and Ignorance were an incongruous pair, who bred two
twin monsters, Anarchy and Despotism, and one of these
was sure to devour the other.   An ignorant people
were only fit to be slaves, and sooner or later they were
sure to be slaves — slaves to superstition, slaves to the
crafty, slaves to the powerful.   They were the prey to
every man who knew more than they did.   They must
either learn to think or remain beasts of burden
through all generations.   And they could not think
wisely without knowledge; and they could not acquire
knowledge unless through the alphabet : by this means
the treasures of the learning of all time were open
for their use.   Those queer, crooked little marks lay
at the base of civilization.   They were the keys of gold
that would unlock the store-houses of the world's accumulated wealth.   I quoted Bacon to them, of whom,
of course, they had never heard, that " a man is simply
what he knows. "   And I could not help but think that
just as Francis Bacon stood, unknown to them, in the
background of history, while his life-work was lifting

even them up to higher levels; so there might be great auxiliary spirits, instruments of God, in the invisible world surrounding us, who were constantly at work for our good, of whose names and very existence we knew nothing. I told them that the brain of man, without education, was a mass of useless pulp; nay, worse than useless, since it might be turned into an instrument directed to the destruction of its owner. I explained to them, as well as I could, the doctrine of Evolution; how, under a divine impulse, the higher rose out of the lower; the greater out of the less; the complex out of the simple; the noble out of the ignoble; the pure out of the impure; the civilized man out of the savage; the Christian out of the brute. I showed them that Darwinism *plus* God was the true philosophy of the new age. I told them that they were the children of the Most High, and, poor and despised as they were, the inheritors of the purposes of God, and that they were His agents to lift up themselves and others. All this, of course, I did not put in these words, but in language which they could understand, with many illustrations and interesting facts. Their attention was rapt and intense. To be sure, the bow of their minds could not long retain its spring, but laughter, or some touch of human interest, relaxed it, and the next instant they came back eagerly for more knowledge. I pointed out to them that all the dark and dreadful sufferings of humanity, during the past ages, were due to ignorant and untrained minds. If the people had known their own interests they would not have been the victims of kings and creeds, to die by millions on battlefields, or on the scaffold, or at the stake.   My auditors were themselves the posterity of captives made in wars among the savage and brutal inhabitants of Africa, and sold as slaves to the whites.   Through this awful gate-way of oppression they had entered into liberty, and, if they were true to themselves, through this they would enter into culture and civilization.   I told them that they must hold no animosity toward the whites for having bought their ancestors from their African captors; they had been released thereby from savagery.   If they had not been thus sold they would have been killed by their own countrymen, according to their cruel customs.   Even slavery was an improvement on murder.   I quoted the wise saying of a wise man, that " we must gather from the past not fire, but light."   We could not hold the by-gone time responsible for its barbarisms.   The past was all barbarism.   The past of their race was dark and terrible — it was the future to which alone they must look.

Then I gave them a brief lecture on astronomy. Knowledge is the accumulation of interesting facts. That which does not interest and benefit humanity is not worth knowing.   You must widen the brows of men by forcing new ideas into their brains.   Thought was the food of the mind, and it grows with what it feeds on. It longs for knowledge as the eye longs for light — it is the sustenance of the soul.

Instead of the savage's conception of the stars and sun and moon — as lamps, hung in the sky to light the steps of men on a universe of earth — I showed that

our globe was a mere speck of matter in a boundless
creation; that every new accession of knowledge increased our conception of the magnitude of the universe.   From the perception, by the naked eye, of a
few thousand stars, we had advanced, by the aid of
science, to the knowledge of a hundred million suns,
each with its galaxy of planets, like our own.   And
now the application of photography showed that
beside these suns, made manifest by the telescope, there
were thousands of millions more.   Indeed, the immense
thought was being forced upon us that this created
universe was illimitable—indeed an universal universe
— boundless as space and eternity.

And then I dwelt upon the inexpressible greatness
of the Architect of all this — that mighty Being out of
the operation of whose Will had flowed all this endless
congregation of suns and populous planets, and comets
and meteors; and all the teeming life of this earth, the
animals and plants, visible to our eyes; and that other
universe of being, revealed to us by the microscope, *
the limits of whose endless variety and minuteness we
have not yet reached, and probably will never reach.
And then I referred to this wonderful Creator, not as
a king on a throne, with a crown on His head, but as a
vast omnipresent *Mind*, permeating all space and all
matter; unresting, unending, untiring; to whom nothing is small and nothing great; who keeps the count
of the motes in the sunbeam, and remembers every
creature that lives, or ever has lived, on earth or in the
heavens.   And I said to them that so vast, so wonderful,
so adorable was this Being that He alone was worthy

of study and contemplation by the thoughtful mind; and that nature, man and all things that are within the universe are entitled to consideration simply because they are part of the outflow of this divine power. I said to them that God was invisible, even as our own minds are invisible; that he had no shape, even as our own minds were without shape; that he was recognized by his works, even as our own minds are known to one another by their influence on matter. That he who helped and made free the mind of man released a part of God from the trammels and thraldom of matter, and gave thought spiritual wings upon which it could traverse the universe.

It is impossible to describe the rapt attention of my audience. Many of my words they did not understand, but these probably were more potent with them than those which they did understand, for the imagination came into play and invested them with powers of which the dictionary knows nothing.

After the exercises were over they still hung around the building in clusters, reluctant to depart, discussing whether I was John the Baptist, Moses, Abraham or the angel Gabriel. They were all agreed I was not Sam Johnsing, the chicken-thief—of that they were certain.

CHAPTER XXIX.

PREACHING AND TEACHING.

> " Will no man say, Amen?
> Am I both priest and clerk?"
> —*Richard II., iv. 1.*

THE barn was a large one, but it would not begin to hold the crowds that assembled every night — for my fame had spread far and wide. One-half the audience were white people. They were given front seats by the deacons, who were proud to have them present. I ornamented the building as well as I could. I covered the walls with bright paper, festooned the stage with evergreens, and hung up pictures, here and there, of the illustrious men who had labored for the benefit of the human race. Back of the stage I suspended geographical maps and chronological charts.

I still pursued the system, with which I had commenced, of mingling instruction with entertainment. I ransacked my memory for anecdotes that would illustrate my lectures; but I always wound up by some words showing their duty to the Creator, and to each other, as a Christian people. Each night I took up, as a subject, a country or nation, and gave as interesting an account as I could of its history, and the character and customs of its people; with extracts from the narratives of travelers, of striking adventures by field and flood. I had gradually collected quite a library, which I kept in a room I had inclosed at one end of the barn, and there I slept and studied and prepared my addresses.

Mary and Abigail and Colonel Ruddiman were often present, and among my most attentive auditors. A number of white clergymen began to drop in. The unthinking multitude came to scoff, and many of them remained to pray. The sympathy of the respectable white people was altogether with me, for my exhortations in behalf of cleanliness, temperance and honesty were having a visible effect upon the colored population. The contributions flowed in freely from both blacks and whites.

A large portion of the whites were as illiterate as the negroes, and the avidity of both for learning was astonishing. I held every day, during the morning hours, a school for the children, at which they were taught to read and write, and similar instruction was given to the adults every night.

I was almost happy. I felt that I was doing good — more good than I had ever done before in my lifetime. My flock loved and almost worshiped me. I realized what a grand task it was to beautify and purify human intellects; to lift them up from groveling thoughts to noble aspirations; to cleanse the temples of all these souls from ignorance and debasing superstitions; to teach them, if not a creed, the vital essentials of religion. The very faces of the children began to improve in consonance with the molding and development of their minds. I was elevating two races. I was doing God's work on earth.

But all this did not pass unnoticed among the ruffianry of the district. I heard rumors that nightly con-
sultations were held on the subject at Mother Bindell's
hostelry, and that indignation shook that classic temple
of white aristocracy to its very foundations. Even the
slatternly wenches were outraged at this attempt to
make the negroes as honest, honorable and intelligent
as white men; and Mother Bindell, while she said
nothing, snapped her mean and cruel little eyes, and
convulsively clutched with her withered harpy hands,
conscious — as a white woman — that the very fabric
of society, built on the distinctions of race and color,
was being overthrown by such radical and anarchistic
proceedings. The loudest in denouncing me was the
new Doctor Huguet. He hated a black man with an
intense fervor. He had special reasons, well known to
himself, for hating me; for he feared that the power
that had made him a white man might at any moment
return him to his original condition. If I was only
dead, that danger would cease; and so he roared and
swore, louder than all the rest, that the negro must be
kept in his proper place — that is, the *male* negro;
and that they must go out and burn down my
school-house, and make an end of me. Nothing
else would satisfy their outraged Caucasian dignity.
And so they all fumed and stormed and howled together. But they attempted nothing, for they well
knew that I had made no utterance to provoke race
antagonisms, and that the sentiment of all the respectable white people, who constituted three-fourths of
the entire population, sustained me in my work, by

voice and purse. But it distressed them, in the midst of their drunken orgies, to think that some one was at work trying to make the negroes around them better men, better citizens and better Christians. It is not to be wondered at that a large part of mankind believe in a personal devil, since there is so much malignity and hatred of all goodness in a considerable share of the population of the world. The doctrine of demoniacal possession, despite the doctors, would seem to have some ground and foundation of experience and reason to stand upon. We so often see evil done which neither profits the doer nor any one else, that one is constrained to look for its source in extra-mundane influences, and to see in the unreasonable and unprofitable wickedness of man the impish instincts of some grinning demon behind the scenes.

CHAPTER XXX.

THE CLOUDS GATHERING.

> " Life is a business — not good cheer ;
>   Ever in wars.
>   The sun still shineth there or here,
>   Whereas the stars
>   Watch an advantage to appear."
>   —*George Herbert.*

IT seemed to me that every day the faces of Mary and the Colonel were more and more gloomy. The Colonel was constantly lost in thought, as if brooding over some great trouble.

One afternoon I was sitting reading in my little room, in the barn, when Mary and Abigail entered. After some conversation, I said to Mary :

" I observe that your father looks troubled and distressed. Is it about money matters ? "

" Yes," she replied. " It is about our home. We are likely to lose it ! "

" How so ? " I asked.

" That miserable creature, Buryhill," she replied, " has been buying up the mortgages, judgments and tax-titles against the place. Many of them he purchased, we learn, at a large discount, the tax-titles at about half their face value, and so he holds claims against the place that amount to about seven thousand dollars. The plantation is worth much more than that, and father has been trying to group all his indebtedness together, in one mortgage, and get out of Buryhill's clutches. But some one has gone to every banker and money-lender in C—— (father thinks it was Buryhill or his agents), and discredited father, so that he cannot find any one who will advance him the money needed. In the meantime Buryhill is harassing father with visits and threatening letters, until he is almost distracted. Recently Buryhill has made a new proposition. He says that he has found out, by chance, that father is heir to a claim against certain real estate, not here, but outside of South Carolina,— but in what place he will not tell,—which is worth nothing to father, because it would require long and expensive litigation to enforce it; but that he, Buryhill, being a lawyer, could take it and make something out of it, and that he will give father $2,000 credit for a quit-claim deed of his title, and take a mortgage on the plantation for $5,000, to be paid in two years. Father is so hard pressed that he is disposed to accept this offer; it would give him breathing-space to look around and see what he could do. But I have objected to his entering into such a contract, on the ground that Buryhill is a dishonest knave, and that we have nothing but his word as to the value of the property which he asks father to convey to him. It may be worth millions. It may be some estate in England. I have read of many such cases. I have argued that, if father is to go into any such trade, he should know beforehand just what he is to trade away. But father is so driven to desperation, by his fears of seeing us all turned out of doors, that my words do not seem to have much weight with him, and I fear that he will do what Buryhill desires."

"Your views of the matter," I said, "are correct and wise. Tell your father to do nothing until he sees me and talks it over with me; and ask him whether he cannot call here to-morrow afternoon, and bring with him copies of all his correspondence with Buryhill, and any marriage-certificates, deeds, wills, letters, or other papers he may have relating to his ancestors, especially to the collateral branches. We must find out where that property is, and what is its value. You may be very sure that it is worth many times what that rapacious shark offers for it. In the meantime tell your father to say nothing about his proposed conference with me. Buryhill is surrounding him with a net-work of wires, and he must not know what your father is doing or intends to do."

Mary's face brightened.

"I am so glad," she said, "that you are going to help us. That is a good idea to find out all we can about our ancestors. There is an old chest in the library, full of documents, many of them yellow with age. I shall search them over to-night, and we will bring with us to-morrow any that seem of value. I begin to see a ray of hope through the thick darkness that surrounds us. Poor father has been so distressed in mind that he has been drinking more wine of late, at table, than is usual with him; and I think Buryhill has used that fact to injure his credit with the money-lenders. I do not believe that he could stand up long against such sordid and debasing troubles. I think he

would rather face loaded cannon than the tricks of such
wretches as Buryhill."

The next day the Colonel and Mary drove over to
the barn.   I brought them into my room and locked
the outside doors, so that we should not be interrupted;
and we had a lengthy conference upon the whole matter.   Mary had brought with her a satchel, full of
papers, and I carefully examined them all: old wills,
deeds, letters, etc.   But a diligent search revealed
nothing that would throw any light upon the subject of
our inquiry.   The direct line of the Colonel's ancestors,
the Ruddimans, had resided, for a century past, in
South Carolina, but the collateral progenitors, inter-
marrying with them, had lived in different States:
North Carolina, Virginia, Maryland and Pennsylvania.
The original stock came from Devonshire, England, at
the time of the early settlement of Virginia; but there
was nothing to show anything about their English
relatives.

I was discouraged.   It would be an endless task to
search the records of half-a-dozen States; and in the
meantime the mortgages would be foreclosed and the
plantation lost.   The Colonel and Mary both saw, by
my manner, that I had lost hope, and their own countenance became very grave and sad.

What could we do?   We could not by any legal
process compel that cormorant, Buryhill, to disclose
what he knew.   To be sure, violence might force it out
of him.   If he saw death staring him in the face he
might tell his secret to save his life.   But this was a
remedy as desperate as the disease, and only to be

thought of in the last extremity. I mentioned the idea, however, to the Colonel, and his eyes flashed with a look that would have made Mr. Buryhill very uncomfortable if he had seen it and understood what it meant. For a strong, honest man, caught in the meshes of a rogue, feels very little compunction about laying his giant paw on the pigmy that has entrapped him, and crushing the life out of his miserable anatomy.

" Yes," he said, " if we had Buryhill in the woods, with a rope around his neck, and a few stout arms ready to haul him up, I think, to save his own life, he would relinquish his secret, and with it his little game of ruining me. Like all scoundrels, he is an arrant coward. Yes, I like that idea!"

" Well, well," I said, " it is time enough to think of that hereafter. But you have not yet shown me your correspondance with him."

The Colonel, like all such free-hearted, unsuspicious men, had retained no copies of his own letters to Buryhill, but fortunately he had saved the communications he had received from him, and he handed them over to me. There were a score of them.

I arranged them in chronological order and then proceeded to read them carefully.

It was curious to observe the change in Buryhill's tone; how the courtesy of the earlier letters graduated into peremptoriness and insolence as he felt more and more sure of his victim.

Then there came another change. I said to the Colonel:

" This rascal did not know about the outside property

when he commenced his correspondence with you. I can put my finger upon the point of time when he first heard of it. The sudden change in manner shows increased respect, and that argues that the estate in question is large, very large. Here he writes you a most friendly letter intimating that the matter can probably be arranged to your entire satisfaction. There is a break of three or four days. During that time the thought has occurred to his scheming brain that you knew nothing of this inheritance, and that he might take advantage of your ignorance and carelessness to get it away from you; and then came the letter offering to give you a credit of $2,000 on your indebtedness, for a quit-claim of the property. He thought you could not possibly extricate yourself in two years, in these dull times, from the $5,000 mortgage, and thus he would secure your plantation and your inheritance besides."

" Oh! the villain," cried the Colonel, his face red with rage; " and this is the man I took into my house and treated like a gentleman! He sat at my table and partook of my hospitality, and was plotting, at that very moment, how he could destroy me — how he could send me to the poor-house — me, who had never wronged or injured him. Why, the highwayman who claps a pistol to your head and takes your purse is a gentleman compared with such a scoundrel. The robber gives you a chance to shoot him down; he offers a life for a life; and he takes but a small contribution out of your abundance. But this modern breed of highwaymen stick their guns over the battlements of law, order and society, and, in perfect safety, strip you of everything you have in the world, and smile upon you in the most friendly fashion, while they rob you. Oh! they are monsters! They should be hunted down and murdered, as we hunt and kill wolves and panthers."

" Well, Colonel," I replied, " these wretches are the result of our modern civilization. There is this great difference between villainy inside the law and villainy outside the law: the fellows in the prisons are the stupid rascals who, in their insatiable selfishness, did not stop to consider the limitations and technicalities of the statutes; but a scoundrel, *plus* a knowledge of the law, becomes a gentleman and a statesman. Buryhill will go to Congress yet; while his victims will be tramping around the land, begging for bread at kitchen doors."

The Colonel grew pale and shuddered.

" But we must match cunning with cunning," I added. " Modern society has no sympathy with hon-esty that permits itself to be outwitted by craft. The knavish, plundering non-producer is respectable; the worthy, ruined producer is contemptible. That is the judgment of the world."

" But what is this ? " I exclaimed.

They both rose and stood over me. I held in my hand one of the last letters written by Buryhill to the Colonel. It had been copied by him in a letter-press, and at the same time another letter had been copied with it, and, by accident, no card-board had been placed between the two sheets of tissue paper, and thus the writing of the second letter had passed through both sheets of damp tissue-paper, and had recorded itself, faintly, upon the face of the letter addressed to the Colonel; but the writing was inverted, running from right to left instead of from left to right.

" In dealing with such a knave as Buryhill," I said, " we must not lose a single point."

I could make out the words " Baltimore, Md.," in the inverted writing, reading backward. We all tried to decipher it. Then Mary, with the quick wit of a woman, jumped up and took a mirror from the wall, and held it before me, and I, holding the letter in front of the mirror, distinctly read in the glass the reversed writing, as follows:

C——, S. C., September 12th, 1889.

Mess. Van Hoesen and Bigelow, Attorneys at Law, Baltimore, Md.

GENTLEMEN: In answer to your valued favor of the 9th inst. I would state that your letter of the 2nd inst., to Colonel Ruddiman, in reference to the expired lease of property in your city, sent to my care, was duly delivered to him; and he begs me to say that business engagements have delayed his reply, and that he hopes to soon send a legal representative to Baltimore to see you and arrange for the delivery of the estate. In the meantime, as the Colonel is likely to be absent from home for some days, he requests that any letters you may send him shall be sent, as heretofore, under cover to this office.

I have the honor to be,

Very respectfully,

Your obedient servant,

CHARLES A. BURYHILL.

" There !" I said, " that tells the whole story ! The man is a greater villain than even I thought him. He received a letter from that law firm in Baltimore, addressed to you, Colonel, under cover to him; he opened it and read it; at once (compare the dates), he wrote you that friendly letter, for he saw that you would soon be beyond his power. Then he began his game to swindle you. If you had executed the quit-claim deed, as he proposed, he would have gone directly to Baltimore, as the owner of the property; for you may be sure that, immediately after receiving that first letter, he thoroughly informed himself as to the precise value of it. But let me congratulate you, Colonel," I said, shaking his hand; " that tell-tale record, made by the letter-press, has saved you; for, beyond doubt, the Baltimore property will more than pay your debts and leave you your plantation free."

Mary's face shone with delight, and she thanked me earnestly for the great service I had rendered them. The Colonel was dazed with astonishment. The relief caused by the good news contended in his honest mind with indignation at the audacious villainy of Buryhill. The latter paralyzed the worthy man. He could not comprehend it. To steal his letter and then lay such a cunning trap for him! He rose and strode up and down the room, muttering imprecations, while every now and then his hand stole involuntarily to his hip-pocket, as if searching for a weapon. If Buryhill had entered at that time the Colonel would have settled their differences by a process not known in the whole cunning catalogue of writs and proceedings enumerated in the statute books; — a process from which there would have been no writ of error, or *certiorari*, or appeal, except to the high court of heaven. Buryhill would have left his rat-hoard of accumulated stealings very suddenly, and gone to mingle his villainy with the demon natures of the invisible world.

We were quiet for a time, thinking, and then Mary broke the silence.

"What had we better do?" she asked.

"I will go and see that Baltimore law firm," said the Colonel.

"No, no," I replied; "you don't know them, and you don't know the situation of the property. They may be honorable men,— for there are lawyers who are an honor to our common human nature,— but, on the other hand, they may be as big rogues as Buryhill, and to approach them without a full knowledge of what the property is, and the legal condition of your claim, would be dangerous: you might fall into the hands of swindlers."

"What shall I do, then?" asked the Colonel.

"I think," I replied, "that it would be better for *me* to go to Baltimore. I will find out a trusty lawyer to help me. I will examine the records in the offices where deeds and contracts are recorded. I have an idea that the property was embraced in one of those ninety-nine-year leases, a good many of which were given a century ago. Buryhill's letter says that it is a 'lease,' and that it has 'expired.' You have given no lease of property in Baltimore, during your lifetime; nor could your father or mother have done so without your having heard something about it. But your mother's grandfather, I see by these papers, lived in Baltimore about a hundred years ago. His name was Ephraim Woodside. We must search the records for deeds to, or leases from, Ephraim Woodside, given about a century since. When we have got the date of the lease, and the description of the property, it will not be difficult to find out its value. As I appear to be a negro, I can move about and make inquiries of other negroes without exciting suspicion."

" What will I do with Buryhill, in the meantime ?" asked the Colonel.

" I will write you a letter," I said, " which you can copy and send to him, saying that you have a chance to secure money enough to pay off your debts, and asking ten days' delay, and intimating that, if you cannot borrow the money in that time, you will probably accede to his terms. This will keep him quiet until I have time to report the results of my investigations at Baltimore; for he will feel sure that, with the skill he will employ to thwart you, you will not be able to effect such a loan as you seek. He will have you shadowed; so do not come here. I will give out that I am sick, and will close up the school for a few days, and have Emeline prevent any one from entering here but herself. I will take with me all the deeds, wills, marriage-certificates, etc., that you have brought with you, and that may be necessary to prove your claim. If everything is right you can borrow money enough in Baltimore to pay off all you owe to Buryhill, and get out of his satanic and poisonous clutches."

" Yes," replied the Colonel, his face shining with renewed hope and happiness; " and then I will call the d——d scoundrel out and shoot him."

" No, no," I said ; " I would not pollute my hands with his black blood. Neither would he fight. You would have to shoot him down like a wild beast, in cold blood. Better expose the wretch and drive him out of the country."

We talked very fully over all the details of my expedition, and it was agreed that I should start the next morning for Baltimore.

I was happy — happy to find that at last, despite my black skin, my active brain could work effectively, and I could achieve something. The sense of power returned to me, and I found myself singing, for the first time since the night of my dreadful transformation.

CHAPTER XXXI.

DETECTIVE WORK.

" Do this suddenly,
And let not search and inquisition quail."
—*As You Like It, ii. 2.*

I TOOK a seat in the car, modestly — near the door. I was well dressed. I had my hair cut short ; I wore a pair of large, gold-rimmed spectacles, not to aid my sight, but to increase the respectability of my appearance. I even fancied that the expression of my face had improved and softened, for the body molds itself to the spirit, even as the shell of the *nautilus* adapts itself to every convolution of the body of the little creature within it. High thought and noble endeavor had banished from eyes and mouth the crafty, cruel and brutal expression which had so shocked me the first time I looked into Sam Johnsing's broken looking-glass.

I was amused to notice how the white passengers avoided me as they hastened into the car. I had the seat all to myself. No one crowded me. Ladies sat themselves down on the seat behind or before mine, and then, perceiving me, rose quickly, with uplifted noses, and hurried off to some other part of the car. I did not grow angry — the ordeals I had passed through had cured me of all that sort of feeling. I had braced myself up to endure.

As the train moved on I indulged in many sad and some amusing reflections. Life is a wonderful panorama, and far surpasses in interest, to the appreciative spirit, anything that can be shown on the mimic stage. As we grow older the brain, when not poisoned by the use of intrusive and destructive stimulants and narcotics, acquires all the sensitiveness of a photographic plate, and receives impressions of character of marvelous distinctness and variety of color. Youth is the period of ferment, heat and passion, and the intellectual apparatus does not reach its perfect work until middle life. The receptivity and fecundity of the brain are then at their best. There is no higher material study than the perfection of the conditions of the mind. It is such a subtle potency that it is a grave crime to injuriously affect it, by putting into the mouth anything that will lessen its harmonious and exquisite action. The mind responds, like a delicately constructed instrument, to every influence acting upon the body; and the body must be neither underfed nor clogged with indulgence, if we would have the godlike harp respond to the finest touches of the angels of the soul.

It is hard to tell, I thought, how far a man is fortunate or unfortunate in his generation. In many respects this is the greatest age this world has ever known. Never before did humanity possess such vast powers over nature; never before was there so much happiness on earth; never before did such huge populations dwell in such a golden atmosphere of peace and enlightenment. And yet all these things may be accompanied by such a denial of spiritual life; by such shallow, dust-grubbing materialism; by such a dead-rot of servility and heartlessness and wealth-grabbing and Mammon-worship, that the fair form of Progress becomes rotten and worm-eaten ; and that which we mistake for the pulsations of breathing life may be but the convulsive struggles of the swarming vermin beneath the infected skin. In the age of Queen Elizabeth there were but five million people who spoke the English tongue; now there are, in all the world, one hundred and twenty millions; but what one name, of this generation, have we to set up against the immortal galaxy that adorned that wonderful era ? Not one! We erect great fortunes; but we do not build great men.

> "Ye have the Pyrrhic dance as yet —
> Where is the Pyrrhic phalanx gone ?
> Of two such lessons, why forget
> The nobler and the manlier one ?"

The individual lessens as the race greatens; independent thought becomes an offense, and strength of character a crime. Society is a great shop, where the millions are turned out after the same pattern — like ready-made clothing. As Pope says, in the *Dunciad:*

> "With the same cement, ever sure to bind,
> We bring to one dead level every mind;
> Then take him to develop, if you can,
> And hew the block off and get out the man."

It is the age of pointless uniformity and immensely prosperous dullness. And all this prosperity is but dust blown in the eyes of Apollo. It hides the face of heaven and darkens the visage of God; when, indeed, there is nothing in the universe but God, and nothing worth thinking of in all this world but God; for prayer is only the contemplation of God, on the bent knees of the soul.

> " In vain, in vain, *the all-composing hour*
>   Resistless falls! the Muse obeys the power.
> She comes! she comes!   The sable throne behold
> Of night primeval, and of Chaos old!
> Before her, fancy's gilded clouds decay,
> And all its varying rainbows die away.
> Wit shoots in vain his momentary fires,
> The meteor drops, and in a flash expires.
> As, one by one, at dread Medea's strain,
> The sickening stars fade off the ethereal plain;
> As Argus' eyes, by Hermes' wand oppressed,
> Closed one by one to everlasting rest:
> Thus at the fell approach, and secret might,
> Art after art goes out, and all is night!   .   .   .
> Philosophy, that leaned on heaven before,
> Shrinks to her second-cause, and is no more.
> Religion, blushing, veils her sacred fires,
> And, unawares, morality expires.
> Nor public flame, nor private, dares to shine;
> Nor human spark is left, nor glimpse divine!
> Lo, thy dread empire, Chaos! is restored;
> Light dies before thy uncreating word;
> Thy hand, great Anarch! lets the curtain fall,
> And universal darkness buries all. "

It is a pitiable spectacle:— the soul of man drowned in the splendors of the flesh; a nation perishing from too much prosperity; the dead, flat waste of ages that make no history. Genius lights, with its crooked talons, upon the mountain peaks of world-shaking convulsions.

It finds no resting-place upon the desolate plains of a money-worshiping, characterless, materialistic age.

And then my thoughts drifted to the people about me, and I could not help but think that each one dwelt in his or her own world of reflections, filled with its own memories and thoughts,— of men and women, and deeds and things,— each one totally differing from his neighbor. And it occurred to me, that if the *aura* of every man's thoughts was made visible, what a sight it would be,—extending far beyond the narrow limits of the railroad car, overlapping each other, and reaching, in some instances, to the ends of the earth. Each individual carries his world of thoughts around him like a great atmosphere. In one case it is pure and bright and tenanted by angels; in another it is dark and gloomy, thick with scowling crimes and threatening demons. The raiment of these people touched as they sat together; they exchanged little civilities of speech; and yet heaven and hell were not farther apart than the realms in which their souls dwelt.

And then I pondered what I should do when I reached Baltimore. I had heard, from some of the members of my flock, of a remarkable negro woman, in that city, by the name of Charity Jones. She was a singular evidence of the intellectual power possible in the race. She was a full-blooded negro, perfectly illiterate, but with the most marvelous intelligence and memory. She knew every black man and woman in Baltimore, their character, history and pedigree for generations past. She was almost equally familiar with

16

the white people.   She was consulted regularly by
both races ; and her wisdom and honesty were as
extraordinary as her memory.   I made up my mind I
would go and see her, and get her to furnish me with.
the name of some bright young lawyer who would help
me in the search of the old records of Baltimore.

CHAPTER XXXII.

CHARITY JONES.

"What complexion is she of?
Swart, like my shoe."
— *Comedy of Errors, iii. 2.*

I FOUND her in her cleanly little cabin, overgrown with vines — a stout, broad-headed, full-browed, elderly negro woman, with a quiet, settled manner.

I told her I desired to consult with her, and handed her a silver dollar.

She looked at me with penetrating eyes, and said:

"You are Doctor Huguet."

I was astounded.

"How do you know that?" I asked.

"Because," she replied, "I have heard all about you; and you have a white man's manner and a white man's speech in the mouth of a negro; and you do not belong here."

"How do you know that?"

"Because I know every negro in Baltimore, and for many miles around it."

"Well," I said, "you are right. I am Doctor Huguet. What did you hear about me?"

"Everything; such strange news travels fast."

"They tell me," I said, "that you are honest. I want you to help me to save a good, true man, who is oppressed by a rascal."

243

She handed me back the dollar, and said:

" I do not need money for that. "

But I pressed it upon her again.

" Tell me, " I said, " the name of a bright, young, white lawyer, honest and honorable, who is familiar with the offices of the courts. "

" What do you want him for ? " she asked.

" Simply to help me hunt up some records. "

She placed her finger to her forehead, and sat a few moments silent.   She seemed to be weighing different men in the balance of her judgment.   At last she spoke.

" The man who would suit you is young Mr. Abel Harrison, of No. —— Lexington Street.   Tell him I sent you to him.   Be frank with him, for he is trust- worthy. "

I was surprised to note the excellent language she used.   It came, I suppose, from her good memory and her intercourse with the whites.

I asked her what was the reputation of the law firm of Van Hoesen & Bigelow.   She gave them a high character for integrity.

I thanked her for her information, and told her that if I needed further advice I should call upon her again.

CHAPTER XXXIII.

MY LETTER TO THE COLONEL.

"I have better news in store for you
Than you expect."
—*Merchant of Venice*, v. i.

THE third day after my arrival in Baltimore I wrote
Colonel Ruddiman the following letter:

MY DEAR COLONEL: Permit me to heartily congratulate you and Miss
Mary and Abigail. The estate which Buryhill would have bought from
you for $2,000 is worth at least $250,000. The lease for ninety-nine years,
made September 1st, 1790, expired September 1st, 1889. When it was
made, by Ephraim Woodside and Belinda, his wife, to Sylvanus Carpenter,
the property consisted of twenty acres of farm-land; the city has since overgrown it, and it is now partly built up, with rows of houses. The present
holders of a portion of it called upon Mess. Van Hoesen & Bigelow
to have them hunt up the heirs of Ephraim Woodside, so that they
could purchase a good title. This is how that firm came to write to
Buryhill. They offer $10,000 for four houses and lots. I think the
property is worth more than that, but I would advise that you
accept their offer; you will thus be able to settle with Buryhill without
going into debt to any one; and you know what a hell of slavery debt is.
And you will, after selling this fraction, still have a vast estate left. I
showed the marriage-certificates of your parents and grandparents to Van
Hoesen & Bigelow, but they were not necessary, for they had already
satisfied themselves, from their own researches, that you are the sole heir
of Ephraim Woodside. They inclose to you with this letter a deed for
you to execute for the four lots. When it is returned to me, I will receive
the $10,000 from them, and deliver the deed. I also inclose a receipt for
you to sign, for the $10,000; please return it to me, so that there may be
no hesitation about paying me the money. I have explained to these gentlemen Buryhill's character and plans. They are very indignant, but they
have promised not to write him anything about my presence here, or your
knowledge of the existence of the estate.

As I am afraid that B. may try to intercept any letters to you, I shall inclose this, and the accompanying papers, to Abigail's address, and shall telegraph her to inquire at the post-office for a letter as soon as it arrives. Please wire me as soon as you receive this letter.

I again heartily and cordially congratulate you on your unexpected and great good fortune. My only grief is that the dread shadow of my own disaster yet hangs about me, but I still have hope — hope, the medicine of the afflicted. I remain,

Your sincere friend,

ANTHONY HUGUET.

CHAPTER XXXIV.

THE COLONEL'S HOUR OF TRIUMPH.

" Say what you will, sir, but I know what I know.
That you beat me at the mart I have your hand to show;
If the skin were parchment, and the blows you gave were ink,
Your own handwriting would tell you what I think."
                                        —*Comedy of Errors, iii. 1.*

ON my return home I brought with me the $10,000 in bank notes and handed it over to Colonel Ruddiman. He could not thank me sufficiently; he said, with tears in his eyes, that I had saved him from ruin. His whole appearance had changed; his eyes were bright, his head erect, and his face beaming with the old smiles of hospitality and generosity. Mary, too, was transformed; for she had deeply sympathized with her father in his distresses, and a heavy dread for him was lifted from her heart. She had never touched my hand since the time of my great calamity; indeed, she seemed always to shrink from my person. Now, with face beaming, she advanced and took my huge black paw and shook it warmly, and thanked me earnestly. It was my intelligence, she said, that had extricated them from their perilous position, and she hoped that the time was not far distant when they could congratulate me on deliverance from the dreadful doom which had overtaken me. Certainly, she said, if prayers could storm the throne of

Grace and waken divine hearts to pity, the day of my liberation was not far distant. Abigail, who was in all the secrets of the family, rushed at me with such impetuosity of joy and gratitude that I thought she was about to throw herself in my arms. But she stopped short in full career and shook me by both hands vehemently.

For an hour we sat and talked, and I gave them all the details of my visit to Baltimore, and they laughed heartily at the humorous incidents which I narrated. And we were very happy. And then the Colonel and Mary and Abigail began to discuss the future, and the improvements they would make in the old homestead; the adjoining lands they would purchase; the new horses and carriage they would order; the help they would give to some of the neighbors, noble-hearted men, who had fallen into the grasp of the usurers, and were threatened with the same fate from which they had themselves just escaped. Oh, what a grand expansibility there is about great wealth! How it enlarges one's capacities for good — yes, and for evil, too! How it broadens one's thoughts, and seems to lift up the very dome of the visible world! The difficulty is, that it is usually obtained by arts which incapacitate the winner for generosity and goodness. This is a world of shameful limitations imposed upon the spirit; but wealth, in worthy hands, widens the scope of our possibilities, and we might fancy that it restores us to that pre-natal condition, ere we were hampered by the flesh and the restrictions of earth, and could do anything and everything which the active spirit willed.

We were very happy, and I forgot for a time — and I think they did, too — that I was a great, hulking black man, and that they belonged to the superior, snow-white, dominant caste.

I proposed that we wreak our revenge on Buryhill, not by punishing his body, but by agonizing his greedy, grasping soul, by the acutest disappointment. I suggested to them how intensely interested he must be in the bold game he was playing, the stake of which was an immense fortune;— how he must tremble as the time approached when he was about to grasp it. And so I prepared the following note, which the Colonel copied, and sent off by one of the servants:

Charles A. Buryhill, Esq.

DEAR SIR: I find that it is impossible for me to borrow $7,000 in C—— on my land. I have been very much disappointed at the poor success I have had in these attempts. I would like to see you at this place to-morrow afternoon at two o'clock, if convenient for you.

Very respectfully, your obed't servant,
WILLIAM B. RUDDIMAN.

P. S. You might bring with you a notary and the necessary papers to close up our transactions. W. B. R.

" Now," said I, " when Buryhill reads that, he will conclude that you are powerless, and that the vast Baltimore estate is his. His joy will be immense. He will live in ecstasy for the next twenty-four hours. To now wrest this prey from between his teeth, when he is perfectly sure of it, will agonize his mean soul more than if you had horsewhipped his body till the blood followed every blow ; for the man's greed is the center and substance of his very soul; and when you tear that property out of his hands, which have, as he

thinks, closed upon it securely forever, you will tear
the very master chords and fibers out of his being.   It
will be royal sport to see the wretch foiled in the
supreme hour of triumph !

" I would also suggest that you invite a party of your
friends and neighbors to a banquet, at one o'clock ;
tell them the story of your good fortune, and do not
forget to whisper to the poor fellows who are under the
harrow that your deliverance is to be their deliverance
also.   Then have them all in the back parlor at two
o'clock,— I will come at that hour,— close the folding
doors and receive Buryhill in the front parlor.   Then,
at the proper moment, I will throw open the doors,
and you will make a speech, pay Buryhill what you
owe him and kick him out of the house."

. All this plan we proceeded to carry out to the letter.

Never did a happier party assemble in the old homestead than gathered next day at that banquet.   It is
true that, at first, there was gloom upon the faces of
many of the guests, for they well knew that the Colonel
was embarrassed and likely to lose his plantation, and
they wondered at the folly and extravagance of the
man who, at such a time, could give such an entertainment and waste his money upon wines and high-living.
But the Colonel was in his element.   Never before did
his face shine brighter; never did he greet his friends
with warmer hand-grasp.   Never did Mary Ruddiman
appear lovelier or happier.   And when the Colonel —
the broad glasses being filled with sparkling champagne
to the very brim — toasted the company, and proceeded to make a speech, in which he told them of his

extraordinary and wonderful fortune, every heart at the table rejoiced; and the uproar of congratulations was terrific. And when he added that his good luck would now enable him to help such of his neighbors as were in the same slough of despair that he had been in, the guests all rose and cheered the noble old gentleman till the house rang, and there were few eyes around the board that were not wet with tears. But when he went on to tell of Buryhill and his knavish tricks, and the disappointment that was in store for him, the joy of those present knew no bounds, and the mirth and fun grew fast and furious; for, of all men, these struggling planters most hated that specious, slippery, oily and successful villain.

At two o'clock, promptly to the minute, Buryhill arrived in his grand carriage, accompanied by a notary public, and driven by a liveried servant. A score or two of eyes watched him, curiously and laughingly, from behind the curtains of the dining-room. As he walked briskly up the walk he looked around him sharply, with eyes of anticipatory ownership; he seemed to make a mental inventory of the repairs and alterations he would require at the end of two years. The Colonel met him and the notary, with the most dejected and long-faced aspect he could assume, and, drawing a heavy sigh, showed them into the front parlor. The guests had in the meantime filed, on tip-toe, into the back parlor. I stood at the folding doors (they mistook me for a servant), where I could see all that transpired in the front room.

Buryhill's manner to the Colonel was all suavity and

courtesy, but he bustled around in a business-like way, impatient to close the matter up and enter into actual possession of his great fortune. He placed the deed, mortgage, etc., on a table.

" Now, Colonel," he said, " you sign here. But we shall need another witness, besides the notary."

" Oh," said the Colonel, " don't worry about that. I will soon find one. But, first, let us ascertain just how much I owe you."

Buryhill was prepared.

" There," he said, " is the statement of each item, with the interest computed until to-day. It amounts, as you see, to $7,138.91. And there is the mortgage with the interest for one year added in, in advance, with the usual commission and charges. It amounts, you see, altogether, to $5,988.98."

" Why," said the Colonel, " that is nearly $6,000 ! "

" Yes," replied Buryhill; " these things run up very fast."

And the Colonel looked exceedingly melancholy.

" I don't see," he said, " how I will ever be able to raise $6,000 in two years, in these dull times."

Buryhill smiled. He thought so too, but he said nothing.

" Couldn't you throw off the commission and charges," said the Colonel, " and make the mortgage for the even $5,138.91 — the interest to be paid at the end of the year ? "

" My dear friend," said Buryhill, " I couldn't possibly think of doing so. The mortgage is drawn in strict accordance with the custom of capitalists. And I don't make a cent out of the matter. I am simply doing this as a friend, to help you out of your difficulties. Any other man would have driven you to the wall."

"But may not that other property," said the Colonel, "be worth more than $2,000 ?"

"No," replied Buryhill; "in fact, since I wrote you my letter, making you the offer I did, I have found out that there is another defect in the title, and I shall probably never recover back a cent of the $2,000 I pay you. But I feel that an honorable man must stick to his bargain, even if he loses by it; and then my friendship for you and your family counts for a great deal with me. Indeed, if a certain person were not so cold and haughty, I think I could see how this whole matter might have been arranged without the payment of a penny. But that is all past now." And Buryhill drew a gentle sigh.

"Make the mortgage $5,000," said the Colonel; "call the outside property worth $2,138."

"Really, my dear Colonel," replied Buryhill, "I couldn't do it. I have put things up to the highest notch."

"How much did you say the whole amount of my indebtedness was?" inquired the Colonel again.

"Here is the memorandum," replied Buryhill— "$7,138.91."

"Well," said the Colonel, looking very miserable, "I suppose we will need another witness."

"Yes, yes," replied Buryhill eagerly, pushing the deed before the Colonel, but so folded that the description of the property did not appear. " Sign here, Colonel — right on this line," (pointing with his finger).

The Colonel rose and looked at the folding doors. That was the signal agreed upon. In an instant the doors rolled back, and Buryhill found himself face to face with a crowd of the principal citizens of the vicinity, who regarded him with no friendly eyes.

" Gentlemen," said the Colonel, " we needed a witness, and it is well to have enough of them. In the first place, I owe this man $7,138.91. There," he said, laying a roll of bills upon the table, " is the amount. Count it and sign these receipts and certificates of satisfaction. The notary will see that everything is regular."

The astonishment of Buryhill was indescribable. His face grew very white, and his eyes wandered from one to the other, as if he could not make out what it all meant. Then he glanced at the pile of bank-notes, and then at the face of Colonel Ruddiman, who, instead of the dejected debtor of a few moments ago, towered before him a very picture of wrath and righteous indignation.

The Colonel pushed the money before the notary.

" Count it, Mr. Hughes," said he; " see if it is right, and make this d——d rascal sign these papers, for we want to get through this business and get him out of this house, which his presence pollutes."

The notary counted the money, and still Buryhill glared around him, a realization of the changed con-

ditions working themselves slowly through his astonished brain.

" Gentlemen," said the Colonel, " you see this miserable wretch standing here ! Public opinion would
justify me if I shot him dead in his tracks. Think of
it ! I received him into my house as a friend; I seated
him at my own table, in the midst of my family and
friends, and, while he was eating my meat and drinking my wine, he was plotting how he could turn me
out of the home of my ancestors, and send me, a ruined
man, to the poor-house. And all this time he smiled
upon me, and drank to my health, and flattered me,
and smiled and smiled again. And in the midst of
hilarity and good-fellowship, while other men's souls
expanded and grew kindly and brotherly, this d——d
wolf was plotting how he could devour me. And what
did he do? " continued the Colonel, waxing eloquent.
" He proceeded to find out every dollar that I owed,
and every incumbrance on my property. Most of it
was held by friends, kindly-hearted men, who would
never have troubled me until times were better, for
they knew they were amply secured and that their interest would be paid regularly. He—this wretch here
—circulated reports that I was hopelessly ruined ! And
that I was an irreclaimable drunkard! He had his
agents at work spreading these reports everywhere, as
I have lately ascertained. And then he proceeded to
buy up the claims against me — mortgages, notes, tax-
titles, book accounts—at as large discount as he could.
And all this time he visited my house and kept up the
appearance of being my loving friend! Oh, the damn-

able villain!"   And the Colonel's hands twitched convulsively, in an ominous fashion.

"At this time an estate which had descended to me
from one of my ancestors, in Baltimore" (here Buryhill's face collapsed and his jaw dropped), "reverted
to me at the end of a ninety-nine years' lease — an estate
worth a quarter million of dollars.   A letter was sent
to me to announce the fact, from a firm of attorneys in
Baltimore, in care of this thief and scoundrel" (Buryhill
started); "but instead of delivering it to me he opened
the letter, read its contents, put it in his pocket, — *my*
letter,— and then proceeded to lay his plans to rob me
of that vast inheritance."

Buryhill grew whiter and whiter and seemed to shrink
within himself.

"He offered me $2,000 for what he knew was
worth $250,000.   If the wretch had had the slight-
est spark of generosity or manhood he would have
given me my home clear, when he knew he was about
to swindle me out of such a vast sum.   But he wanted
the quarter of a million in Baltimore, and he wanted
everything else I had in the world.   Why, as he came
up the garden walk yonder, this very day, I saw
him carefully observing my Jersey cattle, in the neighboring field; and I could see he was devising how he
would get hold of them also, for unpaid interest, when
the poor, old, drunken Colonel, at the end of two years,
was turned out of house and home.   Oh! I can
scarcely keep my hands off him!"

Buryhill recoiled before the glaring eyes and menacing attitude of the old soldier.

" Why, even here, and now," he continued, " while he believed that I was ready to sign a deed that would give him a vast fortune, for a mere pittance, he refused to abate a single dollar of his claim.   If it had not been for yonder poor man," said the Colonel, pointing to me, where I stood in the doorway, " yonder poor negro,— for such he appears to be,— I should have been utterly lost and ruined."

Buryhill turned and looked at me with keen and curious interest.

" And now," continued the Colonel, " sign those papers, and leave this house before I lose control of myself.   I had intended to call you out and shoot you down, but you are not worthy of any honest man's bullet. . I had thought of having my negroes horse-whip you within an inch of your life, but cooler coun-sels have prevailed.   I have exposed you in the face of the whole people.   If you can continue to live in this country after to-day, you have a tougher hide than even I give you credit for."

Buryhill by this time had recovered his self-posses-sion.   He had not spoken a word in reply to all the torrents of abuse poured out upon him.   They did not worry him one-tenth as much as the thought that that quarter of a million dollars was lost forever, and that the Colonel was out of his power.   His eyes, constantly traveling that circle of wrathful counte-nances, kept reverting to me, as if wondering how one so ignorant-looking could have outwitted him so com-pletely, and puzzling his head to know how I had dis-covered his precious secret.   And then, I could see, he indulged in some calculations as to how much of that $7,138.91 was profit, and he took some slight share of comfort out of his mental arithmetic. He picked up the roll of money, in his usual bustling, busy way, and proceeded to count it, with great care; occasionally holding a bank-note up to the light to make sure it was not a counterfeit. Having finished this task, he buttoned up the money in his breast-pocket, and, scrutinizing the papers which the Colonel had had prepared for him, he signed them. Then, rising with a brisk smirk on his face, he said :

"Colonel, permit me to congratulate you on **your** good fortune. Mr. Hughes, I guess we had better be moving. Gentlemen, good day to you all." And he waved his hand in a half circle around the scowling group. But as he moved toward the door I could see that there was a quickness in his step and an alertness in his manner that betrayed trepidation.

But Mr. Hughes held back.

"Mr. Buryhill," he said, "you can go back alone. I prefer to walk back to C——."

"All right," replied the imperturbable rascal as he stepped into the hall. The next moment I heard a scuffling noise, and, pressing forward with the rest, I saw Dr. Magruder holding him by the back of the neck, and inflicting a series of kicks upon his person, every one of which lifted him from the porch, while he struggled and howled.

"You infernal rascal," cried the Doctor, emphasizing every third word with a kick, "you are a disgrace (kick) to your birth-place (kick) and your calling (kick) and your race (kick). Take that (kick)! and that (kick)! and that!" (a culminating kick).

Here the Doctor's wind gave out, for he was rather pursy, and the exercise he had taken was violent; but still he held on to his victim.

"Gentlemen," said he, "I am ashamed of this creature; I am ashamed of him as a Northern man. The North is a land of heroes — the war proved that. I want you to understand that it produces very few such scoundrels as this. They are the latest fruit of our 'commercial age;' of the 'business era,' proudly so called, which now dominates politics, religion and everything else; in which, if a man steals enough and keeps out of the penitentiary, he becomes an aristocrat. God help the country where such Dead Sea apples grow on the Tree of Knowledge."

And the Doctor accentuated this last generalization with another kick which sent Buryhill flying down the steps. Here Captain Braynton and one of the Colonel's sons were waiting for him, and they passed him on to his carriage and his waiting servant in livery, by a succession of rousing liftings from the earth, so rapid that his feet did not rest on *terra firma* half the time. He looked like a fallen angel traversing space, with his disturbed coat-tails standing out behind him as a poor substitute for wings.

At last, sore and furious and swearing vengeance, he clambered into his vehicle, and the intelligent colored man, who fully comprehended the whole situation, and appreciated his master thoroughly, drove off as fast as his horses could travel.

CHAPTER XXXV.

ABIGAIL HAS A PROPOSAL.

"She'll none of the Count; she'll not match above her degree, neither in estate, years nor wit. I have heard her swear it."

—Twelfth Night, i. 3.

HOW glad I was to get back to my scholars, and how glad they were to see me! There had been desolation enough in their hearts during my absence. They had been very solicitous about my sickness, and had hung around the barn night and day. Never did Roman conqueror, returning with the trophies and spoils of plundered provinces, receive a warmer welcome than I. And it was a pleasure to me — a great pleasure, to set all those intellects going again, and see the effect of the trooping armies of knowledge entering their brains. Really, learning is like charity: " it blesseth him that gives and him that takes."

One old man, who had been a faithful scholar at seventy years of age, had died during my absence, but his widow and his children were all there. I had observed the old man's eagerness for knowledge, tottering as he was on the very brink of the grave, and I asked myself whether our mental acquisitions in this world were carried away with us into the next? Why not? It must be the thinking principle that is immortal, and memory is surely part of the thought-apparatus. In fact, without memory there cannot be self-consciousness. We either retain our knowledge, or we live not.

The old man's death set me to thinking what a strange, temporary world this is. Death is always busy around us, and his darts fly thicker than the sun-beams. Try to recall the faces of those you have known, who have crossed the dark river, and what an innumerable caravan recollection summons up ! What a banquet we would have if we could sit down with the dead !

Indeed, it has sometimes seemed to me that we are all voyaging together over a rough sea, on a loosely constructed raft, full of holes. You turn to speak with a friend, and, lo ! he is gone, in the twinkling of an eye; — not a bubble left of him. You turn to another, and, as you converse with him, he drops out of sight, into the great deep, before your very eyes. You be-gin to realize that this wonderful structure, called Life, is made, not to carry its passengers, but to drown them; and that, but for the new souls which constantly clamber painfully up its rickety sides, it would soon be sailing tenantless over the dark waves. And you commence to study the loose, shifting planks be-neath your feet, half-submerged in the water; and to watch, with intense interest, every tremor in the fabric. The wonder is, you think, that the precarious structure does not altogether dissolve and sink in the billows of time, leaving only lifeless fragments in the midst of a dead universe.

One evening, as I looked out through the twilight,

waiting for my scholars to assemble, I saw two figures,
a man and a woman, riding through the sunset toward
me.   At last they stopped, and the man turned back,
while the woman rode forward.   It was Abigail, looking very bright and handsome, as she reined up her
black pony and dismounted.

"What, Abigail!" I said, "is that a lover?   Who
is he?"   For I felt a deep interest in the fair girl.

She blushed and laughed and looked confused.

"Yes," she said, and her laughter grew merrier;
"yes, I have had an offer of marriage."

"Who is it, Abigail?"

"Can't you guess?"

"No, indeed," I replied.

"It was from yourself," she said.

"From myself?   What do you mean?"

"From Doctor Anthony Huguet," she replied with
a mischievous smile.   "Yes, from your body, but not
from your soul."

"Do you mean that miserable wretch who has taken
my place in life?" I asked.

"Yes," she said laughing, "but you should not
speak thus of one's lover."

"Has he really offered you marriage?" I asked.

"Yes, indeed," she replied; "he has hung around
our place for weeks, pestering me every time I went
out of the house.   First he made me unworthy pro-
posals, and I struck him with my riding-whip across the
face.   Then he grew more desperate, and to-night, as
he rode over here with me, he proposed to marry me.

He said he would make me a white lady, and one of the richest and greatest in the land."

"And what did you say?" I inquired anxiously.

"I laughed at him. I told him he was not Doctor Huguet, but Sam Johnsing, the chicken-thief. And that he was likely, at any moment, when the heavenly powers relented, to go back into his own body, and then you would return to your true form, and"—here she blushed deeply—"you would repudiate such a marriage, for your heart was devoted to Mary. He got very angry at this, and said you would not trouble anybody very long, and he muttered and swore. I really think he means you some mischief. Then he saw you sitting here and rode off."

"Do you think you will accept him, Abigail?" I asked, to test her.

"Oh, no," she replied; "I would not marry him if he were the last man in the world, and if I knew that he would remain Doctor Huguet to the end of his life. The creature has no soul. He has fallen in love, as he would call it, with my person. He wants to possess me, and in his passion he would sacrifice his social position as a white man to the gratification of his feelings, and then he would throw me away as a worthless incumbrance. His skin is temporarily white, but his heart is blacker and fouler and falser than any negro in the whole land. He is a low, bad man, and I would sooner—yes, a thousand times sooner—die unwed than merge my life with that of such a creature. I would rather marry a black man, whom I loved and respected, than share wealth and social distinction with that wretch." Then she added: "But there is no future for me but to live and die an old maid." Here she laughed again. "But that is not the worst fate in the world. I have seen a great many sweet and lovely women — and useful women, too — who will never enter into matrimony. Single blessedness is better than double wretchedness."

And yet I knew that life, warm, pulsing, throbbing life, beat through every artery of her fair body, and that this was only the cold philosophy to which she had schooled herself. And my heart pitied her. Her soul was high and noble; and, educated and bred in the midst of kind friends, there was not a taint of servility or sordidness in her nature.

Alas! poor Abigail — bright and cheery and lovely and lovable — little did I think, as she looked back from her seat in the saddle, and laughingly waved me adieu, what a dark doom was even then suspended over her head. But life is like the heavens: we never know what storms and thunderbolts may come out of it; we never know how soon the many-tinted cloud-wreaths which adorn, like picturesque scarfs, the drapery of the dying day, may turn into black and horrible tempests and lay cities low. The Fates that preside over the destinies of men seem to love the very grotesqueries of fortune. Now they lift up the half-fed boy to a throne; and anon they send forth the king a beggar and a wanderer on the face of the earth. At one moment they squeeze the heart of splendid success until it sheds streams of blood; and anon they make the soul of the unutterably miserable to sing aloud for joy. And there is no science of meteorology that will tell us what is on the way to us out of the overhanging skies of our lives. We can only bow reverently to the unseen forces, and take all that comes with a stout heart.

CHAPTER XXXVI.

MY MIDNIGHT VISITORS.

"Strange that, where Nature lov'd to trace,
As if for gods, a dwelling-place,
And every charm and grace hath mixed
Within the paradise she fixed,
That man, enamored of distress,
Should turn it into wilderness.
Strange that, where all is peace beside,
There passion riots in her pride,
And lust and rapine wildly reign
To darken all the fair domain."
— *The Giaour* (*Byron*).

IT was a few nights after my interview with Abigail that I found a vast multitude assembled at my school-house. Every bench was occupied; crowds stood in the aisles and looked through the doors and windows. It seemed to me that the whole population, black and white, of the neighborhood, had turned out to listen to me. There was a time when such an assemblage would have flattered my vanity, but I had been so chastened by humiliation that all such feelings had long since departed from my breast. For I kept repeating to myself: How little a thing is glory? It consists simply of thoughts of you in the minds of others; and in a short time those others will be dust, and their very names have perished. And what is immortality? Who were the great men that lived before Agamemnon? Lost! Lost! And the day will come when the earth's generations will have forgotten Alexander and Napoleon. Fame ? Fame is nothing. We leave nothing behind us on this earth that is permanent, except our influence for good or ill; that goes on, visible to God, but invisible to men — a force in the affairs of humanity, spreading like a great, undying ripple in the sea of mind. Big or little, eminent or obscure, we each contribute to that intangible net-work of earth-forces, forever renewing themselves with every new brain that is born into the world. Fame ! No; let us do our duty.

I preached peace and charity to that vast assemblage. I told them how beautiful was gentleness ; how hideous and barbaric was cruelty ; how quickly goodness sprang up at the summons of goodness ; how prolific evil was in begetting evil. I showed how transitory life was, with all its bigotries and passions and little, petty interests. I quoted to them the remark of the great German, " that only mankind was the true man." I drew a picture of death — not the judgment day of flame, but the momentous act of taking rank in the invisible world, clad in the atmosphere of our deeds on earth. The segregating of the good from the bad ; the repulsive crowding together of the evil with the evil ; and then the beginning of new careers of work and influence upon the minds of those yet dwelling in the flesh, for blessing or for ban. And I spoke of the suddenness of the great summons of death :

> " The gambler, reckoning gains, shall drop a piece,
> Look down — and there see death ! Look up — there God !"

Charity — Charity — divine Charity, was the theme of my discourse — brotherly love — pity for the unfortunate. I said to them that I did not expect black men to become white men, or white men to turn into black men ; but there was room on God's footstool for them all. The blue flowers in the meadow did not quarrel with the red flowers. The oak tree grew peacefully beside the maple. The orange did not ask God why he made the laurel. Death was not a thing to be dreaded, if man lived right.

> "For modes of faith let graceless zealots fight :
> He can't be wrong whose life is in the right.
> In Faith and Hope the world will disagree,
> But all mankind's concern is Charity."

Death was as natural as life ; there was nothing horrible about it. It was superstition that had invested it with terrors and hobgoblins.

Let the mantle of Christian charity cover the differences of race and social conditions, for under it all men could dwell together in peace and happiness.

I then took up the subject of the evening, the French Revolution. I showed that even the excesses of that dreadful time had been caused by a thousand years of oppression, which had unfitted men for peaceful self-government; and that the "Reign of Terror" itself was due to the machinations of outside despotism, determined to discredit liberty; and that the money of Pitt and the English aristocracy had paid for the extravagancies of Anacharsis Klootz and the Goddess of Reason.

It was nearly eleven before the audience dispersed

to their homes, and midnight before I had fallen to sleep in my little room in the barn. I well remember how brightly the moonlight shone in through my window and fell in a flood of mellow glory over my bed. It was a peaceful, lovely night — a night in which to thank God for the privilege of living.

How long I had slept I know not — perhaps an hour. I was awakened by a great pounding on the door of the barn. I looked out through the window and saw a group of horses tied to some trees near at hand. I went to the door and opened it. I was at once seized by several men. I looked around and perceived that I was surrounded by a group of about twenty men, wearing white masks over their faces. Those who had hold of me led me out into the road.

A tall young man, who seemed to be the spokesman of the party, said to me :

" You d——d rascal, what do you mean by teaching the niggers to read and write, and preaching to them ? "

I was perfectly undaunted. Life was not so bright or hopeful that the threatened loss of it could intimidate me. I thought my hour had come,— and my release with it.

" Can *you* read and write?" I asked him.

" Certainly," he replied.

" Are you any the worse for it?" I asked.

He struck me a severe blow in the face, which brought the blood, and replied:

" Do you compare me with the niggers, you black whelp?"

"There is no negro in this country," I said, "who would strike a prisoner, unable to defend himself. You are a white coward, and a disgrace to your race."

"Kill him," shouted a little man, whose figure I thought I recognized.

The tall fellow advanced on me with a bowie-knife in his hand, but one of my captors struck his arm up and said:

"Stop, Harry! You know our agreement: there was to be no murder."

"Kill him," repeated the little man, fiercely, drawing a revolver.

But another of the party grasped him around the arms, and said:

"None of that, Doctor! You know how the people feel around here; there will be trouble if you kill this man."

A number of others echoed this sentiment.

"We want you to leave this heah country," said the tall fellow they called Harry. "Will you go?"

"No!" I replied, emphatically.

"Then we will kill you," he replied.

"What do I care for death?" I answered, calmly. "My life is more dreadful than any death!"

There was silence for a moment or two after this strange answer.

"What do you mean by teaching the niggers? Don't you know that this is a white man's country, and that no niggers can rule over us? What do you mean by making them know as much as white people?"

"My every word has been scanned," I replied, "and

you know I have never uttered a syllable to set race against race. I have always argued that politics should be a thing apart from race, and should have no connection with the color of the skin. My teaching has made the negroes better laborers and better citizens."

" But this is a white man's country, I tell you," he replied fiercely, " and the niggers are beasts of burden, and must be kept in their places. That is what General Lee and Stonewall Jackson fought for."

" Do not profane the names of those great men," I replied, " by connecting them with such midnight maraudings as this. They were gallant soldiers. Do you think they would, if alive, stand by and see twenty men assault one, no matter what was the color of his skin ? Can you imagine them, after spending a night in the company of black women, attacking a negro for teaching whites and blacks to read and write? No, no; you dishonor them by speaking their names out of your foul mouths, reeking with the smell of Mother Bindell's whisky. They did not fight for Slavery. They fought for State Rights and Liberty as they under- stood them. Both of them wanted the Confederate Government to arm the blacks and make them free, on condition that they fought for the South. If their advice had been followed the result might have been different. They were great men, broad-minded and humane, religious and philanthropic. They were nursed at black breasts and they had no hatred for the poor negroes. But you! Your highest aspirations are to get drunk and kill school-teachers."

They were furious. They gathered in a group

a short distance from me, gesticulating wildly and arguing. I could hear the small man they called Doctor insisting that I must be killed at once, while others, in lower tones, spoke in favor of moderation. Then they whispered together. I thought the end had come when they surrounded me in a body. One burly fellow with a quick jerk tore my night-gown from me and left me stark naked. A dozen hands seized me and dragged me to a tree and securely tied me to it, with my arms around the trunk.

" Now," said the tall fellow, " will you agree to quit this country at once, if we let you go?"

" No!" I shouted.

" Then let him have it," said he; " give him a bull's dose!"

And instantly a great whip, with many knotted lashes, encircled me with a fierce, stinging blow, and I could feel the blood starting out of the skin and trickling down my back. I never winced. I shut my teeth and determined to die ere I would cry out. Again it fell — and again — and again — and again. The wounds crossed and re-crossed each other. The lashes cut into places already raw. The pain was dreadful. One ruffian relieved another. At length a merciful insensibility came to my relief. I had fainted.

In the gray of the morning some negroes found me, still tied to the tree; my back a revolting mass of wounds; my whole body cased in dried, caked blood, down to my very heels.

They tenderly released me, carried me in, and placed

me upon the bed, and one hurried off for the physician. The news spread like wild-fire. In an hour a thousand persons, whites and blacks, had gathered. All were indignant; the blacks sullen, scowling, threatening. I was their brother. I had suffered for them. They whispered together, their features working with rage.

I heard of the dangerous aspect of things as I lay writhing in pain. I sent for the leaders. They swarmed into my room, and through the doorway and the windows I could see a vast array of convulsed and angry faces.

" Men," I said, " black men, it is true I have suffered these great wrongs because I tried to serve you; because I would not desert you; but those who did this thing do not represent the great, humane, honorable white race of the South. They are ruffians, cowards, scoundrels, drunkards, debauchees. Rum is at the bottom of all this, as it is at the bottom of most of the evil-doings of the world. But look at the white people gathered here. They know I have not deserved this treatment. They are as indignant as you are. They are sorry. They grieve for me. They are your brethren and neighbors. Your hearts are one. Do not let your just wrath cause you to lift a finger in violence against any man. God has all this business in his keeping, and He will repay these men to the uttermost. In a few days these wounds will heal, and I will be well again, and ready to renew my work, never to quit it until I die. If you love me, do not seek to revenge me."

18

It was wonderful to see how the rage faded out of their dark faces as I appealed to their better natures; and they filed out, their voices thick with sobs, muttering, " God bless you!"

And day after day, and all night long, they kept watch and ward around me, lest my enemies should renew their assault.

CHAPTER XXXVII.

I HEAR BAD NEWS.

"Yet the first bringer of unwelcome news
Hath but a losing office, and his tongue
Sounds, ever after, as a sullen bell,
Remembered knolling a departed friend."
—*2 Henry IV.*, *i. 1.*

THE news of the attack upon me spread far and wide, and provoked universal indignation. The Colonel and his sons were fierce. Miss Mary and Abigail came and offered to assist in nursing me, but I told them I needed no assistance, beyond the soothing lotions which the doctor had prescribed. I was soon sufficiently recovered to be up again, and the fourth night after the attack I was able to meet my flock in the school-room. An immense crowd greeted me and gave me a perfect ovation. The women especially were very emotional and received me with wet eyes.

I counseled peace. I told them the assault upon me was made by some of the foolish, dissipated young men of the vicinity, with intent to drive me away; and I hoped, when they saw that it was impossible, they would look into the matter, and become satisfied that I was really doing good to all the people, and give up their unreasonable hostility to the civilizing influences which I had invoked. I said I did not propose to pros-

ecute any of them, although I knew the names of some
of my assailants, despite their masks.

Ben, who had been from the first one of my most
devoted night-scholars, and was making excellent
progress, told me that the morning of the attack on me
his new master had been brought home by the coach-
man, near day-break, very drunk and in a terribly bad
temper. And he also told me something which set me
to thinking, namely, that Buryhill had twice been at
the house, and had held long interviews with the so-
called Doctor Huguet. I knew that Buryhill had no
natural affiliation with such a creature as Ben's master,
and it augured no good for me that these two enemies
of mine had found each other out. I knew that what
the brutal and shallow mind of Sam Johnsing lacked
the cunning villainy of Buryhill would supply. It was
a formidable combination. But what did I care? Death
would only release me from hopelessness. As the days
and weeks and months sped on, and left me still under
the dreadful spell, I had lost heart. I began to fear
that God had forgotten me. I should not take my own
life, so long as there was any good to do on earth, but
I should not shrink from death. Let the blow fall when
it would, I was ready for it.

Although my back still smarted and stung, I delivered
my address as usual, to an audience more than ever in
sympathy with every word I said. The negroes fairly
worshiped me. Had I not suffered agony and shed
my blood for them? I was, indeed, the Angel Gabriel,
or Moses, or Abraham, or John the Baptist, or all of
these rolled into one. I was the perpetual miracle

which had come out of the wretched carcass of Sam Johnsing.

At the close of the exercises Colonel Ruddiman and the young ladies accompanied me into my little room. The Colonel told me that the District Court met the next day but one in C———. He would probably be foreman of the grand jury, and several of his neighbors were members of it, and they had resolved, in view of the foul attack made on me, to bring in an indictment against Mother Bindell for keeping a disorderly house, send her to prison and close up the filthy den. There would be a big fight over it; but the respectable part of the community were determined that the influences which were corrupting and ruining the young men of the neighborhood must cease; and if they could not do it by the peaceable processes of law they were determined to do it by force — yes, if they had to burn Mother Bindell's foul habitation over her villainous old head.

Things were evidently drawing toward a culmination. As I looked out of my window, before going to bed, I saw my faithful body-guard of black men, with guns on their shoulders, marching up and down in the moonlight, keeping guard over their beloved teacher.

But the next day came the saddest surprise of all.

It was about five o'clock. I was sitting at the door of the barn reading, when, from a cloud of dust in the distance, I saw a horseman emerge, riding furiously. As he drew nearer I saw that it was Colonel Ruddiman.

I rose to meet him. He was greatly excited. His face was pale and he was covered with dust.

"What is the matter, Colonel?" I cried, thinking of Mary, and my heart in my mouth.

"Abigail is gone!" he replied.

"Abigail gone!" I exclaimed. "How? Where?"

"We don't know. Mary sent her, this morning, with a delicacy she had prepared for Mrs. Braynton, who has been sick for some time. She was to have returned at once. The Braynton house, you know, is only about a mile from ours. She did not come back. We thought nothing of it, supposing she had stayed to talk to Mrs. Braynton. But, at noon, one of the field hands, passing through a piece of woods, between our house and Capt. Braynton's, found, on the roadside, her hat and a torn fragment of her dress, while the ground showed marks of a struggle and the tracks of several feet. I at once started every one out to search for her. They did not find her, but they discovered traces of a carriage and horses, not far from where the hat was found. She had evidently been carried off. I am on my way to town to notify the police; for in all probability the carriage was driven to C——."

"Do you suspect any one?" I asked.

"No," he said.

"Had she any lovers?"

"None that we know of."

"Then you did not know that the so-called Doctor Huguet has been following her up, and offered her marriage the other day, and she refused him."

" No," replied the Colonel, very much surprised; " that is the first I have heard of it, or Mary either."

" Then there is where you are to look," I said. " Go to his house — or, rather, my house — in town; and also ransack Mother Bindell's. The villain has undoubtedly abducted the poor girl."

The Colonel drove off hurriedly.

And so the unhappy Abigail had made me the confidant of secrets which she would not entrust even to Mary. What did it mean?

I was greatly distressed,

CHAPTER XXXVIII.

THE PLOT THICKENS.

"That night a child might understand
The de'il had business on his hand."
— *Burns.*

THE whole country was aroused and searching for Abigail. The poor girl was greatly beloved by all who knew her, black and white. She was so amiable, and modest, and beautiful, that she had no enemies among rich or poor. Her abduction, coming upon the heels of the midnight attack upon myself, had aroused the whole population to a high pitch of indignation; and the young prodigals and lechers, who were supposed to be responsible for both acts, kept out of the way, at least in day-time, of the respectable people. Colonel Ruddiman and his friends had visited my house in C——, but Ben assured them that she was not there, and that his master had not been at home for several days. Report said that he and Buryhill had been seen together at the latter's house. A party had also visited Mother Bindell's, and had searched the house from cellar to garret, without finding any clew of the missing girl.

Then came the news that Mother Bindell had been indicted and arrested for keeping a disorderly house, and that Harry Sanders and another wealthy young reprobate had gone upon her bond to appear and stand her trial, and she had been released and had gone back to her vile home. Buryhill had appeared as her attorney, employed, it was said, by Doctor Huguet. The young men were loud in their threats against Colonel Ruddiman and all those who had taken part in the attempt to break up their rendezvous, and the vicious part of the community buzzed and hummed and swarmed like a disturbed wasps' nest. There was evidently some directing intelligence behind the scenes, encouraging them and making them bold and insolent. It looked as if a collision was about to occur between the respectable and the profligate elements of society. The saloons were full of wrangling, swearing crowds, and the obsequious landlords smiled and smiled, as they filled the glasses and pushed them over the counters for the endless strings of thirsty customers. Every disreputable resort in C—— regarded the indictment of Mother Bindell as a threat against itself, and the excitement was correspondingly great. On the other hand, the white planters were banding together and arming themselves, and riding hither and thither ; they were old soldiers, who did not talk much, whose bite was always worse than their bark; — men upon whom danger acted like strong drink, stimulating their faculties; and who had not forgotten the smell of gunpowder in their nostrils since the days when they rode, hungry and half-clad, through fen and forest, in defense of their principles. Even the negroes were profoundly disturbed ; but they were generally without weapons and lacked leaders.

CHAPTER XXXIX.

FLAME AND DEATH.

> "Farewell! I know the next news that they bring
> Will be my death; and welcome shall it be:
> To wretched men death is felicity."
>
> *—Edward II. (Marlowe).*

I FEEL certain that my hour draws near.

Last night I dispensed with my usual lecture. I was too much distressed at the sad news of Abigail's disappearance to talk to the multitude, and they were too much wrought up over the rumors that floated everywhere to give me their usual attention. They gathered in knots and talked in whispers, and a great many remained around the barn until morning.

I know that some great event is about to happen to me. What it is I cannot tell. How do I know it?

I have seen Him again!

Yes. Last night I closed down the curtains to keep out the moonlight, bright almost as day, and I soon fell asleep. How long I slept I have no means of knowing. I awakened with a great start, my heart beating violently and the sweat breaking out from every pore. What was it that filled the room? Moonlight? No; it was the same soft, hazy luminosity I had beheld once before—a substance rather than a light. Where the moonshine crept in, in streaks, beside the closed curtains, and touched it, the moon's rays appeared sepulchrally white compared with the warm glow which filled the chamber. And then, under my astounded eyes, it began to repeat what I had seen before. It gathered itself together against the farther side of the room, brightening as it receded, and then, awe-struck and terrified, I beheld the central light forming itself slowly into that same grand, marvelous countenance—

THE FACE OF CHRIST.

That unutterable, that indescribable face!

But the threat had gone out of the great thoughtful, pitiful eyes; and the mouth, the sweet mouth, smiled upon me. Yes! Blessed be God! It smiled upon me! Upon me, the most wretched of men; the poor, unhappy, broken-hearted negro. And then a dark shadow, as it seemed to me, crept around the luminous head, and the shadow grew and expanded, not suppressing the light, but filled with the light, and yet a darkness painted on the light; and still it grew until it spread far beyond the narrow boundaries of my chamber into infinitude; and then it began to resolve itself into small forms — into millions of faces — faces brown, yellow, pale, black, but none of them white; faces of men, women and children; of the young and the old; of the gray-haired grandsire and the little infant — millions upon millions of faces — and every face looked into mine and smiled upon me!

And the great eyes glanced around at the innumerable multitude, and said:

" WHOSOEVER DEALETH MERCIFULLY WITH THE

LEAST OF THESE IS NUMBERED AMONG THE BELOVED OF GOD."

And as he spoke the vision began to fade away, and in a little while it was gone, and I was alone in the darkened chamber. And again, methought, I heard a murmur, like the rustle of a vast host of soft wings; and then followed faint, delicious, unearthly music, that faded away in the distance, and died out in silence.

I know that my release is at hand.

But how will it come to me ? Shall it be through the gates of death ? Shall I part from my beloved forever ? Do spirits know each other beyond the grave ?

And I fell upon my knees and prayed fervently to God, that, after all my months of agony, He would not send me down to the dark grave, but would give me back the best and noblest of women.

This morning I taught my school of little ones, but my thoughts were far away.

At noon came the news that Abigail had returned home. Nothing more than that. She had been seen to pass along the road and enter the Ruddiman house.

It was four o'clock. I was reading. A shadow fell upon me. I looked up.

It was Abigail!

My God, what a change!

The fair face was pallid and swollen and distorted; the mouth rigid and set; and the eyes, in which you could not discern the pupils, wore a baleful expression, hard, terrible, sullen, threatening.

I rose and took her in my arms. I kissed her. I understood it all. I could only cry :

" My poor, poor, dear, dear Abigail ! "

I offered her refreshments. I begged her to be seated. No; she stood there rigid, tearless.

" Abigail," I said, " where were you ? "

In a strange voice, that sounded husky and far away, she replied :

" In the Bindell barn, bound, gagged and covered with hay, while they ransacked the house for me."

" Where are you going ? "

" I came to bid you farewell," she said, in the same impassive way, " for I loved you — loved you well enough to have married you, despite that black skin. It is over now. Good-by."

" No, no; you must not go," I cried, holding her hands, " you are not to blame for the sin of others. Your soul is pure, pure as the mountain snow."

The expression of bitterness deepened around her mouth as she slowly hissed out:

" There was a fraction of negro blood in my veins, and that justified the white scoundrels in carrying me off, to become the plaything of their lust. My seven-eighths of white blood was nothing. They would never have dared such villainy with a girl of pure white ancestry. I suppose it is all right in the eyes of God. Society will pardon them. No one will pity the octoroon ! "

" No, no, Abigail," I cried, " your friends love you deeply, warmly; they honor you. I love you. I honor you. *I have seen the Christ again !* I am forgiven.

The day of my tribulation is almost at an end. We will all be happy together yet. I will carry out my first promise to you. You shall go where all taint and discredit shall fall from you. I will kill the man who breathes a word against your good name. You live in our hearts, and our arms shall surround you forever."

Her face relaxed and softened, but she cried out:

" No, no; I must go. I am polluted, disgraced, ruined; an unworthy thing — fit only to be cast out on the dung-hills of the world — a poor negro — a "——

But she could not speak the word.

"Abigail," I said, " stay here with me until Colonel Ruddiman comes. He will, I think, be at the lecture to-night."

" No," she said; " I have a duty to perform. I must go. If you are liberated and I live, I may come back to you. But I must go now."

I had no right to detain her. I did not know her purpose. I kissed her as I might have kissed my own child, and wrung her hand, and parted from her, alas! forever.

I never saw her again alive, save once, and then but for a moment, in the midst of a dreadful scene.

The time had come for my lecture.

There was a great multitude around me as I stood up to speak.

" My friends," I said, " there is something within

me tells me that I shall never address you again in this flesh — in this school-house."

Sobs broke out all over the room, and hundreds wept aloud. My own voice choked, and I could scarcely proceed.

" My friends," I continued, " let us not grieve over anything the future may bring forth. We are all in the hands of God, and He who made us can neither forget nor forsake us. We may die, but we do not pass out of His kingdom. Wherever we go, God is there — for He is everywhere.

" The poet tells us that ' the voices of dying men enforce attention like deep harmony.' My premonitions assure me that from the brink of the grave I speak now unto you; and I would have you treasure up my words as long as you live, for they are the words of one who loves you, who has toiled for you, and has suffered for you.

"We live in troubled times. Storm and danger brood over us. Violence and rapine — perhaps death — are around us. Crime is bursting out like a volcanic ebullition, hot with the flames of hell.

" To the white race I would preach mercy and charity. I ask them to give the humblest and low-liest a chance in the great, fierce battle of life. Do not trample on the man who is down.

" To the black race I would preach patience and wisdom. The negro's remedy is not in violence. Six millions cannot go to war with sixty millions. He who steps outside the law invokes all the overwhelming powers of government upon his own head, and they crush him. The prejudices of race are not to be dissipated by grouping the people into the separations of race-politics. The curse of our land is party slavery. It is worse for the negro than the old physical slavery. God have mercy on the man who permits another to do his thinking.

> " ' First slave to words, then vassal to a name,
> Then dupe of party; child and man the same:
> Bounded by nature, narrowed still by art,
> A trifling head and a contracted heart.'

" The race, whatever its color, which gives itself over unanimously and unconditionally to any one political party, incurs the hatred of the organization it opposes and the contempt of the organization it serves. The one has nothing to hope from it; the other has nothing to fear from it. The one feels that it can never gain it; the other that it can never lose it. The former persecutes the race for their unreasoning hostility; the other despises them for their unreasoning fidelity. The first feels that it cannot placate them by doing them justice; the other that they will not revolt under any amount of injustice. They become a target for the abuse of all men; a wall behind which scoundrels hide to steal; a faction without a friend or an advocate.

" The perpetual dread of the South is a race war. When the negroes all mass themselves together, in solid political phalanx, it looks, to the whites, like a black army ready to march to battle. Every passion in the white man's breast rises at the challenge, ready for the conflict; — race, home, wife, children, prosperity, self-government, liberty, shriek in his ears their clamorous appeals for protection. He seizes his rifle,— he marches, — he murders.

" What is the remedy?

" *Let the black men break ranks!* Let them dissolve into the community. Let them divide politically on other lines than those of color. Great economic questions are arising which have nothing to do with the old struggles. A tidal wave — a great passionate cry for justice, for prosperity, for liberation from the plunderers, for each man's share of happiness and the fruits of civilization — sweeps, high-mounting, through the hearts and brains of the whites of the South. They are gathering in a vast army, with principles for banners and ballots for weapons. The black man's interests are the same as theirs. He needs prosperity, growth, opportunity, happiness. So do they. He wants to see the robbers struck down. So do they. He desires all that civilization can give him — all that belongs to him. So do they. Will he join with his white brethren to rescue the land from poverty and ruin? Or will he stand afar off, in solid, unreasoning, sullen, threatening array, to perpetuate the race-prejudices which are destroying him? When he breaks his own ranks and moves, in solid column, with part, at least, of his white friends and neighbors, they will perceive that his ballots are bullets, as potent as their own to kill injustice. Their own interests will compel them to defend his rights. The day of persecution and cruelty will end. In every intelligent white man the intelligent black man will find a defender; and the reign of peace and love and brotherhood will begin in the

19

South, yea, in the whole land.   And if the negro does not then rise to the topmost heights of culture and education and material prosperity, it will be his own fault.

"I pray God that the hearts of this congregation may be joined together, black and white, in bands of mutual love and charity that shall endure through all trials and tribulations.   Let no race hatreds divide you.   Remember that you are children of one father; that 'he made of one blood all the races of men that dwell on the face of the earth;' that Christ died on the cross, not for a particular complexion, but for all men; that his religion is not the religion of a race, but of mankind.   In the name of God and God's charity——"

The sentence was never finished.   There was a rattle of fire-arms through the doors and windows.   Men threw up their arms and screamed and fell.   There was uproar and confusion.   A dreadful panic came upon all, and they rushed to escape.   My God! what a horrible scene followed !   The whites were allowed to depart unharmed, but the negroes, men, women, and even children, were shot down as they fled, until they lay scattered around, inside and outside the building, in groups, dead and dying, groaning and shrieking for mercy.

I stood there immovable.

"Yes," I said quietly to myself, "it is through the gates of death."

The place grew suddenly lighter.   The miscreants had fired the building, and the red flames and dense smoke rose toward the heavens.

Then I felt myself seized by many hands; I was dragged out of doors. As I was haled along I saw that there were a hundred or more around me, all wearing white masks. But among them I saw the chicken-thief; and in the background a figure was skulking, evidently giving orders, whom I recognized, by his shape and size, as Buryhill.

I was under a tree. The conflagration lighted up the whole scene with a blood-red glare that drowned the white moonlight. The screams of the wounded in the barn, as the fire reached them, were dreadful to hear. The mob was wild with rage. All their eyes were centered on me. My hour had come. No power on earth could save me. I knew it.

" Quick! the rope!" cried a voice of command.

One end was thrown over a projecting limb; the noose was around my neck, and a score of men struggled for the privilege of seizing hold of it.

" Up with him! Up with him!"

The rope tightened painfully and cut deep into the flesh as my great weight began to rise from the ground. It had slipped to the back of my neck. I was choking, but still conscious. The whole dome of my brain was alive with spouting cataracts of sparks, of a hundred colors, veritable rainbows of fire. My eyes seemed to be pressed out of my head.

" Give it to him!" cried some one, and I heard the rattle of pistols, and felt stinging sensations in different parts of my body as the bullets struck me.

Doctor Huguet stood directly in front of me, and but a few paces distant. With my head bent down, by the position of the rope, I looked straight at him. His mask had fallen off, and his face wore a delighted, fiendish, devilish expression. He had a pistol in his hand; he raised it slowly and took deliberate aim at my heart. I saw the flash. I felt a sharp blow on my breast. In the same instant a white figure — a woman — darted out from the background of the crowd, rushed swiftly forward and smote him fiercely with a glittering weapon. He fell. And then all was darkness.

CHAPTER XL.

BORN AGAIN.

"Some safer world in depths of woods embraced,
Some happier island in the watery waste,
Where slaves once more their native land behold,
No fiends torment, no Christians thirst for gold."

— *Pope.*

OH, how painful it is to exist. Pricking, stinging sensations tingle through every nerve ; a horrible weight is upon my chest ; violent pains dart through my head ; my eyes are throbbing and burning.

Is this the world beyond the grave ? Better oblivion than such torments.

What am I ? A spirit damned ?

Can this be hell ? Into what variety of untried being have I fallen ?

I hear a voice speaking; it sounds a great ways off, though it is near at hand :

" Keep the windows darkened, and these cold cloths to his head. I will return in an hour."

And a voice replied:

" All right, sah ; I'll 'tend to it."

It is the voice of Ben ! I would know it among ten thousand !

" My God ! Where am I ? "

Something was over my eyes. It was a wet bandage. I pushed it up and saw Ben !

I looked around me.

I was in my own bed-room at C—— !

I looked at my hands.

My God! I am back in my own body!

Glory be to God! Glory be to God forever!

And I shouted aloud.

I understood it all in a moment.

In the very instant of death the transference of souls had taken place, and the spirit of the chicken-thief had passed to its dread account, flying before the bullet from his own pistol!

He had killed himself! He had committed suicide! And the merciful Christ had restored me to my own — to my home, to my name, to my body, and to my love!

And Ben stood watching me obsequiously, but with hate glittering in his small, black eyes.

"Ben, Ben!" I cried, opening wide my arms. "Don't you know me? Don't you know your old friend! I have come back. I am Doctor Huguet indeed!"

There was no mistaking the manner, the words, the sentiment, the enthusiasm! And in an instant my black servant was locked in my arms, in one long, fervent embrace.

"Oh, massa, massa!" he cried, the big tears streaming down his face, "I knows you! I knows you! You *has* come back! And that d——d nigger is gone foreber! Bress de Lord! Bress de Lord!"

"Quick, Ben, quick," I said, "bring me pen, ink and paper. Have the fastest horse in the stable saddled. I must write to Mary. Have a messenger ready to take it at once."

"Won't you hurt yourself, massa? You are cut, you know, but de doctor said it was only a flesh woun'. But you must be car'ful."

"Oh, I am strong, Ben! A thousand lives are throbbing in my veins. Quick, the paper! Mary must not have another hour of misery."

What I wrote I do not remember. It was one long, passionate burst of delight and love and hope. The very words burned with kisses, and the sentences were like embraces. My soul flowed out from my pen in ecstatic raptures. It cried: "Come to me, come to me, come to me! The world is ours and made for us alone; it is ours forever!"

"Quick, Ben, quick, the messenger! He must bring her back with him!"

And when Ben took the letter out of my hands I fell back exhausted.

CHAPTER XLI.

VENGEANCE.

"There's danger in the lion's wrath,
  Destruction in the tiger's jaw;
  But worse than death to cross the path
  Of man, when passion is his law.
  Woe, woe to those who strive to light
  The torch of truth by passion's fire!
  It guides not; it but glares through night
  To kindle freedom's funeral pyre."
                    —*The Song of the Bell* (*Schiller*).

FAST and far, that fateful night, from that scene of terror and horror and death, lit by the massed flames that towered and roared to the skies, rode the messengers, black and white. From house to house and cabin to cabin spread the dreadful news of cruel crime. Even to Colonel Ruddiman's distant dwelling-place, gloomy from Abigail's fate, came the awful tidings with which her name was mingled. Then was there hurrying in hot haste, and arming, and mounting and speeding of messengers, right and left, to summon those who still slept in the fair moonlight, unsuspicious that death and flame had been at work in the holy calm of that peaceful night. And then, through lane and wood, and past slumbering field and copse and hedge and homestead, quick thundering on galloping feet, gathered the clans, until Col. Ruddiman's trampled lawn swarmed with armed men. Silent and grim they were. No oaths resounded. They spoke in whispers.

And stealing along the narrow, beaten paths, from white-washed cabins, came dusky figures on foot, who joined them, bearing guns and clubs and scythes— darkness that moved like shadows in the shadows, portentous in their silence, dreadful in the glare of their white eye-balls.

A clustered group of leaders held counsel together, speaking below their breaths; and then all rode away, the old man of many battles at their head, the quick-footed shadows running by their side, swift almost as horses, silent as the moveless trees. A ghostly, speechless cavalcade it was; now buried in the dark gloom of the overhanging forest, now sweeping out into the white moonlight, far streaming along the beaten, sounding road. An instinct told every man, horseman and footman, what their destination was, though no one named that dark den of infamy, that sink of sin, where innocence had been cruelly slaughtered, where ruffians had gathered to plot rapine and murder against peaceful men and women and little children.

Fast they rode and fast they ran. The whole night seemed alive. There to the south the red embers of the school-house still warmed the blushing sky. No one slept; but from every house and cabin, white and black, young and old, afoot or on horseback, the streams of life swept out, like rivulets, down every cross-road and narrow lane, to join the rushing torrent of grim and silent men who poured down to the red ocean of vengeance. And in all those hearts there was but one thought — Death! And no man turned his head aside to think of aught else than — Death. With eyes straight forward they rode on, and on, and on.

" Halt! " The word was passed in whispers along the line; and there, some distance ahead, they saw a house and barn, at a cross-road. How tenderly, like a mother's love, the soft moonlight fell upon them, and hid the traces of shabby dilapidation. How sweetly the whole scene slept in the silence of the night, as if under the smile of angels! Oh, merciful Nature! that covers with the same flowers the dust of the assassin and the hero. The ruffians, their hands still bloody with the cruel murder of defenseless creatures, men, women and little harmless children, slept the sleep of justified righteousness, and the kindly night threw her mantle of peace and loveliness over their foul abode.

But Justice and Vengeance are at hand ! See how the cavalcade separates. Some stand still ; others move on ; they divide to the right and to the left, until the sleeping household is encircled and surrounded, and behind every tree and fence and bush rifles are pointed, concentering on the doomed house.

But look ! A gray head is thrust quickly out of one of the windows. The old cat sleeps lightly. There is an exclamation of alarm. Lights are lit and flash from room to room, and the forms of men and women — many of them — hurriedly pass and repass the windows. The whole house is aroused. They know their danger.

And then a strong voice cries out :

" We will let the women come out. We make war on men only."

It is the Colonel who speaks. There is silence! The lights go out. They are consulting. And then the front door flies open, and a motley crew, half-naked, carrying bundles of tawdry finery in their arms, rush out, terrified, and scuttle away, squawking, to the timber, like a flock of foul wild geese.

But Mother Bindell comes not forth. No; the fierce old demon is seen bearing a light from room to room, with bottle in hand, distributing whisky among the men, to strengthen them for the fight. And then the light is extinguished, and all is silence.

The same strong voice speaks out again:

" Are you ready to surrender ? "

The answer is a volley from the windows, and two men fall wounded.

And then, with a great rattling, crackling report, comes the reply, and the house is encircled by a wall of fire.

The besieged have the advantage: they are sheltered and in the darkness; while their assailants are almost unprotected, and exposed, in the white glare of the full moon, to be picked off by the skilled marksmen, who do not waste a shot. Several of the attacking party are killed and many wounded. They are having the worst of it. But still the fight goes on. A half hour passes—a half hour of terrible battle.

Dr. Magruder and Berrisford are with those who are keeping watch over the back part of the building. They are sheltering themselves behind the old barn and firing as opportunity presents itself.

And now a singular thing happens.

The Doctor notices a smell of burning hay.   Men's senses are acute at such a time.   The wall of the old barn is full of cracks and crevices.   He peers through one of them.   There is a light within the barn.

" Berrisford," he said softly, " come here.   What do you see ? "

" Hush ! " whispered Berrisford. " It is white ! " And a superstitious thrill ran through him.

" It is a woman," said the Doctor; " I see her more clearly now, through the smoke. "

" What is she doing ? " whispered Berrisford.

" She has kindled a fire in the barn, and now she is tying a rope around a great mass of hay."

" By heavens," said Berrisford, as the flames flashed up; " she has stuck a pitchfork into it, she lights it, she lifts it up, she rushes toward the door.   *It is Abigail !* "

The Doctor sprang forward to save her at the risk of his own life.   He was too late.   Out through the open doorway, right toward the house, across that hell of flying bullets, into the very jaws of death, she ran swiftly, bearing the great blazing, roaring mass, high above her head, like a banner.

" She means to fire the house," said Berrisford.

Yes; straight to the back door she ran, and flung down her burning burden against it.   And then she began to walk back, as calmly, as unconcernedly as if she had been upon a quiet country road near her own home.   But she had proceeded but a few paces when the fire of the defenders of the house, who well understood what she had done, was concentrated upon

her, and she staggered and fell backward — dead, with
a smile of triumph upon her face.

And then the door flew open, and a gray-haired
woman, with blazing eyes and harpy hands, rushed out,
and tried to scatter and stamp the burning hay. A
dozen rifles cracked, and she fell headlong among the
roaring flames, which leaped and danced and roared
above her — exulting over her as a thing fit only to be
utterly annihilated. Door, wall, window, cornice, everything is now aflame, and the fire-demon grasps and
gnaws and devours, until the whole house is lashed in
its red and mighty arms; and every board — reeking
with years of sin and shame — is sucked into the vortex
of the horrible destruction.

And now, dimly through the smoke, begrimed and
bloody figures dart suddenly out, as if to escape. But
they cross not the dreadful circle around the conflagration. Here and there, illy-defined heaps, casting black
shadows in the glare, lie upon the ground, moveless.
Lives they once were, loved by mothers; now they are
but dust-heaps. And, like an evil spirit, that exhausts
itself and can do no further harm to man, the great conflagration pauses; but it casts down, with its last strength,
walls and timbers and rafters and roof into the red furn-
ace of the cellar, where the coals glow portentously —
like a veritable hell — where stood so long that house
of hell.

And then a negro, on a farm horse, without a saddle,
rode up to Colonel Ruddiman.

" Massa!" he said, " dat man, de Doctor, what Abigail stabbed, he's not dead.   Dey said he was.   But de knife glanced on his ribs, and he am alive."

" Who told you that?" asked the Colonel.

" Ben sent me word," said the other.

" Then," said the Colonel, "we had better finish this morning's work.   I want five men to accompany me to C——.   The rest might as well return to their homes. Gentlemen," he said courteously, raising his hat to the multitude, who had gathered around him, " you have done a good work.   You have cleaned out a foul nest.   You have revenged the murder of the noblest man in this world, and the ruin of one of the bravest and best and truest women that ever lived.   I thank you in the name of outraged virtue and society.   Let us now disperse.   But will some of you look after the dead and wounded?   And will you make a litter and carry the remains of poor Abigail to my house?   Let there be no more violence, but let each man go quietly to his home."

CHAPTER XLII.

MY GREAT SORROW.

> " Yet now despair itself is mild,
>   Even as the winds and waters are ;
> I could lie down, like a tired child,
>   And weep away the life of care
>   Which I have borne, and yet must bear."
> —*Shelley.*

"BEN," I said, " how did I come here?"

"Well, you see, dey tells me dat dat nigger, Sam Johnsing, who had your body, he j'ined with Buryhill to kill you and burn de school-house; you know all about dat. And just as dey swung you up, Abigail, who was mos' crazy, she run out and struck Sam wid de Colonel's bowie-knife, and down he drapped, and never moved. And dey all thought he was gone dead, suah ; and Harry Sanders he gets a carriage and brings him home. And den, from what you tells me, just as you died your soul went back into your own body, but I 'spects de spell was on you yet, for you neber stirred nor spoke until de doctor comes, and he feels your pulse and looks at your breast, and he says, says he, ' He's not dead — he's fainted; he's got 'gestion ob blood in his head. It am only a flesh woun'.' And den you sits up in de bed and opens your arms and cries, ' Ben, Ben ! ' and den, bress de

Lord ! I knows you !' I knows you ! But I tinks, massa, you's talkin' too much."

" No, Ben," I said, " I am feeling much better. Joy has cured me. I think I will get up and dress instead of sitting here in bed."

There was a clatter of horses' hoofs entering the brick path that led to the house.

" Quick, Ben," I cried, " look out of the window, and see if it is Miss Mary."

Ben put his head out of the window.

" No, sah," he said; " it's Colonel Ruddiman and Doctor Magruder, and two or three oder white gemmen."

" Show them up, Ben," I cried; " I am so glad to see them."

Before Ben could leave the room there was a noise of hurrying feet upon the stairs, the door was flung open with a bang, and there stood Colonel Ruddiman, his eyes blazing with rage and his face black with dust and smoke.

" Oh, you infernal scoundrel !" he shrieked, " I have got you at last ! Ravisher of women, murderer of men, take that !"

I was paralyzed by such a salutation. I had not noticed, so astonished was I by the look upon his face, that his hand held a revolver. But Ben saw it, and, as the Colonel fired, quick as a flash, he flung himself before me, and the bullet meant for my heart entered his body, and he fell against me, with his arms outstretched, shrieking:

" Don't shoot, massa, don't shoot. Dis am de real

Doctor Huguet come back agin. De nigger am gone, massa. Don't shoot! Don't shoot! Dis am de white Doctor Huguet, for suah."

Here the blood poured in a flood from his mouth, and fell all over me — the rich, red, royal blood of honesty and love. His weight bore me back against the head-board. Great, convulsive tremors ran through him; his eyes turned up in his head; but even in the death agony I could feel him spreading out his arms to protect me.

"My God!" I cried, "see what you have done! You have slain the noblest heart in the world."

The Colonel stood there, with a pistol in his hand, a deadly, implacable look upon his face. He raised the revolver again.

"Don't shoot!" I cried; "I am the real Doctor Huguet."

Great heavens! I thought, am I to die now, just as life and love open before me again?

The Colonel's dark face relented not. The pistol slowly rose to the level of my head. The dead weight of Ben held me down and rendered me helpless.

"Stop, father, stop!" came a wild cry from the door, and Mary rushed forward and struck up the out-stretched arm, and the bullet entered the ceiling.

"Father, are you crazy? Would you kill your dearest friend? Read that letter!"

And, handing him a paper, she sprang forward and threw her arms around my neck and kissed my pale face. The living and the dead embraced me.

"Shoot now, if you will," she cried; "but you must kill me first."

20

Doctor Magruder and the others entered the room and came forward. The Colonel read the letter; then he dropped the pistol, and tore his hair with both hands, and cried out, like one distraught :

" My God ! What have I done ? What have I tried to do ? "

And then he fell upon his knees and grasped the hand of poor Ben, and cried :

" Doctor ! For God's sake, be quick. Is there life in him ? Is there hope ? "

Doctor Magruder stepped forward and took up Ben's arm. But he shook his head, and said softly :

" He is dead."

They lifted him from off me, and laid him out upon my bed. Poor, poor, dear friend, he had died to save me! And then I remembered that " greater love hath no man than this : that a man lay down his life for his friend." His face was black, but his soul would shine in heaven whiter than the wings of angels.

I forgot my love; I forgot everything ; and I fell upon him and wept aloud.

" My poor, poor friend," I cried, " where thou art buried I shall be, and our dust shall mingle together through all the ages. You gave your life that I might live. You gave me everything you had—for life is everything."

They lifted me up and carried me to a sofa. I had fainted.

When I returned to consciousness Mary held my hand in hers, and the Colonel, with red eyes, sat near me. He, too, had been weeping.

And then they told me the dreadful story of poor Abigail's fate, and all the awful tragedy of the early morning — that tale of fire and blood, and ashes, and vengeance.

And oh, I was so weak and tired and worn, that even love and hope were passionless in my heart. I had gone through fearful ordeals. I had been the plaything of Deity.

Sleep ! sleep ! Oh, if I could only sleep !

CHAPTER XLIII.

THE END.

> "Last scene of all,
> That ends this strange, eventful history."
> —*As You Like It, i. 7.*

A WEEK has passed. The dead are buried. The wild passions of the time have subsided, like the moaning ocean after a great storm.

In another month Mary and I are to be married. The world opens bright and beautiful before us. It is happiness merely to live.

Have I forgotten the lessons I have learned ?

No; no; they will never depart from my memory. My heart is softened by the miseries I have endured and the scenes I have witnessed. I have walked in the Valley of the Shadow of Death. I understand now, as I never did before, the feelings of the proscribed and wretched.

Mary and I have talked it over. It was at the graves of Abigail and Ben, where they sleep, side by side, in the white man's cemetery, on the top of a breezy hill, that looks out far and wide over the beautiful land. There, hand in hand, we agreed that I should devote my fortune and my life to the up-building of the negro race in this great America— this grandest and noblest of nations. Mary enters, heart and soul, with deep religious fervor, into all my plans and purposes.

I shall erect school-houses, I shall provide teachers, I shall employ good men and women to work goodness in the land. I shall labor to enlighten minds, to enkindle souls, to sweeten tempers, and to lift both races out of the slough of bigotry and intolerance. I shall preach mercy and good will and peace on earth to men, for the great Gospel of Brotherly Love is the true solvent in which must melt away forever the hates of races and the contentions of castes.

> " Humanity moves onward:
> Where to-day the martyr stands
> To-morrow crouches Judas,
> With the silver in his hands.
> Another cross stands ready,
> Another fagot burns;
> But the shouting mob of yesterday
> In silent awe returns,
> To gather up the ashes
> For History's cold urns. "

THE END.

CÆSAR'S COLUMN

A Story of the Twentieth Century.

By EDMUND BOISGILBERT, M. D.
[IGNATIUS DONNELLY]

This wonderful book was first issued in June, 1890. The
name on the title page was Edmund Boisgilbert, M. D., and
it was given out that this was a pseudonym. The leading
magazines and reviews, with one exception, and many of the
great newspapers entirely ignored the book, and everything at
first was against its success. It created the most profound in-

terest, however, among those who read it, and soon became talked about. JULIAN HAWTHORNE, BISHOP POTTER, FRANCES E. WILLARD and others spoke highly of it, and CARDINAL GIBBONS praised it as an example of the highest literary form. OPIE P. READ summed up its charm in these words: "*It will thrill a careless reader of novels, or profoundly impress a statesman.* It is gentle as a child and yet it is rugged as a giant." In six months "Cæsar's Column" passed through twelve editions, and considerable guessing was done as to the real name of the author, among those prominently named being Judge Tourgee, Mark Twain, T. V. Powderly, Robert G. Ingersoll, Chauncey M. Depew, Benj. F. Butler and others. In December it was finally announced that Ignatius Donnelly, author of "Atlantis," "Ragnarok" and "The Great Cryptogram," was also the author of "Cæsar's Column." Mr. Donnelly had escaped general suspicion because his previous writings are more distinguished by laborious industry and wide information than by the qualities that go to make the creator of romances.

"In 'Cæsar's Column' Mr. Donnelly takes as his text the dangerous tendencies of our age and gives a picture of what the world will be a hundred years from now, if the spirit of invention and material progress remains the same and the moral spirit of society moves along in its present channels. The San Francisco Chronicle aptly says: In a startlingly original and fascinating novel he presents a profound study of sociological conditions.

WHAT THE CRITICS SAY.

"A Gabriel's trump."—FRANCES E. WILLARD.

"A very extraordinary production."—RT. REV. HENRY C. POTTER.

"The effect of an honest purpose is felt in every line."—*Pioneer Press.*

CÆSAR'S COLUMN—WHAT THE CRITICS SAY.

As an example of the highest literary form it deserves unstinted praise."—CARDINAL GIBBONS.

"A wonderfully fascinating book. It will hold the attention of the world as no other book has held it for years."—*Chicago Saturday Blade.*

"'Cæsar's Column,' in *its vivid portrayal*, will lead many to realize the many dangers to which our country is liable."—HON. WM. LARRABEE.

"I was unable to lay it down until I had finished reading it. It should be read by every farmer in the land."—H. L. LOUCKS, *President National Farmers' Alliance.*

"Bellamy looks backward upon what is impossible as well as improbable. 'Cæsar's Column' looks forward to what is *not only possible, but probable.*"—MILTON GEORGE.

"I have read 'Cæsar's Column' twice and am convinced that it has been *written in the nick of time.* * * * I predict for the book an immense sale and a world-wide discussion."—CORINNE S. BROWN, *Secretary Nationalist Club, Chicago.*

"The story *is most interestingly devised and strongly told. It is not the work of a pessimist* or an anarchist, but rather of a preacher who sees the dangers that all thoughtful men see in our time, and, appreciating the importance to humanity of maintaining what is good in existing systems, utters his warning as a sacred duty."—*Free Press.*

"The book points out tendencies which actually exist and are in need of cure. It warns us with vehemence and force of the necessity of guarding our liberties against the encroachments of monopoly and plutocracy, and of disarming corruption in government by every device that a vigilant ingenuity can supply."—GEORGE CARY EGGLESTON. in *New York World.*

'*The most remarkable and thought-provoking novel* that the disturbed industrial and social conditions of the present have produced. * * * The purpose of this book is to arrest attention—to make men think wisely and act justly, and with dispatch. The write· holds it as a signal of danger before the on-coming train. Will the warning be heeded?"—*The Arena.*

"The author writes with tremendous feeling and *great imaginative power.* The picture gives in startling colors what would be the case if many of our business methods and social tendencies were to move

A KENTUCKY COLONEL

By OPIE P. READ.

A SYMPOSIUM OF OPINION.

THIS is pre-eminently an American book by an American author. *Book Talk* says of it: "In these days of endless foreign importations in the line of literature, when readers are constantly hobnobbing with lords, dukes,

The Colonel.

and princes in English novels, and characters with unpronounceable names or undefinable morals, in Russian, French or Italian fiction, it is an unmistakable relief to pick up a book like 'A Kentucky Colonel.'"

HON. HENRY C. CALDWELL, who is not only one of the greatest of American lawyers, but one of the best of literary critics, says: "I have never read a better story. It is *the most beautifully written*, the *most striking in character*, and upon the whole *one of the most thrilling and yet chaste pieces of fiction* that has been produced in many a day. It will create a sensation."

"A novel of remarkable power and interest."—*Spirit*.

"A notable contribution to recent literature."—*Book Buyer*.

"A KENTUCKY COLONEL"—SOME OPINIONS.

"The sketches of Southern life in this book are exquisite"—*Book Chat.*

"The book does not read like a romance. It seems to be a record of an actual experience."—*New York Herald.*

"Full of action and vigor, with descriptions of scenery that are always poetic and sometimes exquisite in their word-painting."—*Chicago Herald.*

"A book the popularity of which will not be temporary. It has virility, tenderness, striking character pictures, and the American flavor."—*Chicago Journal.*

"Mr. Read is by no means a realist, but his characters come nearer that ideal than the studied and overwrought efforts of Howells and James."—*Atchison Champion.*

"If the author has not actually known the people he writes of in his romance, he makes one feel that he must have known them, and no literary art can do more."—*Louisville Critic.*

"Mr. Read's genius finds its best examplification in this delightful book, which equals in human interest and surpasses in dramatic finish any of his previous productions."—*Chicago Evening Post.*

"In 'A Kentucky Colonel' I find *the best and brightest pictures of Southern Life.* That young fellow *Savely*—what a type—and how many of them went down during the war."—ALEX. E. SWEET

"A sparkling gem among recent literature. The characters live and breathe a perfect mirror of Kentucky life, from the backwoods revivals down to the recipe for making a mint julep."—*Northwestern.*

"The book will interest, not merely for its plot, but for the bold character-drawing. Mr. Read does nothing by inference. His figures are solid and imposing, and as sturdy in action as they are bold in outline."—*Boston Globe.*

"There is a rich vein of true humor and of healthy and vigorous sentiment, and it has a fresh and breezy atmosphere which is heartily welcome in view of the hot-house character of much of our fiction."—*Philadelphia Record.*

"The deepest thinker and the most progressive of all the writers of humor in this country is Opie P. Read. * * * His writings are

"A KENTUCKY COLONEL"—SOME OPINIONS.

fresh, sparkling, witty, agreeable, and so pleasant that he is of more service to humanity than are scores of long-faced teachers and preachers."—"BRICK" POMEROY.

"It is a novel that bears on every page the seal of authenticity. It is realism, it is romance, it is photography, and it is caricature. * * * What we most like it for is the sincerity of its coloring. Of the many stories, short and long, of Kentucky life, it gives the most realistic pictures."—*New York Independent.*

"'A Kentucky Colonel,' the latest novel to have the name of big-bodied, big-hearted, genial Opie P. Read on its title-page, is having an immense sale. It is a powerful piece of fiction and the best of his productions to date. It will be read and enjoyed long after its author has passed away."—*New York Journalist.*

"'A Kentucky Colonel' will be read and appreciated by the scholar, for as a work of art it is highly pleasing; and it will be read and appreciated by the people, for it is pure, is pervaded by a moral atmosphere most refreshingly wholesome, and is intensely interesting from beginning to end."—*Little Rock Republican.*

"One reads it from first to last with keen delight, and sighs when the end comes. The tale is so simply and sincerely told, the men and women who wander through the pages are so evidently men and women, with so true a tang of the Kentucky soil, the humor is so local and unaffected, the pictures of nature so delightful, that the book is closed with the comfortable sense of time well spent."—*Chicago Inter Ocean.*

"So beautiful, so chaste, so full of simple, rugged honesty and pure, wholesome sentiment, that no one can read the book without being bettered. * * * The book is full of a gentle humor that has just enough tart in it to make it appetizing. Some of the word-painting is almost sublime, and everywhere there is that broad, sweet touch of tenderness that is a part of the author's very self. * * * There is not a single dull line."—*Am. Commercial Traveler.*

"A delightful novel. Kentucky has been productive of an enormous quantity of self-assertive, self-respecting humanity, which has been the theme of the floating humorist and paragrapher; but unfortunately the type has not heretofore been fixed in permanent literature. 'A Kentucky Colonel' is an attempt to do this, and it is certainly not an unsuccessful attempt. The simple, stalwart honesty of the Kentucky

"A KENTUCKY COLONEL"—SOME OPINIONS.

man, the unaffected naturalness of the Kentucky woman, both proof in their honesty and naturalness against the inroads of artificiality and convention, are exhibited in a style as honest and natural as the subject. Mr. Read feels the force of the Colonel's remark when he proudly speaks of his daughter as a 'Blue Grass girl, suh, not afraid to be natural.'"—*St. Louis Post-Dispatch.*

"I don't think I ever saw a more truthful portrayal of character. The story is *new, strong in every point, and cannot help being a success.*"—HENRY CLAY LUKENS.

"Your 'Kentucky Colonel' has taken my household by storm. It is *a delightful story admirably told—a great pen picture* which I, as a Kentuckian, pondered over at times until I had to shake myself back into every-day life."—WILL VISSCHER.

"A KENTUCKY COLONEL" IS PUBLISHED IN ONE LARGE 12MO VOLUME, OF 342 PAGES.

CLOTH EXTRA,	-	-	- $1.00
PAPER COVERS,	-	-	- .50

Sent by mail to any address on receipt of price.

F. J. SCHULTE & CO., PUBLISHERS, CHICAGO.

AN INDIANA MAN

By LE ROY ARMSTRONG

ONE VOLUME 12MO. CLOTH, EXTRA, $1.00. PAPER, 50 CTS.

F. J. SCHULTE & CO., Publishers, CHICAGO.

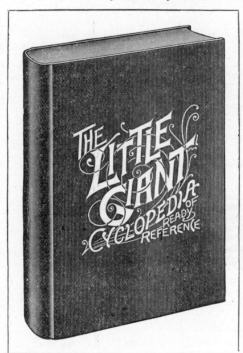